INCONSPICUOUS

A Circle City Mystery

M. E. May

M&B Literary Creations

M&B Literary Creations

Cover Art by Julie Kukreja, Pen and Mouse Design

Printed in the United States of America
10 9 8 7 6 5 4 3 2

Books by M. E. May

The Circle City Mystery Series

Perfidy

Dedication

To my friend, Tricia Zoeller, I give my thanks
for her encouragement and steadfast friendship.

Acknowledgements

As in *Perfidy*, Book One of the Circle City Series, I want to acknowledge those who serve and protect the great city of Indianapolis—the men and women of the Indianapolis Metropolitan Police Department. I am especially grateful to those in the department who have been willing to answer my technical questions about the IMPD's policies and procedures. Their assistance is very valuable and greatly appreciated.

Thanks go out to my beta readers Tricia, Claire, and Judi for reading my first drafts and letting me know what worked and what didn't. I also want to acknowledge my colleague and award winning author, Robert Goldsborough for reviewing the final draft. It was a thrill to have him read and review my work.

Of course, I wouldn't be able to get through all the publishing highs and lows without my husband, Paul; my children, Brian and Marie; and my four wonderful grandchildren, Kodey, Kaleb, Kameron and Gustin. Their encouragement and support mean the world to me.

"Come walk with me through the mist into the
frightening unknown elements of the human mind."
—M. E. May

Chapter 1

Her dog barked as Penny Flanders' alarm clock buzzed. That was strange. Lucy, her German Shepherd, rarely barked this early in the morning. This time of day Penny normally found Lucy sitting next to her bed patiently staring at Penny, waiting for her to wake up. Lucy considered it her job to assist her master in waking, if the alarm didn't do its job. Penny lay in bed bleary-eyed and confused until she heard Lucy yelp in pain, then whine pitifully.

Now wide-awake, she lay perfectly still, listening intently. Realizing there was an intruder in the house, she slowly rolled to her left and got out of bed. Quietly, she crept to the door. She heard footsteps on the stairs and knew it was only a matter of time before the intruder reached the bedroom. Panic rose in her chest as Penny slowly closed and locked her bedroom door. Then she propped a chair against it hoping the police would come before the intruder managed to get in.

Grabbing her cordless phone from the bedside table, she decided to hide in the master bathroom. Penny locked the bathroom door and called 9-1-1. She sat down on the side of the tub and held the phone to her ear waiting for it to connect.

Silence. It wasn't ringing.

She held the phone out looking at it as though it had offended her. Pushing the off button, then the on button, she placed the phone to her ear hoping for a dial tone. Nothing. Her heart started pounding like a timpani drum and she feared the sound of it would betray her location.

She berated herself for leaving her purse downstairs with her cell phone in it, stripping her of options. Sure Lucy was dead, Penny trembled at the thought of being next. Something acidic rose to her gullet. She swallowed hard to stop it from going any further.

The bathroom had no window for escape. Even if she went back to the bedroom, it was a long drop from the second story to the ground. No way could she do it without injuring herself, giving the intruder an advantage. If she had just listened to her brother when he advised her to get a roll up ladder in case of a fire, she could have escaped and roused a neighbor.

Bang!

Penny jumped and a new wave of terror flooded her veins. She thought she might die of a heart attack before the intruder had a chance to get to her.

Crash!

That had to be the bedroom door coming down. Penny sat frozen on the edge of the tub unable to move or speak, praying God wouldn't let her go out like this—murdered in her own home by a stranger.

She could hear the intruder banging and scraping as he climbed over the debris. Then he called to her in a singsong voice.

"You mustn't lock yourself away. Not like when you did it to me. It's very unpleasant, isn't it? But at least *you* have water. Come out now. Come out and see me."

This was bizarre. Lock him away? Come out and see me? What the hell was he talking about? Do I know him?

He pounded on the bathroom door. Penny leapt and ran to the far side of the room. She hit the wall as though she could vanish through it like a ghost. It didn't work. With her back to the wall, she slid down to the floor, tears of terror in her eyes.

"Open the door," he demanded, in a louder, angrier voice. "It's very tiresome for me to have to break it down when you know I'll get in one way or another."

Frozen with fear, she couldn't open it even if she'd wanted to do so.

"Have it your way."

Crash!

Penny ducked and threw her arms over her head as the door slammed down and small pieces of wood and metal pelted her. She didn't want to look at the monster.

"Don't hurt me," she pleaded. "Please, don't hurt me."

"I wouldn't think of it." His voice was deep and sinister. "Unlike me, you won't feel a thing."

Chapter 2

Homicide Detective, Erica Barnes, stood outside the doorway of the two-story frame house watching Patrol Officer Lloyd try his best to keep the reporters behind the crime scene tape. CSI techs were searching for evidence from the grounds.

Her partner and shift supervisor, Detective Brent Freeman, had just arrived on the scene. Detective Bays had Freeman sign the log sheet then he and Erica went in through the open door.

"Who found the body?" This is how Freeman often greeted his partner. They'd been working Homicide together for the past five years.

"Bays and Samuels were the first responders," said Erica. "I spoke briefly with Bays. He said the dog walker found the victim. She's over there, sitting in the living room with Kendall. She's pretty shaken up."

"I'm sure she is," Freeman agreed. "Probably not more than twenty-five, is she? Expecting to drop in and take the dog for a nice walk. Instead, she finds her employer murdered. By the way, where is the dog?"

Erica checked her notes. "Dog walker found the dog just inside the back door, unconscious. Vet just took her away. Said he'll call us with an injury report later. Looks like the back door is where the bastard entered.

"Victim is Penny Flanders, age 32. Happened in the master bedroom upstairs. Again, first on the scene were Patrol Officers Donovan Bays and Anne Samuels. Bays said the dog walker was hysterical. Samuels asked her to have a seat in the living room while they secured the scene. Bays checked the perimeter and started a log. Samuels stayed close to the girl until Kendall arrived. I haven't been upstairs yet, but I hear it's a mess."

"Okay, Barnes, sounds like we've got a lot of work to do," said Freeman. "You're the lead on this one, where do you want me to start?"

"I'll go see how Kendall is doing with our witness. You get started upstairs. I want you to get your observations down before the death investigator moves the body and the crime scene team starts collecting evidence."

Erica appreciated her long-time partner and shift supervisor's show of confidence and respect. She headed towards the living room as he ascended the stairs.

The young blonde-haired woman sat on the couch wiping her eyes with a tissue as she conversed with Detective Chennelle Kendall. Erica hated seeing someone so young affected by such horrendous cruelty. After nine years on the force, six of them in Homicide, she still wasn't used to the depraved actions of some who dare to call themselves human beings.

Detective Kendall arose when Erica entered the room. She was tall, slender and dark skinned with silky black hair and dark eyes. Erica always thought Chennelle looked more like a fashion model than a homicide detective.

"Detective Barnes, this is Felicity Harden," said Kendall. "She was employed to care for Miss Flanders' German Shepherd. Miss Harden, this is Detective Barnes who is also from the Homicide Unit of the Indianapolis Metropolitan Police Department. She's the lead detective on the case and I'm sure she has a few questions for you."

"Okay," said Felicity, sniffing and clearing her throat.

"Kendall, go keep an eye out for the death investigator and show him or her upstairs."

"You got it," Kendall said as she headed for the front door.

"I won't keep you long, Miss Harden. I know this has been a very difficult ordeal," Erica began. "You've probably already told Detective Kendall and the other officers your story. I am sorry to have to ask you to repeat it, but it's very important."

"Well, like I told Detective Kendall, I always walk Lucy between 2:00 and 3:00 in the afternoon, Monday through Friday, while Penny is working. She usually leaves the house at about 7:30 in the morning and is back by 6:30 at night."

Felicity stopped, her lips quivering as she wiped the stream of tears from her cheeks. "This afternoon, I got here at about 2:10. When I walked up to the back door, I could see the glass was broken and the door was ajar. I wasn't sure if I should come in. I was scared someone might still be in the house, but then..." She paused again, closing her eyes momentarily.

"Please take your time, Miss Harden," said Erica. As upset as Felicity was, Erica wanted to keep her calm and focused so she'd remember more details.

"I pushed the door open a little and I saw her lying there. Lucy I mean. At first, I thought she was dead. Then I realized she was breathing, but unconscious. I was in such a panic I couldn't remember the vet's number, but I had it in my cell phone. I knew the vet made emergency house calls so I called him. Before they took her away, I heard them say Lucy has a concussion, a broken hip, and possibly some internal bleeding." She began to sob in earnest. It was obvious she was very fond of her charge. "I hope I wasn't too late for her, too."

"I'm sure she'll be fine," Erica assured her. "What happened after you called the vet?"

"I don't know why, but I picked up Penny's kitchen phone to call 9-1-1. There was no dial tone, so I used my cell again." Felicity took in a deep breath before continuing. "It was so quiet in the house I thought the intruder must have left. While I was talking to the 9-1-1 Operator, I started walking through the house. I saw Penny's purse on her desk as I passed her home office. I knew she must still be here. Then my cell phone battery died. I wished I'd listened and got out of the house like the 9-1-1 Operator told me. I shouldn't have gone upstairs," she choked, her eyes widening in horror.

Her voice became louder and more hysterical. "I found Penny on the bed. And her eyes! Oh my God, what he did to her eyes! I'll never stop seeing them as long as I live. How could someone do this to her? What sort of sick son-of-a-bitch does something so, so...?"

Erica shook her head. Even after all these years on the police force, she still had no satisfactory answer to such a question.

"To your knowledge, did Miss Flanders have any enemies? Ex-boyfriend, angry neighbors?" asked Erica still trying to keep Felicity focused.

"Penny never talked to me about her personal life. I liked her, but she was my employer. I walk dogs for a lot of people in the neighborhood. I've never heard anyone say anything nasty about her."

"Thank you, Miss Harden. You're free to go now. We'll have an officer escort you home."

"Don't bother, Detective," said Felicity. "I only live a couple of blocks from here. It was such a nice, sunny day I decided to walk over." She stood, backpack in hand.

Erica motioned for one of the uniformed officers. "I want you to escort Miss Harden home." Then Erica turned to Felicity. "Miss Harden, one or more of those reporters outside might follow you and corner you. For your safety and peace of mind, I insist you be escorted home."

"Okay," said Felicity. "I hadn't thought about the reporters."

"Also," Erica said as she touched Felicity's arm, "please don't talk to anyone but the police about what you saw today. The details of a murder scene are very important in helping us capture a perpetrator. If the press gets a hold of this information, it could cause widespread panic or copycat murders. Do you understand?"

"Yes," she said, tears welling in her eyes once more. "I don't want this to happen to anyone else. Penny didn't deserve to die that way. It's horrible! I just want to forget it."

"Come along, Miss Harden. I won't let anyone harass you," stated the officer as she took Felicity's arm, guiding her to the front door.

Erica then turned to see Kendall approaching from the living room. "Did you talk to the first responders?" Erica asked.

"Yes," answered Kendall. "Samuels and Bays had everything under control when I arrived. Bays kept the reporters away until we could get more officers in here to make sure no one crossed the line. I don't understand how they found out so quickly."

Erica spotted Patrol Officer Donovan Bays with an officer she'd never seen before. "Bays!" she shouted. "I need to ask you a few questions."

"No problem," said Bays. "Have you met my new partner?

Erica shook her head.

"This is Patrol Officer, and rookie extraordinaire, Anne Samuels," Bays said. "Samuels, meet one of IMPD's finest Homicide Detectives, Erica Barnes."

"It's a pleasure to meet you," Samuels said.

Erica nodded in acknowledgement noting Samuels' enthusiasm.

"Samuels has dreams of becoming a top-notch homicide detective someday," said Bays. Erica saw Samuels redden with embarrassment.

"It doesn't hurt to have ambitions," said Erica, trying to encourage Samuels while admonishing Bays for embarrassing his partner. "Now, it's my understanding, Bays, that you inspected the perimeter while *you*, Samuels, stayed in the house with Miss Harden."

"That's correct," stated Samuels. "She was extremely upset, of course. I couldn't blame her. She'd just found Miss Flanders' dead body. She kept going on and on about Miss Flanders' eyes. How she'd be having nightmares about them for the rest of her life."

"Is that all she said to you about it?" asked Erica.

"Yes," Samuels responded. "Bays had gone out to check the perimeter and it took a while for me to get Miss Harden to stop crying so I could understand what she was saying. I went upstairs to tape off the inner crime scene area as soon as Detective Kendall arrived."

"Did you find anything outside, Bays?" asked Erica.

"Some shoeprints and some nosey reporters," said Bays, crinkling his brow in disgust. "I was just about to mark the area where I found the prints when two reporters and a cameraman came running up to me asking what happened. Next thing I knew they'd tromped all over our shoeprint evidence. I threatened to arrest them for obstruction if they didn't get behind the tape. They unhappily complied."

Erica hated reporters. They had absolutely no respect for anything or anyone except themselves and the glory of the story.

"Did you ask them how they found out about this so fast?" asked Erica.

"Yeah, but all I got was their standard *freedom of the press* and *we don't reveal our sources* bullshit. I did get their names though, in case you want to question them later." He flipped through the pages of his notebook. "Here we go—Andrea Atkins and Jesse Lane from the local NBC station, and Peter Elliott, reporter for the *Indianapolis Star*."

"Thanks, Bays," said Erica. "I just may have a little talk with them later. Let's get upstairs, Kendall."

"Right behind you," said Kendall.

"You spent some time with Miss Harden. Do you think she could have been involved in this?" Erica asked while they ascended the stairs.

"No way," Kendall replied. "She was way too upset. This was definitely a one man show—the strong man that is."

"You can say that again," said Freeman from the top of the stairs. "Wait until you see what went on up here."

"Holy crap!" blurted Erica as she approached the bedroom door. "The damn door's off its hinges! This guy use a battering ram or something?"

"Damn close," Freeman told her. "Victim must have locked herself in there, because he did the same thing to the bathroom door. Snapped the poor girl's neck like a toothpick. Patel said it was quick, she died instantly."

"Any signs of sexual assault?" asked Kendall.

"Patel still hasn't finished her preliminary exam," stated Freeman. "Let's go ask her."

Erica and Kendall followed Freeman around the debris, entering the bedroom cautiously. Erica could see the bathroom door had indeed been smashed in as well. The victim was laid out consistent with someone placed in a casket. It appeared she was dressed in clothing the killer brought with him. The dress had a flowered pattern and was much too big for the girl. It was definitely not a style someone in her thirties would wear. Her hands were lying on her stomach holding a single red rose. As they came closer, Erica saw what had caused the look of horror in Felicity Harden's eyes.

The killer had used an overabundance of makeup on Penny Flanders' face. But it was her eyes which almost caused Erica to heave her lunch. The perpetrator had sewn Penny Flanders' eyes open with some sort of heavy black thread. He had also written *SEE ME* across her forehead with something comparable to an eyeliner pencil. Erica wondered if this was a message for the victim or for the police.

"So what we got here, Doc?" Freeman asked.

Dr. Padma Patel, Death Investigator and Forensic Pathologist, was just finishing her exam of the body. She was a petite woman who pulled her silky, dark brown hair into a tight bun at the nape of her neck. The doctor sighed and shook her head.

"There is bruising which occurred before death. The ones on her arms are most likely from the killer grabbing her from the front. See the finger impressions," she said while pointing. "Then there's some bruising across her chin, like the killer was gripping it." Dr. Patel pointed to the area in question.

"There is also bruising on the base of the skull indicating her head was wrenched. I can feel the broken vertebrae. Further examination in the morgue will give us the details. My guess would be she died due to cervical damage in the neck region. You can see the finger imprints on top of her left shoulder and the finger imprints on her face with the thumb impression on her left cheek and the four fingers on the right cheek. There may be fingerprints on the body. I'm going to talk to Mark Chatham about having his fingerprint expert check the body before I take her so the evidence is not compromised by transport and refrigeration."

"I hope her death was quick," commented Kendall.

"Very," said Dr. Patel. "Any suffering would have been prior to death, and was most likely psychological in nature. He was very strong to have broken down two doors, so it wouldn't have been any problem at all for him to kill this small woman."

"How soon will we be able to get a preliminary autopsy report?" asked Erica.

"I've got two autopsies on the table now," Dr. Patel answered. "Unless any more such killings are committed for me to investigate, I should be able to do this one tomorrow morning. I think it will be simple, but you never know. I'll give you a call when I've completed it."

"Was there sexual assault?" asked Erica.

"There may have been, but I must examine the body thoroughly in order to say for sure."

"Thanks, Doc," said Freeman. "Oh, yeah, one more thing. Make sure our victim's special features are kept secret. We don't want the press getting hold of our killer's M.O."

"Of course, Detective," Dr. Patel said with a smile.

As they walked away, Erica nudged her partner, speaking in a low tone. "How come she lets *you* call her Doc? She has a fit if any of the rest of us does."

"I guess it's just my charm," Freeman smirked.

"Yeah, right," Erica retorted. "That's why you're still single."

Before the last word left her mouth, she knew she'd stung him. Freeman frowned and turned away. A year and a half ago, after the funeral, Mandy Stevenson broke up with him and he'd been avoiding relationships ever since. This was okay with Erica. In her opinion, he fell in love too hard, too fast. Brent had wanted to marry Mandy, but she couldn't bring herself to marry a cop. Instead, she'd be marrying Dr. Maxwell Thornton next month. Erica was relieved the breakup hadn't affected Freeman's relationship with Mandy's father, and their boss, Major Robert Stevenson, Commander of the Robbery and Homicide Division.

Erica turned to see Mark Chatham, Shift Supervisor of the Crime Scene Investigation Team, entering the room.

"Hey, Barnes, Freeman," said Chatham. "Wow, what a mess. What do we know so far?"

"I hope you brought the troops," responded Freeman.

Chatham scanned the scene. "Since he kicked in the door, we may find a shoe print on it. Hey, Parelli! You like jigsaw puzzles?"

Erica and Brent turned to see a tall woman with shoulder length, chestnut hair and brown eyes approaching. Sophia Parelli was new to the Forensics Department.

"You know I love a challenge, Mark," she said with a smile, pulling on her latex gloves. "I just need to figure out the best way to get these pieces back to the lab without further damage."

"We'll leave you to it," said Erica. "Kendall, you stick around and help Chatham's team. Freeman and I are going to look for next of kin."

"Will do," she said.

"Chatham, when can we get together to go over crime scene photos and evidence?" asked Erica.

"The shape this place is in, it'll probably take at least eight hours to do a thorough job. I can get you a preliminary report early tomorrow afternoon. Let's say…1:30?"

"Sounds good," said Erica. "Will that work for you, Freeman?"

"That'll work," answered Freeman. "I've got to be in court at 9:00 a.m. tomorrow, but should be out by then. Maybe by the time the meeting's over, the autopsy will be complete. Ready to go downstairs to search her office, Barnes?"

"See you tomorrow afternoon," said Chatham, picking up his camera.

Chapter 3

While searching the victim's desk, Erica found an envelope addressed to Penny with a birthday card inside. The card was signed *Love you always, Mom and Dad.* The return address on the envelope was for a Dylan and Jean Flanders. She and Freeman left the crime scene through a deluge of reporters and headed for the Flanders' house. Hoping none of the reporters were following, Erica continued to watch over her shoulder to make sure of it.

The Flanders lived in a small, red brick ranch style home in Speedway, not far from the Indy 500 racetrack. As they pulled in the driveway, Erica couldn't help but admire their efforts to maintain such a beautiful front yard. The trees and bushes were neatly trimmed and spring flowers were in bloom along the front of the house.

When Freeman knocked on the door, Erica heard a dog barking on the other side.

"Get back Ranger," said a stern female voice. The door opened and a plump woman of about sixty years was standing there holding back a German Shepherd. "What can I do for you?" she asked.

Both detectives showed the woman their badges and Erica introduced herself and Freeman. "Is your husband home, Mrs. Flanders? We need to speak with both of you."

"Yes he is," answered Mrs. Flanders, worry lining her face. "Come on in. Ranger won't bite. He likes the police. He used to be one until he got too old. My husband retired from the gas company a couple of years ago and thought he'd be good for protection." Mrs. Flanders was speaking conversationally; however, Erica could hear how her voice quavered.

"I remember you, Ranger," said Erica, scratching him behind his ears. "We worked together on the Campbell case when I was still in uniform. I didn't know you'd retired."

After receiving a strange look from her partner, they followed Mrs. Flanders to the kitchen. There sat a stocky man with gray hair chopping onions.

"Dylan, these detectives have something they need to talk to us about."

"What can we do for you?" asked Mr. Flanders frowning.

"Could we all sit down for a moment, please?" said Erica.

"Oh, God," said Mrs. Flanders, a sudden look of panic on her face. "Something's happened, hasn't it? Is it one of our kids?"

"Please, Mrs. Flanders," said Erica, gesturing for her to sit in the chair next to her husband.

"Mr. and Mrs. Flanders," Freeman began. "We are here to talk about your daughter, Penny."

"Did something happen to her?" asked Mr. Flanders, holding his wife's hands as she began to shake.

"I'm afraid so. There isn't any easy way to say this, sir," said Freeman lowering his eyes. "Your daughter was murdered early this morning in her home."

Mrs. Flanders screamed then burst into hysterical, heart-wrenching sobs. Mr. Flanders looked at Freeman in disbelief. "Are you sure?" he asked.

"Yes. I'm sorry, sir," said Freeman. "We just came from her house. I know this is a bad time, but we'd like to ask a few questions, if you feel up to it."

"Give us a minute," said Mr. Flanders, turning to his wife. "Jean. Jeannie honey. I can handle this, if you want to go lie down."

"I can't believe this is happening," she sobbed. "Why would anyone murder our sweet little Penny?"

Mr. Flanders pulled his wife toward him and let her cry.

"Is there anyone we can call for you," offered Erica, trying to find some way to help them through their suffering. "You mentioned you have other children."

"Penny was our youngest," said Mr. Flanders, voice shaking and tears welling up in his eyes. "Our address book is in the living room by the phone. You'll find my sons' names in there. Keifer, Dorian and Ian. Same last name, of course."

Erica rose from her chair and retrieved the phone book. She wrote down the names, addresses, and phone numbers for Penny's brothers. She called each of them in turn, but only made contact with Ian since he'd already arrived home from work. Erica had to leave messages for the others. Luckily, Ian only lived a few blocks away and was there within minutes.

"Mom! Dad!" Ian shouted as he burst through the door.

"In the kitchen, son," his father responded, his voice cracking.

"A Detective Barnes told me to come right away, said there was an emergency. What's going on?" Ian asked, his face wrinkled in anguish.

"Mr. Flanders, I'm Detective Brent Freeman and you spoke with my partner, Detective Barnes." Erica stood to shake his hand. "We are from the Homicide Division and have some bad news."

"What is it?" Ian asked, his voice increasing in volume.

"Your sister, Penny, was murdered in her home early this morning," answered Freeman.

"No," he exclaimed. "This can't be happening. Mom? Dad?"

"I'm afraid it's true son," said his father, tears streaming down his face still holding his wife. "We were waiting for you before we answered any questions."

"Questions? You're not interrogating my parents under these circumstances," shouted Ian.

"With all due respect, sir," said Erica, "we would be glad to wait a day or two. However, if there's anything any of you can tell us to help us find her killer, the sooner we know the better."

"I don't think my mother can handle this right now, Detectives," said Ian. "Dad, does Mom have any sedatives she can take?" His father took Ian's mother out of the room.

Ian sat down hard in a chair. "Penny? How could anything like this happen to Penny? She was a sweetheart. Everybody loved her. Detectives, this had to be a stranger. My sister didn't have any enemies or crazy ex-boyfriends. We were all very close. If she had a stalker or anything, she would have told us."

"She may not have known someone was watching her," said Erica.

"I didn't think of that," said Ian. "What about Lucy? Where was Lucy?" Ian paused momentarily running his fingers through his auburn hair. "Dad got her for Penny the same time he got Ranger so Penny would have protection."

"Although she's still alive, I'm afraid Lucy was attacked by the killer first," said Freeman. "She's at the Westside Veterinary Hospital."

"How did Penny die?" asked Ian.

"The killer broke her neck," said Freeman.

"Is that it?" asked Ian. "He just came in and broke her neck, for the fun of it?"

"We don't know what the motivation was at this time," answered Erica. "We do know her death was quick and she didn't suffer. We're waiting on the autopsy results for more details about what happened and for a definitive cause of death. Our forensics team is going through her house now, looking for evidence. They're the best. We'll find out who did this to your sister."

"I sure hope so," said Ian bitterly. "Mom and Dad weren't planning to have any more kids after Dorian was born. Mom really wanted *him* to be a girl. Then they *accidentally* got pregnant with Penny when Dorian was four. They finally got their little girl, and now...."

"I'm so sorry, Mr. Flanders," said Freeman.

"We all loved Penny," said Ian. "She was so tiny when she was born. We all thought of her as our miracle baby." Ian stood abruptly nearly sending the chair across the room. He walked over to the kitchen window staring out into the back yard. "You'd better hope you find this bastard before we do."

Erica could tell he was trying to hide his tears.

"Detective Barnes and I won't trouble you any further today," said Freeman. "Here is my card in case you think of anything else you believe might help us in this investigation."

"When can we see her?" asked Ian.

"You'll have to call the Coroner's office to make arrangements," said Erica. "The medical examiner is hoping to do the autopsy tomorrow morning. Unless she finds something undetectable from her initial exam, it should go rather quickly."

"Thank you, Detectives," said Ian. "I'll see you out."

They stopped at the door momentarily. "Remember, Mr. Flanders," said Erica. "If you think of anything, even if you feel it's minor or unimportant, give us a call. It could help us in this investigation."

"We'll do whatever it takes, Detective Barnes," said Ian. "*Whatever* it takes."

Chapter 4

The following morning Brent Freeman rushed into the Homicide Department flushed and breathing hard. Nearly late for his court appearance, he went directly to his desk and started leafing through papers.

"Aren't you supposed to be in court?" asked Erica.

"Yeah," he said, more testily than he'd intended. "I've just got to find one more thing...ah, here it is."

"This is the gang banger case, right?"

"Yeah. It's the one I investigated by myself last year when you had the flu. I'm one of the prosecution's first witnesses," said Brent. "It wasn't hard to prove with all the DNA evidence. I heard this prosecutor is new and hungry. This is her first solo homicide case. Should be a slam dunk for her."

"Is she pretty?" Erica said with a sideways glance.

"I don't know," he said, scowling at her. "I talked to the bald-headed guy when the case first started, so I haven't even met her. I think her name's Ralston. I doubt they would have given her this case if they didn't think she could handle it."

"Well, at least you're all purty in your best suit and tie."

"Cut it out," he retorted, irritated by her jab. "I've got to go or I'll be late. See you in the conference room at 1:30."

"See you then." He heard Erica say behind him as he scrambled from the room.

Brent made it to the courtroom just in time to find there were two others testifying ahead of him. He'd hoped to be number one or two so he could get back to work. He hated having to sit around and wait to testify, but it was all part of the job.

Forty-five minutes later, it was finally his turn to take the witness stand. He walked swiftly up the aisle smiling at Judge Norman Jackson. Judge Jackson was one of the fairest judges Brent had ever known and felt confident this trial would go smoothly. He stepped up to the witness stand to be sworn in. As the bailiff stepped aside, he saw her for the first time. She was beautiful and tall with rich, blonde hair falling delicately over her shoulders. The navy blue suit and light blue silky blouse she wore brought out the sparkle in her brilliant blue eyes. Her round, perfect face was angelic. He stared at her like a deer in headlights.

"Did you hear the question, Detective Freeman?" the prosecutor asked.

He awoke from his trance realizing he hadn't heard a word she'd said. "I'm sorry, could you repeat the question?" Brent said through his embarrassment.

"I asked if you were the primary investigating officer in this case."

"Yes," Brent answered.

"Please tell us, Detective Freeman," she said in a very professional manner, "what evidence was found to lead you to draw the conclusion the defendant, Hector Fuentes, was the one who shot and killed Franklin Henderson?"

"Franklin Henderson was shot at close range with a gun owned by Hector Fuentes," stated Brent. "Also, we found a foot print in the victim's blood near the place where the victim was shot. It matched a pair of shoes we later found in Mr. Fuentes' closet. Those shoes were taken into evidence by the Indianapolis-Marion County Forensic Service Crime Scene team and tested. The blood evidence on them was found to be a positive match to the DNA collected from the victim, Franklin Henderson."

"Did you recover the weapon used to kill Franklin Henderson?"

"Yes," answered Brent then watched her walk towards the evidence table. He saw her pick up a gun and bring it to him.

"Detective Freeman, is this the gun you recovered?"

"Yes," he replied. "It's a Sig Sauer P220. The Ballistics Unit test fired this weapon and found the bullets taken from the victim were fired from this gun."

"Where did you find the gun, Detective?"

"I found it in a dumpster behind Fagen's Jewelry Store, approximately 1,000 feet from the victim's body. It was wrapped in a jean jacket and flannel shirt. Forensics later determined through DNA analysis that the jacket and shirt belonged to Hector Fuentes. Forensics also found gunshot residue and blood spatter on the clothing. DNA testing showed this blood belonged to the victim, Franklin Henderson."

"So, Detective, was there any reason for you to believe anyone besides Mr. Fuentes used that gun to kill Mr. Henderson?"

"No," answered Brent.

"Did you find Hector Fuentes had a motive to kill Franklin Henderson?"

"During our investigation, we discovered Franklin Henderson and Hector Fuentes had an altercation a week before the killing. The patrol officers who responded to that altercation discovered Hector Fuentes' sister, Yolanda, had been dating Franklin Henderson secretly. I verified this after speaking with Miss Fuentes."

"Sort of a Romeo and Juliet story?" she quipped.

"Objection, your Honor," said the defense attorney as he jumped from his seat.

"Sustained," said Judge Jackson. "Miss Ralston, you will stick to the facts of this case. The jury will please disregard the reference."

"Sorry, your Honor," she said, turning her attention back to Brent. "Detective Freeman, was there anything else that might have made you suspicious of Mr. Fuentes?"

"Hector Fuentes told Franklin Henderson to quote, *keep your black ass away from my sister or I'll kill you*, unquote, according to Officer Donovan Bays."

Fuentes' stout attorney shot up out of his chair like a rocket. "Objection, your Honor," he shouted. "This is hearsay."

"Miss Ralston you should know better," stated Judge Jackson. "And you, Detective Freeman, have testified in enough courtrooms to know you cannot quote another officer in this manner. Objection sustained, the clerk will strike Detective Freeman's reference to what Officer Bays said from the record and the jury is instructed to disregard it. Proceed with your questioning, Miss Ralston."

"I have no more questions for this witness, your Honor," she said, gliding effortlessly back to her seat.

"Does the defense have any questions for this witness?" asked Judge Jackson.

"Not at this time, your Honor. However, we would like to reserve the right to recall the witness at a later date."

"So noted. You're dismissed, Detective Freeman," said the judge. "It's nearly noon so I suggest we break for lunch. Court will resume at 1:30 this afternoon." He tapped his gavel then everyone rose as the judge vacated his chair and left the courtroom.

Brent hung around on the pretext of asking Miss Ralston what she thought of his testimony. If he was lucky, he might convince her to have lunch with him and perhaps even discover her first name. He watched Miss Ralston place her files and papers into her briefcase then saw her turn her head slowly to peer over her shoulder.

"Detective Freeman," she said with a smile and a glint in her eye. "Are you waiting for me?"

"Well, I was just wondering if I did okay on the stand." He immediately realized how lame it sounded, but it was too late to take it back. "I mean, I hope the hearsay stuff didn't damage the case."

"You did very well. I doubt the jury will disregard anything," she whispered smiling at him with those luscious lips and pearl white teeth. "Is that all you wanted to ask me?" she asked raising an eyebrow.

"Actually, Miss Ralston," he began.

"Natalie. You can call me Natalie," she said. "Would you like to catch some lunch with me, Detective?"

"Brent," he said in surprise. "You can call me Brent, and yes, I'd love to have lunch with you. Although, I probably should have asked you instead..."

"Come on Brent," she laughed. "It's the twenty-first century. Let's grab a quick bite downstairs. As you heard, I've got to be back here at 1:30."

"Sounds like a plan," he said. "I've got to be in a meeting at 1:30 myself."

They went to the cafeteria and ordered tuna sandwiches, chips and soft drinks. They found a clean table in a quiet corner in the back.

"So, how long have you been in the prosecutor's office?" asked Brent.

"About a year," answered Natalie.

"Then why is this the first time I've seen you?" he asked. "I'm sure I wouldn't have forgotten you."

"I'll take that as a compliment, Detective," she said taking a small bite of her sandwich. She smiled seductively as she chewed and swallowed, then licked some mayonnaise off of her index finger sending chills down his spine. "I've been around, just not allowed to prosecute homicides until recently. We all have to pay our dues, you know."

"I guess so," he said, beginning to sweat a little. "So this is your first murder trial?"

"I've assisted on a couple, but this is my first opportunity to be first chair," she said. "I started with some misdemeanor robbery and battery cases. I guess the boss liked my style, because you usually don't get to be lead prosecutor on a homicide case until you've been with them for at least 18 months."

"I can tell you're really good," Brent said.

She leaned in close. "That's not the only thing I'm good at," she whispered then took another bite of her sandwich, followed by a slow sip of soda.

Brent blushed as he stared at her with his mouth wide open. "How dumb is this Fuentes character?" he said, flustered. "Throws his clothes in the dumpster, but keeps the shoes."

She laughed. "I guess he didn't want to toss those $200 Jordans in the garbage."

Knowing they probably shouldn't discuss the case any further, he finished eating while she talked about why she wanted to be a prosecutor. Her voice and her gorgeous blue eyes mesmerized him. He broke eye contact momentarily to glance at his watch. It was 1:15 already.

"Oh, wow, time flies doesn't it?" he said. "I've got to get back for my meeting and court will be starting again soon."

Natalie reached in her purse retrieving a business card and pen. She wrote something on the back of the card then held it up for him to see. "Official business," she said as she showed him the front of the card then flipped it over. "Unofficial business," she said, handing it to him. "Call me. I'd love to finish our conversation when we have more time."

He watched as she picked up her belongings then sauntered out of the cafeteria. Brent sighed, his heart thumping. He couldn't believe she'd given him her number without a lot of games. Natalie Ralston was definitely different.

Chapter 5

Erica watched Brent enter the conference room with a huge smile on his face. She squinted at him with curiosity. "Hey, what's going on? You don't look like a man who just spent three plus hours in boring court room proceedings."

"What? There a law against a guy smiling?" Brent smirked.

"Okay, who is she?"

"Who's who?" he asked, feigning innocence.

"You know perfectly well who," Erica snapped. "I know that look, Freeman. I've seen it before. Cough it up!"

"I just had a very pleasant lunch with the prosecutor, Natalie Ralston. That's all."

"Damn it, Freeman! You're already in love."

"I didn't say I was in love. I said we had lunch."

Before Erica could retort, Mark Chatham, Sophia Parelli and Chennelle Kendall came in with files and photos for the board.

"We'll finish this conversation later," whispered Erica through clenched teeth.

"What you got there?" Brent asked Chatham.

Chatham slid the folder of crime scene photos across the table. There she was again, Penny Flanders all laid out on her funeral bed with her eyes sewn open, glazed over by death.

"We tested the makeup and compared it to what she had in her bathroom. He used her eyeliner pencil to write the message on her forehead. No fingerprints on the pencil except hers," said Chatham. "Her eyes were sewn open with a thick nylon thread the bastard must have taken with him. We didn't find the thread or the needle on the premises."

"We were able to salvage enough of the two doors to determine he'd definitely kicked them in," began Parelli. "Nothing else was used as a battering ram. We photographed the dirt footprints we found on the carpet. We discovered they were left by a size nine and a half athletic shoe called Thunder Kicks."

"Never heard of them," said Brent.

"People who study martial arts wear them," said Erica.

"Oh, yeah. You would know Miss Brown Belt Barnes," Chatham sniggered.

"I'll have my black belt pretty soon, so watch out!" she said with a grin.

"Okay, okay, let's get back to the evidence," said Brent, steering everyone back to the job at hand.

"The only fingerprints found at the residence belonged to the victim and the dog walker so he must have worn gloves," said Parelli. "This was further supported when no fingerprints were found on her body despite the fingerlike bruises she sustained."

"Dr. Patel sent the clothing Flanders was wearing to Brian Palmer who's going over them now. Brian's preliminary findings show no blood or hairs on the sheets except for the victim's and of course a few dog hairs. We did recover the nightgown she was wearing before he re-clothed her. Palmer said there was a little human blood on it—like a nosebleed or something. The blood type matched the victim's, type A-positive. DNA will tell us for sure, but the lab results could take a while with the backup they're experiencing right now. There was also some fecal matter and urine on them. That's probably what she was wearing at time of death. Hopefully, those clothes will reveal something more than the obvious."

"Kendall, I'd like for you to go see Dr. Patel this afternoon," said Erica. "Find out if she's completed the autopsy or at least if she knows whether Miss Flanders was sexually assaulted. Great job everyone. Keep me posted on the clothing, Chatham."

Chatham nodded then he and Parelli departed, leaving the files of photos and reports. Erica took the photos and started arranging them on the board.

"Is there anything else before I go visit the good doctor?" asked Kendall.

"No, I'm going to finish this and Freeman can go through the reports," said Erica. "Come back here when you're finished."

"Sure thing," said Kendall as she left the room.

"Okay, Freeman," said Erica. "Spill it!"

"Sorry," he said with a smirk. "Got to get back to work."

"Fine! Be that way," she answered in a huff. "I'm going to go back to my desk and make some calls."

"Later, Barnes," he called after her as she went out the door.

***

Detective Kendall found Dr. Patel in her office looking grim and filling out paper work. Of course, Dr. Patel often looked grim. Chennelle knocked on the open office door and Dr. Patel looked up motioning for her to come in.

"Good afternoon, Dr. Patel. Detective Barnes asked me to stop by to see whether the autopsy was complete on Penny Flanders."

"Ah, yes," said Dr. Patel. "Very unpleasant. This is one sick individual."

"Were there signs of sexual assault or semen to collect?"

"Yes and no. The sexual assault occurred post mortem; however, a foreign object was used, not a human organ. The vagina and the rectum were severely battered and stretched and have several tears. I also found what appears to be a wood chip lodged in the cervix. Thank God he waited until she was dead."

"I wondered why there was so little blood at the scene."

"Since her blood was not circulating after he broke her neck, the blood found on scene probably occurred during the sexual assault," stated Dr. Patel. "There would still be blood in the tissues he tore. There was also urine and fecal matter found in the bathroom close to where I believe she died. Control of those functions is lost at death."

"Chatham mentioned that," stated Chennelle, gulping.

"You may want to ask Mark Chatham if they found tissues in the blood from the bathroom. The killer may have committed the assault in there before he dressed her and placed her on the bed. There is a pattern consistent with the ceramic tile of the bathroom floor on her right side indicating she was lying there for a while. Post mortem lividity did not set in completely until she was placed on her back. Also the dress was slit up the back to more easily put it on her, as they do at funeral homes."

"I hope the eye stitching was done post mortem as well," stated Chennelle.

"Most definitely. There would have been more blood caught in her eyebrows and eyelashes if it had occurred before death. I believe we would have found more defensive wounds or something under her nails. No one could have endured such pain without automatically trying to push the assailant's hands away. I saw no signs she tried to defend herself."

"Maybe she couldn't," suggested Chennelle.

"There were no marks to show she was bound in any fashion. She had definitely expired prior to this injury. I took out the threads and sent them to the lab along with some coarse hairs I found in the vagina, the wood chips, and some tissue samples. If we are lucky, some of the killer's DNA will be in these samples."

"Your initial assessment is correct? Miss Flanders died from a broken neck?"

"Yes, that is correct," answered Dr. Patel. "This killer was apparently very strong and knew precisely what he was doing. It was probably very quick and relatively painless."

"Thanks, Padma. I'm going back to the office to relay this to Barnes and Freeman. Thanks for bumping this one up a bit."

"No problem," Dr. Patel said as Chennelle headed towards the door. "I should have a written report ready by late tomorrow afternoon."

After returning to the Homicide Department, Kendall met with Barnes and Freeman in the conference room. She reported the details of the autopsy explaining the tests yet to be run. Chennelle watched as Barnes' face began to turn red.

"Holy Mother of God," exclaimed Barnes. "What an f'ing psycho!"

"You've got that right," agreed Chennelle. "I really don't understand necrophilia. What kind of pleasure could anyone get out of raping a corpse? It makes no sense."

"Some people just don't think like we do," stated Freeman.

"What's next?" asked Chennelle.

"We'll talk to some of her co-workers and friends, and try to get a picture of her life," said Freeman. "This doesn't seem like the type of murder involving someone she knew. It's more likely a stalker. Someone who admired her from afar—watching her, studying her routine and then striking when he felt the time was right."

"So you definitely think she was targeted?" asked Barnes.

"Yes. He sounds too organized to have just picked her at random," answered Freeman. "He was much too neat and precise about what he did to our victim. Even if he was a stranger, I bet he's been watching her for a while."

Chennelle cast a concerned look at Barnes, and then at Freeman. "You think we've got a serial killer here, don't you?" she asked.

"Killings like this one don't normally appear so well-planned at the beginning," stated Freeman. "I'm afraid there may be other practice victims out there we don't know about. We'd better be prepared."

Chapter 6

Day three of their investigation had been exhausting. Erica and Brent had made the rounds questioning Penny Flanders' colleagues and neighbors. No one they spoke with could think of anyone who might want to hurt her. She was friendly and always the first to lend a hand. She rarely consumed alcohol and didn't smoke. The All-American sweetheart meets Godzilla—and loses.

They would be meeting with the team again this afternoon to go over the results of the testing on the evidence collected by Dr. Patel. As they walked into the large conference room, they found Kendall going over a file.

"Got something new there, Kendall?" asked Freeman.

"It's just Dr. Patel's official report. I guess I was hoping something new would jump out and present itself. You know, like you see in the movies. All of a sudden some clue comes along; the cop has an epiphany and solves the case."

"We can only hope," said Erica with a faux dreamy smile.

"Right," Kendall chuckled. "So, did the two of you find out anything today?"

"Ms. Flanders was squeaky clean and everybody loved her," answered Freeman. "She apparently spent most of her free time volunteering at the no-kill animal shelter on the west side."

"So, nobody had any idea who could have done this to her?" asked Kendall.

"Nobody," the partners chimed in.

"Same here," stated Kendall.

Mark Chatham arrived with Dr. Brian Palmer. Palmer was one of IMPD's best DNA experts. In fact, he was overzealous about his work to the point of being irritating.

"Hey, Palmer, it's good to see you," Freeman said, shaking Dr. Palmer's hand.

"Good to see you as well, Detective. You may be even more thrilled to see me once I give you my latest news," Dr. Palmer said cheerfully. His discoveries always gave him an air of excitement. "First of all, the organ tissue samples we received did not have any detectable foreign human DNA. However, we did find something we believe was from her dog."

"What?" Erica exclaimed. "You've got to be kidding."

"Oh, no," said Dr. Palmer with surprise in his eyes. "I would never joke about something so serious. And, oh my, you didn't think I meant seminal fluids, did you?"

"No, Palmer," Erica said in disgust. "Her dog is a female."

"Oh, sorry," he said, blushing. "The hairs Dr. Patel found in the vagina were dog hairs. My assumption from the presence of these hairs is whatever the killer hit the dog with to render her unconscious was used for the sexual assault."

"The vet said Lucy was struck with something cylindrical from the appearance of the wound to her head," said Chatham. "He also found a small wood chip in the wound and sent it over. Under the microscope, we found it to be the same type of wood as the chip Dr. Patel found lodged in Miss Flanders' cervix. Parelli and I went back to search the crime scene a second time to see if we could find a wooden object fitting this description. We searched every inch of the house and surrounding properties. We found nothing which could have made those wounds on the dog or the victim. We figure the killer took it from the scene."

"Go on Dr. Palmer," said Erica, seeing Palmer anxiously bouncing on the balls of his feet. "What about the dress? Did you find anything there?"

"Funny you should ask, Detective Barnes," Palmer replied, his face brightening. "This perpetrator seemed to be very careful not to leave fingerprint evidence at the scene or seminal fluids on the body; however, he wasn't so careful with the dress." Dr. Palmer left a pregnant pause, pulling everyone's eyes upon him. "I found several long hairs on the dress which appear to be female, but not the victim's. Miss Flanders' hair was dark brown. The hairs found are gray at the roots and a lighter brown on the remainder of each strand. Tests showed the hair was dyed. This is why I think it's probably female," he shrugged, "but these days you just never know. When we have the DNA results we'll know the sex for sure and then my assistant will put them through our DNA database first. If we don't find it there, I'll have her run it through CODIS."

"Did you find anything else?" Erica asked impatiently. She was all too familiar with how Dr. Palmer liked to drag out his findings for his audience.

"Ah, yes," he said dramatically raising his right index finger. "I recovered two short brown hairs and some skin cells. The short hair could be male or female, but we won't know until the tests are complete. Lab's been a little backed up, but I'm hoping to get the results to you in a week, week and a half."

"What about the shoe print?" Kendall asked Chatham. "Have you been able to trace it to any particular store?"

"There are too many problems with tracing it. It was a shoe size nine and a half, which is a very common size," noted Chatham. "Then there are so many martial arts schools and supply stores along with the online stores. It would be a miracle to identify our killer this way. However, when you find the killer, we'll be able to match the print evidence to his shoes."

"Well, Dr. Palmer," said Erica, "let us know when you find out whether or not there's a hit on this DNA. In the meantime, Forensics will go over the collected evidence with a fine tooth comb and my team will continue the interviews. The DNA evidence will be big," said Erica. Of course she regretted saying this when she saw the huge grin it put on Palmer's face. His need for constant affirmation of his genius got on her nerves.

"Alright then," said Erica. "Let's get back to it."

Chapter 7

Back at her desk, Erica was typing her report from the interviews she and Freeman had conducted. The telephone rang and Freeman picked it up. "Homicide, Detective Freeman," he announced.

He blushed and Erica saw him turn to avoid her stare. "I don't see any reason why I shouldn't be able to help you with your problem," he said. "I'll meet you there at 6:30 sharp. See you then." Freeman hung up the phone with a smile.

Erica was still staring at him when he turned back to face her. She knew the call had to be from Natalie Ralston.

"What?" he said.

"Was the lady prosecutor on the phone?" she asked, grinning broadly.

"As a matter of fact, she was."

"Be careful," she said looking at him sternly. "Take your time with her. Enjoy dating for once. Don't fall so hard, so fast this time."

"Yes, Mother," he said.

"I'm serious, Brent. I don't want to see you get hurt again."

"Well then, don't watch," he said.

"I give up!"

"Good. I'd rather have loved and lost than never loved at all," he said as he waved his arms around like a Shakespearian actor.

"You're so full of crap!" she exclaimed. "Fine. Just don't come running to me when Miss Cutesy Prosecutor breaks your heart. Let's get started on these phone calls. You take the phone company. I'll start with my instructor, Masashi Nakamura, to see if he knows which retailers sell Thunder Kicks around here."

She felt a twinge of guilt. Erica didn't really mean what she'd said about not being there for him. Oh, she meant the part about him being full of crap, but personal or otherwise, she would always have his back.

Erica dialed the number for the Takeda Martial Arts Academy. The phone rang four times.

"Takeda Martial Arts Academy, this is Claudia. How may I help you?"

"May I speak to Sensei Nakamura?" Erica asked.

"He's with students right now. May I have him call you back?"

"Alright then. Please tell him Detective Erica Barnes from the Indianapolis Metropolitan Police Department called. He has my number."

"I'll make sure he gets the message."

"Thank you," said Erica then she hung up the phone. "Masashi's going to call me back. So, where are you taking her tonight?"

"We're meeting at St. Elmo's."

"Very fancy," she commented. "Just make sure you wear something nice. At least make a good impression so she knows you clean up well."

"I wear a suit every day. How much more *cleaned up* can I get?" They grinned at one another and she knew there were no hard feelings about her mothering.

It didn't take long for Freeman to contact the phone company and request the records he needed. He typed a few more notes, closed the file folder, and looked at his watch. It was after 5:00 already. "Hey, Barnes. You good with me leaving now?"

"Yeah. I'm going to wait here for Masashi's call. Shouldn't be much longer," she said staring down at her paperwork.

Freeman stood up and grabbed his jacket. "See you tomorrow."

"Sure," she said. "Have a good time." She watched him walk away with a little more bounce in his step than usual. She shook her head knowing he was not going to take her sage advice.

***

Brent entered St. Elmo's Restaurant in his best blue dress shirt and navy Dockers, a look of which even Erica Barnes couldn't disapprove. He canvassed the area trying to spot Natalie when the hostess approached. She was a young pretty brunette with a toothy white smile and long legs.

"Hello sir," she said smiling. "Are you Brent Freeman?"

"Yes," he said in surprise.

"A Miss Ralston is here and said you should be arriving soon."

Brent smiled and nodded.

"Come this way please," she told him.

He followed her, looking around, until he saw Natalie waving at him just a few tables ahead. It was an intimate corner of the room and Natalie looked stunning. What she did for the little black dress should probably be illegal. It set off her silky blonde hair and her sparkling blue eyes perfectly.

"You look great!" he said.

"So do you."

The waiter came by to ask if they wanted drinks and Brent ordered a nice Bordeaux. They were looking over their menus quietly when Brent had a tingling sensation of being watched. He looked up to see Natalie staring at him.

"You have the most unusual eyes," she said. "It's like looking into soft pools of caramel."

"Thanks," he said, shifting in his chair.

He'd eaten at St. Elmo's several times and always ordered the New York strip steak, medium with a baked potato and house salad. When the waiter came with their wine, they ordered their meals. Natalie ordered the Indiana Amish Chicken with green beans and a wedge salad and Brent ordered his usual steak. As they sipped their wine, Natalie continued to gaze into Brent's eyes.

“I hope you realize I’m not usually this forward with men I’ve only known for a day,” she commented.

“I really don’t know you well enough to be jumping to any conclusions,” he said squirming.

“What I’m trying to say is, I’m rarely this attracted to someone so quickly,” she said, with a sweet expression of admiration. She glanced down at her hands; fingers intertwined on the edge of the table.

“I’m sorry if I embarrassed you,” she said. “I’m coming on too strong.”

“No, no,” he insisted. “I’m just not used to so many compliments all in one sitting. It’s actually kind of nice.” He reached across the table, touching the top of her hand to reassure her.

“Okay, then,” she said. “Let’s get to know one another. How long have you been working in the Homicide Department?”

“Six years in Homicide, seven on the force,” he replied.

“That’s a long time to have to deal with some of the worst things humans can think of to do to one another.”

“I guess so,” he admitted. “We just have to try to do the best we can to focus on catching the S.O.B.s. Dr. Patel tells people she became a forensic pathologist because the dead need a voice. I guess it’s why Erica and I have done it so long. She and I have worked together for five years now.”

“I’ve not had the chance to meet her yet.”

“She’s good people,” said Brent. “She’s always got my back.”

“That’s good,” Natalie said, looking at her hands again.

“It’s like having an annoying older sister around irritating the crap out of me all day,” Brent said. Natalie looked up again smiling. “I think she’s seeing someone, but she won’t admit it. I’ll catch her one of these days. Maybe you can help me.”

Natalie laughed. “Sounds like fun!”

The waiter brought their salads. They continued their ‘getting to know one another’ conversation through dinner. Brent disclosed what it was like to grow up with three sisters, one of which was his twin. And he listened when Natalie told him how she would have welcomed a sibling or two. They discussed their reasons for choosing their current occupations in more depth. They laughed, they smiled, and they looked deeply into one another’s eyes. Then the waiter interrupted this wonderful repartee by asking if they would like to order dessert.

“I can’t eat another bite,” Natalie declared, patting her stomach. “You go ahead if you must, but nothing for me, thanks.”

“You can bring the check,” Brent told the waiter. “I’ll walk you to your car as soon as I pay the bill.”

“Uh...about the car,” she said coyly. “I had a friend drop me here...so, um...would you mind terribly taking me home?”

“Of course not, I’ll be glad to drive you home.”

Her blue eyes twinkled as she sipped the remainder of the Bordeaux from her glass.

Once the check was paid, Brent helped Natalie with her jacket, sliding it up her well-toned arms then slipping it over her shoulders. She turned and he saw the sensuality in her eyes. She took his hand as they walked out of the building and strolled in the direction of the car.

During the ride to Natalie's apartment, they continued to talk about their lives, families, and work. Brent became more at ease with her, laughing and sharing.

When they pulled into the parking lot of her apartment complex, Natalie asked, "Would you like to come up for some coffee?"

"I'd love a cup of coffee," he said.

He exited the car, and quickly walked to the passenger side and opened the door for her. She handed her keys to him. He unlocked the apartment door and turned to see her staring at him. He took her in his arms, pulling her close, kissing her deeply. He felt her hands glide up and down his back, heat rising between them.

She pulled back and whispered, "Let's go inside before the neighbors start gawking." Then she took him by the hand and led him inside, closing the door behind them.

Chapter 8

The phone rang. The caller ID showed it was Masashi Nakamura. "*Konnichiha,* Sensei," Erica said when she picked up the receiver.

"How is my favorite student this fine evening?" he asked.

"Actually, I'm working on a case where we believe the killer may have used some form of martial arts to murder his victim. He kicked down the door, broke the victim's neck very skillfully, and we found prints from a pair of Thunder Kicks. Do you know of anyone who sells them in the area, particularly the northwest side?"

"Those particular shoes are quite popular. You may have much difficulty finding the source. This may be especially difficult if it is a common size."

"I was afraid you'd say that, Sensei."

"I am so sorry I could not have been more help to you," Masashi apologized. "However, usually the only way one would have learned to kill with such a move would be through training with combative experts. This could possibly narrow your search."

"I don't know why I didn't think of that," she said.

"Because young one, you are only using the skills taught to you by your police academy. You must sometimes look deeper within yourself and go with your feelings, rather than logic."

"Thank you, wise one," she said respectfully.

"You are most welcome. If there is anything else I can do to help, please let me know."

"I will," she replied. "I will see you in class on Saturday morning."

"I look forward to it, young one."

Before leaving for the day, she called Dr. Palmer's office and left a voice mail message for him. "Hey, Doc," she said. "Once you've gone through CODIS with those DNA results, try military records as well. Our guy may have learned some of his moves as part of some special combat group."

Seems like a good time to go home and soak in a nice hot tub of bubbles, she thought. Then she cleared her desk and smiled, as she anticipated a relaxing evening at home with her secret lover.

It was past 7:30 p. m. when Erica finally entered the parking garage. She was walking towards her car when she heard someone call her name.

"Detective Barnes," he called again. "That is you, isn't it Detective Barnes?"

Erica turned to see Peter Elliott, the *Indianapolis Star* reporter. Crap! Damn annoying reporters.

"How are you, Detective?" Peter asked politely.

"Tired. It's been a long day," she snapped.

"I'm sure the murder of Penny Flanders has been difficult. Poor young Miss Harden was terribly shaken."

"You didn't hassle her with questions, did you?" Erica blurted.

"Oh, no. She was so sweet and so upset. I just couldn't. Besides, one of your officers insisted on escorting her home that day. None of us had a chance to talk to her. She's not left her house since it happened."

"So Mr. Elliott, are you really concerned about my well-being or is there something you want to ask me?"

"Is there anything new you can tell me about the Flanders case? Any leads yet?"

"I'm not at liberty to discuss this case with you, Mr. Elliott. You know the rules."

"Can't blame me for trying," he said with a boyish grin. "Would you like to get a bite to eat with me?"

This was a question she hadn't expected. "Thank you for asking, but a nice hot bath is waiting for me along with some tasty leftover spaghetti."

"Okay, maybe another time. Have a good evening," he said then turned and walked away.

Erica watched until he was out of sight. She wanted to make sure he was long gone before she got in her car. She didn't like how reporters suddenly appeared out of nowhere and the next thing you knew they were right in your face. She watched as he disappeared around the corner.

As Erica drove towards her apartment complex, she couldn't help remembering what Masashi had told her about going with your gut instead of always relying on logic. The encounter with Peter Elliott had spooked her for some reason, so she kept looking in her rearview mirror to make sure he didn't follow her. She kept telling herself she was being paranoid, but Masashi's words kept ringing in her ears.

As she left her car, she continued to look around. Then she shook her head and retrieved her mailbox key from her purse as she entered the building.

"Well, hello again," said an all too familiar male voice.

Erica dropped her purse, fear taking over. She jumped back reaching for her gun. "Are you following me?" she demanded removing her hand from her weapon. There by the mailboxes stood Peter Elliott.

"I could ask you the same thing, Detective. Do you live here?" Peter asked, but didn't wait for an answer. "I live on the third floor, apartment 315. I was just about to retrieve my mail." He glanced at the names on the boxes. "Oh, I see you live in 215. Isn't this a wild coincidence?"

"Yes, isn't it," she said without taking her eyes off of him as he opened his mailbox.

"Guess I'll see you around then," he said grinning.

She watched Peter take the stairs two at a time until he disappeared. When he was out of sight, she picked up her purse then put the mailbox key in the lock. Before she could turn the key, someone grabbed her from behind. She dropped her purse again; swiftly gut punching her attacker with her elbow knocking him to the floor.

"Uncle, uncle," he yelped, holding his abdomen, rolling on the floor.

"Oh, my God, Ben," she exclaimed. "I'm so sorry!" Erica bent down to see if he was alright. "I didn't realize it was you!"

"I hope not," he said, trying to catch his breath.

"There was this reporter who showed up in the parking lot at work, and then he was here and told me he lives here, and I was spooked and then..."

"It's okay, Erica," Ben coughed. "I should have known better than to grab you from behind. Can we get up off of the floor now before all the neighbors come out and see how you kicked my ass?"

"Okay, sweetheart," she said and kissed him.

"Maybe I should let you kick my ass more often."

"Shut up and get up," she said ruffling his sandy blonde hair. "Let me get my purse and mail."

"At least I know I don't have to worry about you being able to take care of yourself." Ben got to his feet, still holding his mid-section.

"Looks like you need a hot bubble bath more than I do, Sergeant Jacobs," said Erica.

"I'm willing to share."

"I just may take you up on it," she cooed.

Chapter 9

Erica was already sitting at her desk when Freeman arrived in the morning. She was concentrating intently on her computer screen and was startled by Freeman's appearance at her side.

"Hey," she said, frowning. "Don't be sneaking up on me."

"I didn't sneak," he protested, plopping down in the chair next to her desk. "What's got you so focused you can't hear my number tens clomping across the floor?"

"I'm doing some research," Erica answered. "Do you remember those reporters who were first to arrive at the Flanders' crime scene?"

"Yeah. What about them?"

"Well, last night when I left, Peter Elliott from the *Star* stopped me in the parking lot."

"Did he want an update on the case?" Freeman asked.

"That's what I thought at first, but to tell you the truth, I'm not sure."

Freeman looked confused. "What are you babbling about, Barnes? Just spit it out."

"Don't get testy with me, mister, or I won't tell you anything!" He frowned at her again, but she ignored him as she carried on with her story.

"When he stopped me, I assumed he wanted information about the case, but I remembered I was the one who asked him if that's what he wanted. The more I thought about it, the more I realized he gave up way too easy."

"Was that it?" asked Freeman.

"No. When I reminded him I couldn't talk about the case, he asked me out to dinner."

"He *what?*"

"I know you're not deaf, Freeman."

"What did you tell him?"

"No, of course. The guy gives me the creeps. He took it well, but then I got to my apartment building and he popped up again."

Freeman sat up straighter and touched Erica's arm. "Did he follow you there?"

"I thought so, but it turns out he lives in my building."

"No shit. Are you sure?"

"Yes," she answered. "Like I said, I've been doing research this morning. I started with my landlord. Peter's been living there for about a month in the apartment above mine. I guess I had no reason to notice him until now."

"Maybe it's just a coincidence. Did you find out anything else about him?"

"He's been with the *Indianapolis Star* for a couple of months. They said he came from somewhere in Montana. Of course, they wanted to know why I was so interested."

"What'd you tell them?"

"I said Peter had been at one of our crime scenes and I was checking to make sure he really worked for them."

"They buy it?" he asked.

"I think so, but you can never tell with the media. So far, I'm not finding him in any of our databases." She sighed, and then changed gears. "So, how'd it go last night?"

"What?" he said.

"Was it that bad?" teased Erica. "You didn't go in jeans and a tee shirt, did you?"

"I would never!" he exclaimed. "We had a great time."

Erica gasped when she saw the wide grin and dreamy expression on his face. "You slept with her?"

"Maybe we should get started on the Flanders case," he said.

"Ah man, you did." She knew he was trying to deflect her comment. "I knew this would happen."

"Can it, Barnes. Let's get back to work."

"You're hopeless," she spewed. "Fine. Mr. Nakamura called back before I left last night. He pretty much told me we're looking for the proverbial *needle in a haystack* when it comes to those shoes."

"Oh well, I didn't think we'd get anywhere with the shoes. Whoever did this could have purchased them anywhere—another city, another state, the internet."

"Did you check to see if the phone records came in yet? Or, were you too busy sneaking up on me to check your desk?" She looked up for a reaction. She'd had plenty of experience teasing a little brother in her youth and Freeman had plenty of experience being on the receiving end from his two older sisters.

Freeman rolled his eyes and walked over to his desk. He found the phone records in a folder. "Here," he said handing Erica some of the paperwork. "You check out these numbers from her cell and I'll do her home phone."

"I thought I was in charge," she said.

"Can it, Barnes," said Freeman. "Just do it."

She smirked as she picked up the records.

***

After a couple of hours, they found there were no calls made to cause them to believe Penny Flanders had spoken to her killer. Most of the calls were to family and friends, her office, the shelter and take-out restaurants.

"Damn it," Freeman swore, flinging the folder onto his desk. "The trail just keeps getting colder."

"I hear ya," she agreed. "I did have an interesting conversation with a friend of Flanders." She paused as she flipped through some pages in her notebook. "A Melanie Carson. I asked if she knew whether Miss Flanders was taking any martial arts classes or dating any men who were. She told me Penny wasn't into men."

"Huh?"

Erica looked at him, one eyebrow raised. "I think you know what I mean."

Then a bright spark of recognition shown in Freeman's eyes just before his face turned bright red.

"Miss Carson wasn't her lover or anything," Erica continued. "To her knowledge, she didn't think Flanders was dating anyone. Flanders broke up with her last girlfriend a couple of years ago. Plus, she never told her parents or brothers about her sexual preferences."

"A good Irish Catholic family like the Flanders probably wouldn't have taken it well," Freeman commented. "Maybe someone she turned down got pissed off and decided to teach her a lesson."

"Doubt it. A guy like that would have done it spur of the moment. He wouldn't have killed her quickly and then raped her with an object. He would have wanted her to suffer the humiliation of taking her against her will before he did her in."

"You're right," he said. "I'm just getting frustrated trying to figure this one out."

"But where would she have met a guy who was into martial arts? Miss Carson said Penny wouldn't have been hanging around with macho types. She abhorred violence of any kind."

"Then looks like we're screwed," Freeman conceded. "Back to square one, I guess."

"Unless," Erica said thinking aloud. "Brent, we need to go to the animal shelter where she volunteered. Maybe she met someone there. They get all kinds of volunteers."

"Sounds like a good place to start," Freeman agreed. "Good thinking, Barnes, let's go."

It took about 20 minutes to get to the west side animal shelter. Upon entering the shelter, Erica could hear the barking of several dogs coming from an area beyond the counter. She noticed two tall cages to her right where several cats resided. Each was perched on a different level of a beige carpeted climbing apparatus.

Freeman walked to the counter and Erica heard a buzzer sound. From the back came a stout woman approximately 50 years of age with graying hair and light blue eyes wearing jeans and a Purdue University sweatshirt.

"Hello," she said her voice sweet and simpering. "Are you looking for a cat or a dog?"

"Neither." Erica said showing her badge to the woman. "I'm Detective Barnes and this is Detective Freeman from the IMPD Homicide Department. We're investigating the death of Penny Flanders and understand she volunteered here."

"Oh, yes," she said, her face falling into sadness. "We heard about Penny. She was one of our most loyal volunteers. She was here every Saturday morning like clockwork. Would do whatever we needed done. She even cleaned out the kennels."

"Sounds like she loved animals, Miss...," said Freeman.

"Oh my, where are my manners. My name is Sherry Wolff. Mrs. Sherry Wolff. I've managed this shelter for 10 years now. Penny was real special. At times I thought she loved animals more than people."

"Sometimes we feel that way too, Mrs. Wolff," Freeman commented. "Do you have many male volunteers at the shelter?"

"Of course," she chuckled. "Men have hearts, too."

"Was there any male volunteer Miss Flanders spoke with often, or who may have been harassing her in any way?" inquired Erica.

"You know, I do think I remember Penny complaining about a fellow who used to come in here on Saturday mornings. I finally told him I really needed him later in the day to keep him from pestering her. He worked Saturday afternoons for a while and then stopped coming. Let me see if I can find his card."

Mrs. Wolff rifled through a box of index cards then pulled one out with a smile of accomplishment. "Yes, here it is. His name is Lee Sellers. This card has his home address and cell phone number. Shall I make a copy for you?"

"That would be great, Mrs. Wolff," said Freeman. "Thanks for your help."

Erica didn't wait until they got back to the office to get in touch with Lee Sellers. She called his cell phone finding him at his office. He worked for the local Coca Cola plant as a supervisor. His shift would be over at 3:00 in the afternoon. He agreed to come to the station as soon as he left the plant.

***

At 3:45 p.m., Erica got the call an officer had placed Sellers in Interrogation Room 3. "If we want to find out if he has any problems with strong-willed women, maybe I should question him, and you can watch," she suggested.

"Sounds like a plan," Freeman agreed.

Freeman went into the observation room to watch the interview. Erica walked into the interrogation room, notepad in hand. Lee Sellers was Caucasian with spiky brown hair dyed blond at the tips, and hazel eyes. She could see Sellers spent a lot of time at the gym by his huge upper arms and chest. It was difficult to assess his height because he'd already taken a seat.

"Good afternoon, Mr. Sellers," she said. "Thank you for coming down here to talk to me."

"No problem." Sellers grinned, looking her up and down. "You're not exactly what I thought a lady cop would look like."

"What did you expect, Mr. Sellers? Buck teeth and a shaved head?"

"No," he said looking surprised, but recovering quickly. "I just didn't think you'd be so good lookin'."

"Cut the flattery. It doesn't impress me. I've got a murder to solve."

"I heard about the Flanders chick," said Sellers. "Too bad, she was a real looker, too."

"It doesn't surprise me that you noticed," said Erica. "It's our understanding you came on to her a little too often at the animal shelter where you both volunteered."

"Who told you that—the old bat who runs the place?"

"I found Mrs. Wolff to be very friendly and kind."

"I didn't mean she wasn't nice. She just needs to mind her own business."

"But she did have to change your schedule because of Miss Flanders' complaints, didn't she?"

"Penny never said anything to me. She said no to a couple of dates, but I thought she was just playin' hard to get."

"I see," Erica commented as she jotted down some notes. "Where were you at 7:00 a.m. this past Tuesday morning?"

"I was at work. My shift starts at 7:00," he sneered.

"Should be easy enough to confirm," she said.

"You're not thinkin' I had anything to do with what happened to her, are ya? I may have been a little aggressive about askin' her out, but I never even knew where she lived."

"Really?" said Erica. "Mrs. Wolff keeps a card box with all the volunteers' addresses right out where anyone could take a look at them. How am I supposed to know you didn't look through those cards to get Penny's address?"

"But I didn't," he spluttered. "Look, Detective, I don't have any trouble gettin' women. I was just attracted to her, that's all. She wasn't important enough to me to look her up."

"I notice you like to work out."

"Yeah, so? I go to the gym every day. Gotta keep up my physique."

"Are you into martial arts?"

"Not lately."

"What do you mean, 'not lately'?" she pushed.

"I mean," he said, a vein popping out in his forehead as his face reddened. "I took Karate lessons for two years, about five years ago. It just wasn't my thing."

"Learn any hand-to-hand combat moves?" she asked.

"Is that how she died? Some Karate blow? Listen, sister, I've had about enough. If you're lookin' to charge me with somethin', do it and get me a lawyer. If not, I'm goin' home."

"Of course you are free to go, Mr. Sellers. Just make sure you don't leave town until we clear you as a suspect."

"I knew it," he fumed. "All you chicks are the same. You're teasers." He stood and glared at her.

Freeman burst into the interrogation room. "Detective Barnes," he said, surprise in his voice. "I thought I had this room booked."

"It's all yours," she said keeping her cool and continuing to stare at Sellers. "Mr. Sellers and I are finished."

Sellers stormed around the table towards the door. He glared at Erica and murmured something under his breath as he walked out the door.

"Did you hear what he said?" asked Freeman.

"Nope," Erica answered holding back the plethora of profanity streaming through her head. "I'm going to check his alibi. The guy has a quick temper. I don't think he's our killer, but he's the best suspect we have at the moment."

"He sounds more like one of those blowhards who thinks he's a lady's man."

"Damn I'm glad it's Friday," Erica said. "I'm going to write this up and head home. What about you? Any plans?"

"Not until Sunday afternoon. Natalie is going to visit her parents in Evansville."

"And Miss Wonderful didn't invite you to go with her? Geez, Brent, you've known her almost three whole days now. What's the hold up?"

"Can it, Barnes."

Chapter 10

Erica sighed in relief and anticipation. It was finally Saturday night. She had a great lesson with Mr. Nakamura earlier in the day. He always encouraged her and told her she was ready for Shodan—first-degree black belt.

While standing in her kitchen, putting the last minute touches on her pork roast dinner, the doorbell rang. She looked through the peephole, and then checked herself in the mirror next to the door to make sure her lipstick was straight and her hair was in place. Putting on her best smile, she opened the door.

"Well, well, Sergeant Jacobs. Please do come in," she said with a sensual smile and a beckoning wave of her hand.

"You don't have to call me Sergeant," he quipped.

"Well, then Ben. Why don't you come on in, take off your gun, and stay awhile."

Erica had been seeing Benjamin Jacobs secretly for about nine months now. Erica had worked with him when Major Stevenson's wife went missing a year and a half ago. Ben and his partner, Tyrone Mayhew, worked the missing person case. Erica became involved when Mrs. Stevenson's bloody car was found implying a possible homicide.

Ben pushed the door shut, took off his jacket, and tossed it on the couch. He took Erica in his arms and kissed her full, luscious lips massaging her back as he held her.

"That was nice," she said as she pulled away, stroking his face. Then she walked with more sway in her hips than usual, glancing over her shoulder as she went back to the kitchen. She was definitely enjoying the attention. "Would you be interested in setting the table for me? The roast is ready."

"I'd be delighted, my dear," he answered. Ben went to the kitchen cabinet, running his hand lightly down the middle of Erica's back as he passed her. She smiled at his touch and the tingling sensation it gave her.

"Is it white or red with pork?" he asked.

"Go with the Merlot."

Ben set the table and opened the Merlot to let it breathe. Erica pointed to the refrigerator where he found the salads she had already prepared. She sliced the roast and served it with a combination of Irish potatoes and carrots which had just the right blend of parsley and spices.

As they sat down to eat, Ben took Erica's hand and kissed it. "This looks great," he said. "You've really outdone yourself tonight."

"Thanks," she said with a warm blush. "You know, Ben, when we were working the Stevenson case, I never pictured you as such a romantic. I'm glad I said yes when you asked me out."

"Me, too. You surprised me as well. I never would have thought you could be so domestic. You're a great cook, a wonderful lover, and my best friend."

"I feel the same way," she said smiling. "We'd better eat this before it gets cold."

Ben and Erica talked about work and how much fun it was to pull the wool over their partners' eyes. "Freeman is so clueless. Of course, I can tell when *he's* in love. He gets this bizarre, dreamy look in his eyes," said Erica.

"Is he seeing someone?"

"He went to testify in court on the Fuentes murder case Wednesday morning and met the new prosecutor, Natalie Ralston. Apparently, they went to lunch after court recessed and he came back all smiley and dazed-looking. That can only mean one thing in my opinion. The following night, they went to St. Elmo's and he spent the night with her."

"Wow, he does move fast," said Ben.

"I know. That's what worries me. I just hope he doesn't fall for her like he did for Mandy Stevenson. He was hurting from his break up from her for months."

"Mayhew suspects something's going on. At first, I was paranoid and thought he might follow me around, but then I realized Mr. Family Man wouldn't have time for such nonsense. I just hope when I get married I have the kind of relationship Tyrone and Jada have. He's so dedicated to her and the boys, *and* to the little one that's on the way."

"Did they have the test done to find out what sex the baby is?"

"They did an ultrasound to make sure the baby was okay, but Jada doesn't want to know the sex. She's afraid if she knew it was another boy she'd be disappointed and somehow the baby would sense it. She says once the baby's in her arms, it won't matter whether it's a girl or boy."

"So is Daddy getting excited?"

"Oh, yeah. Like I said, he's big on his role as father and husband. Do you ever think about having kids, Erica?"

"I've thought about it," she said tentatively. "I guess I'm just not sure how it would fit in with a career in police work, especially if both parents are cops."

"I see what you mean. It's hard to think of leaving them without a father. Like you said, it's something both of us would have to give a lot of consideration before jumping in."

They finished their dinner, cleared the table, and when Erica had placed the last dish in the dishwasher, Ben came up behind her and hugged her. He moved her hair gently away, kissing the nape of her neck.

Caressing her shoulders, he continued to kiss her neck, sending chills of pleasure through her. Turning her around slowly until their eyes met, his gaze filled her with love. Passion pulsed through her and she ached for him.

She ran her fingers through his thick, sandy blond hair then down his neck to his shoulders, and his chest. The excitement was building in her and she shivered as he pulled her closer. She could feel his passion growing.

"I think I'm ready for dessert," she said playfully taking his hand, leading him to the bedroom.

In the doorway, he pulled her close once more, kissing her passionately. "Can I stay tonight?" he asked.

"I think that's a fabulous idea."

Chapter 11

Marilyn Novak had finally decided to get back into life and go out for some fun. Since her divorce two years ago, she'd been depressed and lonely, but afraid to test the waters. It was Saturday night and her best friend, Phoebe, had convinced her to meet her at the local pub.

They were sipping their second round of Cosmos when a good-looking man with wavy auburn hair and deep blue eyes approached. He was smiling at Marilyn. She was taken aback by the attention. The proverbial butterflies tickled her stomach.

Phoebe excused herself to go to the bathroom. Marilyn was glad it was semi-dark in the room so this young man wouldn't see her blush. Her heart was racing. She didn't know what to say. It had been years since she'd done anything like this.

"Hi," he said. "My name is Keith."

"Nice to meet you, Keith," she said.

There was a long pause. He raised an eyebrow. "And you are?"

Panic struck her, realizing she'd already done something stupid. "I'm so sorry!" she sputtered. "Marilyn. My name is Marilyn."

"I've seen your friend in here a couple of times, but I don't recall seeing you. I know I'd remember a pretty woman like you."

Very slick, she thought, as she flushed with pleasure. Logically she knew this was a line to get into her pants, but she loved the ego boost.

After some time and conversation had passed, Marilyn realized Phoebe hadn't returned from the bathroom. She looked around and spotted her at the bar talking to a couple of men, flipping her long blonde hair flirtatiously. She started to think her best friend had set her up for a night of guilty pleasures. It had been more than two years since she'd indulged in sex. She had a feeling Keith would definitely fit the bill. He was very attractive, or at least that's what her third Cosmo was saying.

"Marilyn. Earth to Marilyn," Keith said.

"Oh, sorry," she said, startled back into their conversation.

"I asked if you might want to get out of here," he said.

"You bet I do. Let's go to my place," she boldly suggested. She caught Phoebe's eye and waved goodbye. Her impish smile and thumbs up told Marilyn this was something Phoebe hoped would happen.

Minutes later, back at her place, Marilyn and Keith were ripping each other's clothes off. She was like a tigress—all her pent up lust boiling. He kissed her so hard she was sure she'd have swollen lips in the morning, but she didn't care. She was into the moment.

When they reached her bed, she turned and yanked the spread from it just before he reached around her. He caressed her breasts while kissing the nape of her neck. She was wet with sweat and passion.

Marilyn fell onto the bed. Keith moved on top of her. She was enthralled with him, ready to experience what she'd been missing for so long.

Then before she knew it, it was over. Keith fell off of her moaning with pleasure while she lay there disappointed. Now what was she supposed to do?

"That was great, Babe." he said.

She supposed this was what he said to all of his one-night-stands.

"What the hell is going on here?" shouted a dark figure in the doorway.

"What the fuck?" shouted Keith. He glared at Marilyn. "You said the ex was dead."

Marilyn sat there frozen with fear, sheet pulled up to her neck. She thought the voice sounded vaguely familiar, but wasn't sure. Who was he, and why was he in her house?

"I can't believe you'd sleep with this guy," he screamed at her. "You're such a slut."

"Look, pal," said Keith, "I didn't realize she had a boyfriend or a husband or anything. She invited me to come over."

"So you're blaming her?" asked the intruder, turning his anger on Keith. "You're the only one I heard groaning. Fuck her and leave her, right? That's what they all do?"

Marilyn was confused. He must have her mixed up with someone else. She'd married her high school sweetheart who was her first sexual experience. Keith was the second. She couldn't move or speak to deny his claims and began to tremble as she sensed the man's anger grow.

"Marilyn, who is this asshole?" asked Keith.

Her mouth and throat had become dry. When she finally answered, her voice was an almost inaudible squeak. "I don't know."

"Liar!" screamed the intruder stepping into the room, but staying in darkness.

Keith grabbed his boxers and started to walk toward the door. "I'll leave you two to sort this out."

Marilyn watched in horror as the intruder slammed his foot into Keith's chest. Keith went down gasping and sputtering, blood spewing from his mouth. She screamed and covered her eyes with her hands, dropping the sheet, revealing her nakedness.

"This is all your fault," she heard the man say to her in a much too calm voice. Then she slowly removed her hands from her eyes turning an upward glance, and meeting the stare of the man beside her bed.

Chapter 12

Erica lay with her back to Ben, his arm draped over her, holding her close. Half asleep enjoying the warmth of his body, she started when her cell phone rang. Blurry-eyed and slightly incoherent, she looked at the alarm clock. "What the…holy crap. It's 7:00 a.m. on a Sunday. This better be an emergency."

As she reached for the phone, Ben asked, "'Sup?"

"Nothing, go back to sleep." He did as she said, rolling to his other side breathing heavily.

Caller ID indicated Freeman. She answered it testily. "You know what time it is?"

"Unfortunately, I do," he said. "We've got another one, or should I say two."

"*Crap*. Hang on a minute." She slipped out of bed, put on a robe, and went to the living room. "Okay, go ahead."

"It's bad, Barnes. One female, one male. Stevenson wants us on this one because there are similarities to the Flanders case."

"Okay. I'll meet you there," she said looking for her note pad. Brent told her he'd pick her up instead and would be there in approximately thirty minutes.

Erica scurried around the apartment picking up Ben's jacket, gun, and keys, depositing them in the bedroom. She quickly washed her face, brushed her teeth, and dressed, dabbing on minimal makeup. She left a note for Ben which simply said:

Sorry Ben, was called out on a case per Stevenson's request. I've left a spare key to the apartment in case you need to leave before I return. Add it to your key ring. I think it's about time, don't you?

Love, Erica.

Not wanting Freeman to stumble onto her romance, Erica decided it best to meet him outside. It was way too much fun keeping him guessing about whether or not she was involved with someone.

While she waited on the sidewalk in front of her building, a sinking feeling someone was watching nearby haunted her. She glanced around the parking lot, but didn't see anyone. She looked up at the windows of the apartment building, but there were no open drapes or blinds.

Glancing around, she looked carefully at the colorful array of parking space occupants. No one sat in the green Focus, the silver Camry, or the yellow Mustang. There was a white Lexus and a red Camaro—both unoccupied. She decided she was being paranoid. There are too many people sneaking up on her these days.

She jumped as she heard a car approaching, turning to see Freeman's blue Honda coming towards her. He stopped and gave her a weak smile as she slid into the passenger seat and took a steaming cup of coffee from him.

"Details," she said simply.

"Like I said before, two victims this time. Kendall is already at the scene. She said it looks like he may have taken the male out first with a swift kick to the chest. Female appears to be the same as Flanders."

"Dress, eyes, broken neck?" she said, horrified at the thought this wouldn't be the last time this occurred.

He frowned. "Afraid so. Sanchez and Lloyd were first responders. They called Chatham and he's sending a team out there. Not sure who the D.I. on-call is, but they asked Dispatch to have someone sent out ASAP."

"What the hell is going on, Brent?" Erica asked. "Could we really have a serial killer on our hands?" She shivered at the idea.

"I expect with this murder being so similar to Flanders, Stevenson will be pushing for them to make the DNA from that case a priority. I also have no doubt the mayor will be calling Deputy Chief Lewis once he hears about this one."

"You realize this means the FBI will be called in."

"Yes. But what can we do? Somebody like this doesn't just materialize out of thin air, does he? Since we didn't find any similar cases around here after Flanders was killed, I suspect he perfected his craft somewhere else."

Erica sipped her coffee as they drove. After a few moments of silence, she turned to her partner and said, "Don't suppose you brought me a donut?"

Freeman looked at her, creasing his brow.

"*What*?" she said. "You didn't give me enough time to eat."

Freeman pulled up in front of the three-bedroom ranch home owned by Marilyn Novak. As they were walking towards the house, Erica noticed Peter Elliott among the news media hounds being kept at bay. To her surprise, he looked directly at her and smiled. She felt uneasy at this contact, but saw him turn away as Major Stevenson approached to give the media a statement.

She and Freeman signed in with Patrol Officer Lloyd, donned gloves and entered the residence. The living room seemed to be intact with no signs of a struggle. The only thing out of place was the string of clothes leading to the back hallway where the bedrooms were located.

"Glad to see you two could make it," quipped Kendall as she came into the living room.

"What do we have so far?" asked Erica.

"The D.I. is Nate Spalding. He's back there examining the bodies as we speak. Said his preliminary assessment would be the male got out of bed to stop the intruder, but met with a kick to the chest shattering the sternum and some of the ribs. He expects Dr. Patel will find bone fragments in the heart and lungs. Poor guy didn't have a chance. Most likely laid there gasping for air and bleeding internally for a while."

"We got an ID on the dead guy?" Erica asked.

"Found a wallet in the jeans over there on the couch," said Kendall. "License belongs to a Keith Gray, age 28; address is on North Keystone."

"So Keith either just moved in or doesn't live here," stated Freeman.

"No signs of him living here. There aren't any men's clothes in the closets or dressers. No photos of him around or in her wallet. However, I did find a credit card receipt dated last night in his pocket for the bar around the corner, The Club. Maybe that's where they hooked up."

Erica walked away from Kendall and Freeman, taking a look around the house. There was a photo on the end table of a young woman with dark, medium length hair with her arm around an older woman whose dark hair was streaked with gray. Erica wondered if this woman could be the victim's mother. In the bookcase were a variety of novels by Anne Rice, Stephanie Meyer, and Laurell K. Hamilton. The victim was into vampires.

"Hey, Barnes!" Freeman shouted, stirring her from her thoughts. "You ready to go check out our victims?"

She took one more sweeping look at the room. Taking it all in, she hoped to get to know Marilyn Novak well enough to determine why the killer chose her.

"Yeah. As ready as I'm ever going to get," she replied. "By the way, Kendall, who called it in?"

"A neighbor, after she heard Novak's mother screaming for help," Kendall said, frowning and shaking her head. "She and her daughter planned to go out for a mother-daughter breakfast before church this morning. Mom's name is Phillis Gates; age 60; lives about 5 miles from here. She tried to call Marilyn several times at round 6:00 this morning with no answer, so she came over and found this mess."

"Where is she now?" asked Erica.

"Ambulance took her to St. Vincent Hospital. She was having trouble breathing and experiencing chest pains. We decided to get her some medical attention, so we didn't have a chance to question her."

They entered the bedroom at the end of the hallway. Sophia Parelli was taking photos, while Nate Spalding was examining the female victim.

"Hey, Parelli," said Freeman. "The new kid in CSI gets Sunday duty, huh?"

"Something like that," she replied. "I'm snapping photos. Jones will be here any minute to check for prints and Black is outside looking for shoeprints and point of entry."

"I expect there to be a nice shoe print on the male victim's chest," interjected Spalding. "It will show up more in a day or so. You'll want to get photos before Dr. Patel cuts into him."

"Are you familiar with the Flanders' case?" Erica asked Spalding.

"Dr. Patel showed me the photos," he answered. "This has got to be the same person. Female's neck appears to be broken in the same manner. She's dressed the same with a red rose in her hand and her eyes sewn open with *SEE ME* written on her forehead in red lipstick."

"We didn't find any nightclothes," said Parelli. "They were probably sleeping in the nude after their romp when the killer came in. No need to bash in the bedroom door this time as it appears to have been open. No dog to warn the victims of an intruder."

"Any other witnesses, Kendall?" asked Erica.

"Neighbors didn't hear or see anything," she answered. "No one knew anything was wrong until they heard her mother screaming in the front yard."

"Well, I guess you know what we've got to do next," Freeman directed Erica.

Erica nodded. They'd have to go to St. Vincent and see how Mrs. Gates was doing. If the doctor said it was okay, they'd interview her.

"Kendall's got this scene under control. Might as well let these guys do what they gotta do; and go do what we gotta do," Erica stated. "I hate hospitals."

Chapter 13

St. Vincent Hospital was located on the far northwest side of Indianapolis off of West 86th Street. Freeman parked the car in the emergency room parking area. Erica cringed as they walked toward the emergency room doors. Unwanted memories of her mother's illness flashed through her mind. They entered to find a relatively empty waiting room and a curly-haired nurse sitting at the trauma desk.

"May I help you," she asked.

Erica presented her badge. "I'm Detective Barnes and this is Detective Freeman. We are investigating a homicide and we understand the victim's mother, Phillis Gates, was brought here."

"Oh, yes," said the nurse solemnly. "She was very agitated. I believe the doctor put her on a heart monitor as a precaution and gave her something to calm her. They don't think it was a heart attack, but the doctor can tell you more about her condition. Sometimes adrenaline can do strange things to one's body, you know. This kind of stressor would tend to produce a pretty high-powered adrenaline rush."

"Is the doctor around?" Erica asked, her temper rising. She was tired of people feeling they had to give long, drawn-out unsolicited explanations. These types of delays chewed up precious time.

"Oh, yes, but he's with another patient right now," she said stiffly. "If the two of you will have a seat in the waiting area, I'll let him know you're here."

"Thanks," said Freeman, taking Erica by the arm and leading her to a chair.

"You don't have to manhandle me," she snapped.

"Apparently I do. If you want to get someone to cooperate, you have to at least fake being nice. Why'd you want to bite her head off?"

"Well, let's see. There's no one out here, not even a family member waiting. Every minute we take in idle chit-chat keeps this S.O.B. out on the street ready to kill again." Her face reddened with anger and embarrassment at being reamed by her supervisor. "I just want to get this over with and get out of here."

"Look, Barnes. I understand why hospitals freak you out, especially this one, but we're cops. We have to come to hospitals every now and then. It's part of our job."

"You may think you understand, but you don't. You never will until you've..."

"Detectives," called the nurse. "Dr. Foster will see you now. I'll buzz you in."

They went through the emergency room doors and a tall, thin man with a light brown mustache and thinning brown hair greeted them. "You must be the detectives inquiring about Mrs. Gates."

"Yes," said Erica. "I'm Detective Barnes, this is Detective Freeman. We'd like to speak with Mrs. Gates, if possible."

"She's had quite a shock," he said. "We've called her younger daughter who lives in Muncie. She should be here soon."

Erica could tell he wanted to be cautious, but she wanted to get some answers. "I understand your concern, but the sooner we can get the information, the sooner we can apprehend her other daughter's killer."

"I'll let the two of you question her, but if she gets overly excited then I'll have to stop the interview. I'll be watching her heart monitor for any signs of distress."

"Fair enough," Freeman nodded.

They followed Dr. Foster into the depths of the trauma center. There were several empty beds, and one curtained off area. "Thank goodness it's quiet this morning," commented Dr. Foster. "I heard there were fifteen emergency cases here last night. There was an apartment fire in Carmel and a couple of nasty auto accidents."

"Bet you're glad you got the day shift," said Freeman.

"Oh, yes," the doctor said as he stopped just outside the curtain. "Wait here, please. Mrs. Gates," Erica heard him say. "There are two police detectives here. Is it alright if I bring them in to speak with you?"

"Of course," answered a quiet, strained voice. "I assume they're here about Marilyn."

"You are correct," he said to her. "You may come in now Detectives." Dr. Foster introduced the detectives to Mrs. Gates and then reminded them not to upset her.

"We're not here to upset her," Erica shot back at him. "We just want to find out who did this to her daughter."

Dr. Foster nodded his understanding, but didn't look too happy about her retort. Erica then turned back to Mrs. Gates.

"I meant what I said," she told her. "We want to find out who did this to Marilyn. We're hoping you may know something that could give us a clue as to who might have done this."

"All I know is Marilyn was going out with Phoebe last night."

"Who's Phoebe?" asked Erica.

"She's Marilyn's best friend since high school. Marilyn's had a hard time getting back out there since her divorce. I was supposed to have breakfast with her. I called her this morning to make sure she was up and getting ready since I figured she'd be out late. She didn't answer so I went over there, and..." Mrs. Gates words trailed off into tears of pain.

Erica patted Mrs. Gates arm, then took her hand. "I know this is very difficult for you, Mrs. Gates. We'll try to make this brief. We found a young man in the house as well. Do you have any idea who he was?"

"No," she squeaked. She took a moment to take a couple of deep breaths. They seemed to help her compose herself. "Detective Kendall told me his name is Keith Gray. I've never heard of him."

"Take your time, Mrs. Gates," Erica told her soothingly. "We aren't in a hurry. Believe me, any little details, no matter how insignificant they may seem are important." She gave Mrs. Gates a warm sympathetic smile and saw Mrs. Gates' face lighten a bit.

"Your mother must be very proud of you, Detective Barnes," she said.

"Thank you," Erica replied trying to avoid getting into her own personal issues. "So, you're sure if Marilyn had been dating this man for a while she would have confided it to you?"

"Yes, I'm sure of it. I know she's been lonely since her divorce."

"Is she still in contact with her ex-husband?" asked Freeman.

"Oh, no. It was terrible. A week after the divorce was final Jake went out rock climbing with friends. I'm afraid he fell. He died before they could get him to a hospital. I'm sure the incident pushed Marilyn into a deeper funk. He was her high school sweetheart and I believe she was still in love with him."

"Do you think her friend, Phoebe, might know something about Keith Gray?" asked Freeman.

"I suspect if anyone would, she would," said Mrs. Gates. "Like I said, they were supposed to go out together last night."

"Do you know how we can get in touch with her?" asked Erica.

"Of course, hand me my purse," she said as she pointed to a bag at the end of her bed. Erica gave the bag to Mrs. Gates, watching her as she pulled out a medium-sized brown leather purse. Mrs. Gates retrieved a small address book and notepad. She wrote down Phoebe's last name, address and phone number on a sheet of paper and tore it out of the notebook before handing it to Erica.

"Mrs. Gates, can you think of anyone else she might have been involved with who could have been jealous of her relationships with other men, or anyone who might have threatened her in any way?" asked Freeman.

"I'm sorry, Detective Freeman. My Marilyn was a wonderful woman. Everyone loved her. She was kind and thoughtful—the perfect daughter. Her father died in a car accident when she was sixteen and her sister was six. She was a tremendous help to me during that awful time," she said choking back tears again. "I just don't know why anyone would desecrate her this way. How could anyone have so much hate in them?"

"I wish I could give you an answer to comfort you, Mrs. Gates," said Erica trying not to tear up herself. "Most of these monsters were made by other monsters, usually abused in some way. It warps their sense of human decency."

Mrs. Gates looked away and Erica motioned for Freeman to follow her out. She thanked the nurse for her help, hoping to make up for her abrupt treatment of the young lady earlier.

"Now we have two squeaky clean victims, whom everyone adored, but someone wanted dead," she said in frustration. "Of course, you noticed they're both brunettes in their thirties."

"Yeah," agreed Freeman. "Thing is, Barnes, I think we're going have to talk to Major Stevenson about bringing the Feds in now. I'm afraid things could get worse very quickly."

"I hate working with the Feds. They always want to take over."

"I don't know about you, but I'm not so sure I'd object to some help right about now," he stated.

"Did I hear something about the FBI?" chimed an unwelcome voice.

Erica turned to see Peter Elliott standing there. Her face turned flaming red with anger. "Look Mr. Elliott, I'm getting sick and tired of finding you on my heels every time I turn around. If you don't stop, I'm going to believe you're stalking me. Not a good way to get police cooperation."

"Well," said Peter in a matter-of-fact voice. "Since you are a public servant and I am a reporter who is just trying to keep the public informed, I doubt you could make a stalking charge stick."

"Back off!" Freeman said, stepping between Erica and the reporter. "We're not going to talk to you about any of our cases."

"You know, the two of you should be nicer if *you* want the cooperation of the press," he countered. "If you're not going to answer my questions, I'll just have to print what I know—the IMPD is bringing in the Feds because they're too inept to solve these two horrendous murders. Maybe that will ease the public's minds."

"You do what you have to do, Elliott," fumed Erica. "But if you have any other questions, direct them to Major Stevenson and quit sneaking up on me."

"Suit yourself," he said, with an insufferable grin. "Have a nice day."

Peter turned to walk away, and Erica came around Freeman ready to strike. Freeman grabbed her arm.

"Not worth it, Barnes," he said quietly through clenched teeth. "So not worth it."

"Just one. Just one good hard kick. We're right here at the emergency room and they aren't busy."

"Tempting, but no," he said. Then they both burst out laughing.

Chapter 14

Erica looked out the window. "Holy crap," Erica said as she stretched in the passenger seat of Freeman's car. "This Phoebe chick would have to live in Speedway *and* this would have to be the first weekend of qualifications for the Indy 500."

"Crime doesn't take holidays or weekends off," he commented with a quick glance at her.

As they drew closer to the Speedway area, the traffic got thicker. She was just glad Brent was the one stuck driving through this mess.

"Natalie's hoping to wrap up the Fuentes case this week," said Freeman. "I'd like to put in a vacation request for the first or second week of June and go on a nice vacation with her."

"And miss the big wedding?" asked Erica, referring to Major Stevenson's daughter, Mandy.

"Oh, I'd forgotten about it," he said, sadness in his eyes. Erica knew he probably wanted to forget about it. "At least I have someone who can go with me now."

"What am I? Chopped liver?"

"That would be like taking my twin sister to the prom," he said, grinning.

"Real nice," she said. "We've got to turn west on 16th Street, then north on Somerset. Her house should be in the third block up." She watched for the house number, spotting it and pointing it out to him.

There was a white Volkswagen Passat in the driveway. Working in the flowerbed in the front yard was a barefoot young woman, with a long blonde ponytail, wearing a hot pink bikini top, denim shorts, purple gardening gloves, and sunglasses. She turned as she heard them approaching.

Standing, she asked, "May I help you?"

They showed her their badges then Erica asked, "Are you Phoebe Briggs?"

"Yes," she said, looking concerned and throwing her trowel into the garden. "Has something happened? Is it my mom, my brother?"

"No, your family is fine. May we go inside where we can talk privately," asked Freeman.

"Of course," she said, taking off the gloves and tossing them on top of her trowel. "Come on in."

They entered the small ranch home and Phoebe excused herself for a moment. Erica suspected she'd be washing her hands and composing herself. During Phoebe's absence, Erica took the opportunity to walk around the living room to get to know the young lady. She had photos of what looked to be her parents and the brother she'd mentioned. She saw photos of Phoebe with a lovely young woman with short brown hair and beautiful brown eyes she knew was Marilyn Novak. She'd seen a similar shot in Marilyn's house.

Phoebe came back into the room with a short towel draped around her neck then sat down in a leather armchair. "Okay, Detectives. What's going on?" she asked, her voice cracking with tension.

Erica looked her straight in the eyes. "Phoebe, I'm afraid something's happened to your friend, Marilyn Novak. Someone murdered her last night."

"Marilyn?" Phoebe said. Her face screwed up in pain and the tears started flowing. She looked around and then stood up, pacing the room, one hand on her hip the other over her mouth.

"Marilyn's mother told us she was supposed to be with you last night," stated Freeman.

"She was," Phoebe croaked. She put both hands on her hips and shook her head. It looked to Erica like she was trying to stop crying, but it was just too much. Phoebe plopped back down in her armchair, put her face in her hands, and sobbed.

Notifications were the hardest part of a cop's job. Erica hated telling people their loved ones were dead. She had a feeling Phoebe might be feeling guilty about letting Marilyn leave the bar without her, but she had to press on. Too often information was lost or forgotten if someone was given too much time to contemplate what they witnessed.

"Miss Briggs," said Erica. "We know this is very difficult for you but we need to know what went on last night."

Phoebe took the towel and wiped her face. "What happened?" she asked hoarsely.

"Do you know a man named Keith Gray?" asked Erica.

"Yes. Dark red, wavy hair. Blue eyes. Kind of cute, but not gorgeous. He left with Marilyn last night." She paused, looking dazed as shock set in. Then her expression changed to a frightened, wide-eyed glare. "Did *he* do this? Did that bastard take her home and kill her?"

"No, no Miss Briggs," said Freeman. "Unfortunately, he was also murdered. Had she been seeing him for long?"

"No," squeaked Phoebe. "Oh, shit! This can't be happening. They just met last night."

"So this was basically a one-night-stand?" asked Erica.

"Yeah," Phoebe answered. "Marilyn was a mess after her divorce. You see, me, Marilyn and Jake, her ex, were all friends since we were kids. In high school, Marilyn and Jake became an item. He was handsome and athletic, but unfortunately had also become something of a narcissist. Totally stuck on himself. She really loved the guy and he was the only man she'd ever had sex with. She was crushed when he asked for a divorce." Phoebe stopped, her face screwing up again.

Erica pressed on.

"So tell me what happened last night, from the beginning," Erica instructed.

"I'd convinced her to go to The Club with me. I hang out there a lot and I'd seen Keith a couple of times. I asked him to do me a favor and talk to her, you know, give her a little ego boost. I didn't know she'd invite him to go home with her, but I was thrilled. She'd been so down on herself these past couple of years, I thought it would be good for her."

Phoebe started crying again, wailing like an injured animal. Her heart was obviously broken. "This is my fault!" she cried. "I'll never forgive myself."

"Phoebe, that's not true," said Erica, touching her shoulder, distracting the woman from her grief. "No one could have prevented what happened."

"Phoebe," said Freeman. "Do you remember seeing anyone else in the bar watching Marilyn? Anyone give you the creeps?"

"Lots of guys were looking at her. She's gorgeous. I just wish she'd believed it. I can't remember anyone who made me feel uncomfortable though."

"Did you see anyone else approach her, maybe when she went to the bathroom or something?" asked Erica.

"No," said Phoebe. "Keith was the only guy she talked to last night. I didn't see anyone follow her or leave when she and Keith took off."

"Detective Barnes and I will leave you our cards," said Freeman. "After you've had some time to sort through, you may remember something you can't remember now. Please call us, even if you think it's too minute to be important. Sometimes those things turn out to be our best clues."

"Okay, I will."

Erica and Brent left Phoebe's house and headed back towards the crime scene. Erica turned to him. "Let's go to The Club and ask some questions."

"Precisely what I was thinking," Freeman said.

Twenty-five minutes later, Erica and Brent entered The Club. It was a typical, quaint neighborhood establishment with lots of sports memorabilia, beer signs, and posters. Behind the dark mahogany bar was a gray-haired bartender. They flashed their badges as they approached him.

"Detective Barnes, Detective Freeman," she announced. "We need to ask a few questions about Keith Gray and Marilyn Novak."

"Yeah, I heard about it. It's all over the news. Not sure how I can help you though. Wasn't my shift," he told them. "I can tell you Keith was a regular, but from the picture on the news I can't say I ever saw the young lady in here before."

"Do you know any of the people Keith hung out with here?"

"Them two down there said they was here last night. Came in for some *hair of the dog* this mornin'. They might know somethin'."

"Thanks," said Erica. "Do you have security cameras?"

"Yeah," he said and pointed to the ceiling to his right. "That one's trained on the bar area and there's one that covers most of the parking lot."

"We'll want to look at those after we talk to those two," said Erica, looking intently at the two men. One was burley, copper haired, and she guessed he'd be about six-two when he stood up. The other fellow was smaller—dark curly hair, a long thin face, and crooked teeth.

"Damn, talk about your one-night stand gone wrong," she heard the burley patron say as he sipped his beer. Erica noticed the news coverage of the Gray and Novak murders was running on the television.

"Poor sucker," said his pal. "Just wanted a little T&A and wound up D.O.A."

"Not funny, smart ass."

"Sorry, it just sort of popped out."

"Hello, gentlemen," said Erica as she showed her badge to them. "I hear you might know Keith Gray."

The redhead spoke first. "My name's Brandon Faulk and this here's Casey Miller. We worked with Keith at the Allison Transmission Plant. He was a good guy."

"So you guys hang out here a lot?" asked Erica.

"Usually Saturday nights," said Casey. "We'd have a few beers. Sometimes we'd come in on Sundays during football season to watch the Colts."

"Either of you ever notice Keith having any problems with anyone here or at work?" asked Freeman.

"No. He was cool," said Brandon. "Everybody liked him, especially the ladies—if you know what I mean."

"Did either of you know the woman he was with?" asked Erica.

They both shook their heads then Brandon said, "Saturday night was the first time we'd ever seen her in here. Keith went over to talk to her then her friend, Phoebe, went to the restroom. Instead of going back to their table, Phoebe came over here to talk to us. Phoebe's a regular in here."

"Yeah," said Casey. "Next thing you know, Keith and the girl are leaving together. Phoebe said her friend really needed to get laid."

Erica raised her eyebrow, and Casey blushed. "Did you notice anyone watching her, or leave at the same time they did?" asked Erica.

"She was really pretty," said Casey. "Lots of guys were staring at her. You know how guys are, when there's a new girl in the joint."

"I can't say I saw anyone acting weird or following them when they left," said Brandon.

"Thanks," said Erica, handing each of them one of her cards. "Call our number if you remember anything you think might help."

"Sure thing, Detective Barnes," said Casey, smiling at her in a way which made her rather uncomfortable.

Erica saw the distinctively smug look on Freeman's face as they approached the bartender.

"Do you record on a disc?" asked Erica.

The bartender nodded. "We usually recycle them every week. I'll go grab the CDs from last night for you."

While waiting for the bartender to return, Freeman glanced over his shoulder toward Casey and Brandon. Then he smirked at Erica. "Woo, hoo, hoo! Looks like Mr. Casey Miller is smitten with Detective Erica Barnes."

"Ah, shut up, Freeman," Erica whispered so the others wouldn't hear.

"Come on, Barnes. He was mooning all over you. He nearly drooled in his beer."

"*Whatever*," she said giving him the dirtiest look she could muster. "We need to get cracking on this case. Again, we have two really nice people. Both were loved by all and no one can imagine who would do this to them."

"I know this is frustrating, but don't let a couple of murders distract you from your chance for true love. Old Casey has a good job, and..."

"Give it a rest."

"No sense of humor. You're working too hard. Since you didn't get any breakfast, I'll take you over to Bahama Breeze for a late lunch after we get those discs. My treat."

"You're on!"

Chapter 15

It had been three days since the discovery of Marilyn Novak and Keith Gray's bodies. The IMPD Homicide Division had earned a reputation for an excellent solve rate. However, this killer was determined to drag their stats down. Erica was aware that most murder victims knew their assailants. Of these murders, most involved love or greed. The murder of these two individuals, along with Penny Flanders had her baffled and fearfully anticipating more.

Erica leaned back in her office chair, staring up at the ceiling. Dear Lord, help me find this guy before he does this to somebody else, she prayed.

She heard a whistle and saw Freeman approaching. He gave her the finger-hook and she knew it was time to head for the conference room to debrief on these latest murders.

She grabbed her notebook and a pen, heading for the conference room. Earlier that morning she'd tacked the latest crime scene photos from the Novak/Gray case up on the board. As badly as she felt for these women, she felt worse for Keith Gray. Although Penny and Marilyn had probably suffered the same psychological terror, Keith Gray had suffered physically as well as mentally.

According to Dr. Patel, Keith had lain on the floor struggling to breathe while each beat of his heart pushed more of his precious blood into his chest cavity. Dr. Patel noted he had several puncture wounds to the lungs from rib and sternum bone fragments. One fragment put a small gash in his heart which bled out causing a slow, painful death. What a horrendous way to go.

When she reached the interrogation room, Erica found Kendall, Parelli, and Freeman sitting at the conference table.

"So in Dr. Patel's opinion, we're dealing with the same killer," said Freeman.

"Everything's the same except for the sexual assault," stated Kendall. "Maybe he was thrown off his game by Keith Gray. Since he normally breaks the necks of the female victims, they are pretty quiet. According to Dr. Patel, Gray would have been making a lot of noise, but unable to do much. This would have continued until he lost consciousness."

"That's what I think, too, Kendall," said Erica, making her presence known.

"Makes sense," said Freeman. "So, what else you got for us Parelli?"

"I brought the reports we have so far from Forensics," she answered. "Several hairs found on the dress were the same as the long female hairs we found on Flanders—gray at the roots, dyed brown. DNA tests will take at least two weeks to determine if they belong to the same person. However, there were also some shorter hairs found. They were about one inch in length and didn't have any roots."

"How many did you find?" asked Erica.

"Eight," answered Parelli. "It's highly unusual to find so many and not one has a root."

"Wig?" asked Kendall.

"A good assumption," said Parelli. "They are human hair, but there are plenty of human hair wigs out there. Cancer patients are particularly fond of them because they look like their own hair."

"Wonder where this guy got all this money," commented Freeman. "Those things aren't cheap."

"I spoke with Marilyn Novak's sister yesterday," Erica said, flipping back a few pages in her notebook. "Her name's Stacy Gates. She attends Ball State University in Muncie, and is a senior majoring in early childhood education. Works part-time at the college. She's ten years younger than Marilyn and says they haven't been particularly close since she left for college. She wasn't sure what Marilyn's love life was like these days."

"She say how her mother's doing?" asked Freeman.

"Yeah, she said it was just an anxiety attack. Mrs. Gates is home now on anti-anxiety meds. I doubt she can give us anything else," said Erica closing her notebook. "She has our number. I'm sure she'll call if she thinks of anything."

"I followed up on Keith Gray," said Kendall. "He checks out. He worked at the Allison plant in Speedway and lived a few miles from the plant in an apartment complex off of Georgetown Road. His parents live in Shelbyville. Nice guy. Nobody knows why anyone would hurt him."

"Same old, same old," said Erica. This was the worse feeling she'd ever had in her career.

"Barnes and I have been over the CDs of the bar and we didn't see anyone suspicious—nobody looking at her or Gray for any unusual length of time," said Brent. "Nobody follow them to the parking lot or left it at the same time. I've given the discs to the lab for further analysis. Maybe they'll see something we didn't."

"We've got to start working on connections between our female victims," said Erica. "We need to check to see if they had dealings with the same painters, tree trimmers, or repairmen. There has to be some connection. This guy is meeting these women somewhere and he's either so inconspicuous no one notices him, or they trust him. They'd never think twice about seeing him or running into him. They certainly wouldn't think of him as a threat."

"I'll start by comparing their phone records to see if there are any numbers in common," said Kendall.

"Good idea. We've got to concentrate on the women," said Erica. "Keith Gray was just in the wrong place at the wrong time. Freeman, you can help me sort through all of the receipts and bank records to see if any payments were made to the same company."

"I take it you all are done with me," said Parelli.

"Thanks, Sophia," said Erica. "Let us know when you get more test results."

"Sure thing. I'll catch you later," said Parelli on her way out.

The three detectives dug into their files to see if they could find any connections.

Three hours later, they still had nothing.

"Oh, this is giving me a headache," exclaimed Erica.

"Second shift's already here," said Freeman. "What do you say we call it a night?"

"You have something going on tonight, Detective Freeman?" asked Kendall, her eyes sparkling impishly.

"Yeah, Freeman," said Erica, happy to have someone to back her up in teasing mode. "Are you and the lady prosecutor going out tonight?"

"As a matter of fact, we are," he said. "We are going out for a bite and then for a walk around the Circle. The weather is perfect."

"Oooowee! You two must be getting serious," quipped Kendall.

"Are you kidding," laughed Erica. "They've been serious since day one."

"You two go ahead and have your laughs at my expense," Freeman said, smiling from ear-to-ear. "I'm outta here!"

Erica watched as Freeman left the room. She started gathering the files, shaking her head and giggling at her partner. She looked over at Kendall who was doing the same.

Kendall looked up at her. "*Seriously*? Are they really that tight already?"

"Yep. Freeman falls hard and fast. Thing is, it looks like she pursued him first, so maybe it will work out for him this time."

"I like working with him. He seems to respect women more than most guys," said Kendall.

Erica nodded. "I guess it comes from growing up in a household full of women. You'd better respect them or get your ass kicked."

Kendall chuckled. "Well, Barnes. I'm going to go home and put one of my frozen diet dinners in the microwave and watch some TV. What about you?"

"I think I'm going to stop off and see my Pop. I've been so bogged down with these cases; I haven't seen him for a while."

"He's a retired cop. He'll understand."

"I know," said Erica, "but I promised Mom I'd look out for him."

"You miss her, don't you?"

"Every day."

Chapter 16

Erica drove slowly down Ferguson Street in Broad Ripple. This was where she'd grown up. She looked at the tall, plush maple trees standing proudly in each yard. Even though she knew they'd grown, they seemed much smaller than when she was a child. Mrs. Calloway's house still stood with its white picket fence and gorgeous rose garden. She still kept the fence whitewashed and the roses pruned at her young age of ninety-two years.

Two doors down was Erica's childhood home. Her father still lived there in the three bedroom golden brick ranch. It was one of the few houses in the neighborhood with a two-car garage. He'd always insisted he and her mother shouldn't have to scrape windows in the cold winters.

A top-notch investigator with the Robbery Division, Michael Barnes retired five years ago. He and Erica's mother, Clara, planned to travel the world. Unfortunately, they only had time to take one trip. When they returned from their Alaskan cruise, a routine physical found Clara had cervical cancer. The only trips they took from that point on were to doctors' offices and the hospital.

The news of Clara's illness devastated the entire family, but Clara always kept a positive attitude keeping the rest of them sane. Erica's brother, Rick, had landed a job in Seattle and moved there with his wife and daughter just before the diagnosis was rendered. This left the majority of dealing with the situation on Erica's shoulders. Rick's absence also left Erica to help her father with his grief as well as find a way to come to terms with her own.

Erica pulled into the gravel driveway, hearing the crunch beneath her tires. She'd stopped at the store on her way over to grab a few groceries for him—grapes, walnuts and a few of his favorite microwavable dinners. She toted the bags to the front door and knocked with her foot. She heard heavy footsteps and stood in front of the peephole. He always looked before he dared open the door.

"Well, look who it is," he exclaimed with a smile which covered his whole face. "Let me take one of those bags."

She gladly relinquished one of them, closing and locking the door behind her. He still hadn't changed a thing. Faded floral curtains hung at the window. The pine paneling still made the room look much too dark. The carpet must be 20 years old now. A green sculptured pile her mother wanted to replace, but never got around to it. The only thing he had done was place a teal and violet afghan over his black vinyl easy chair, most likely to keep it from pinching his legs where the upholstery was cracking. He absolutely refused to get rid of the chair.

"So, Pop, how's it going?" she asked.

"Well, I saw the doc a couple of days ago. He said my cholesterol is up a bit and if it gets any higher he's going to put me on another damn pill. I told him I already took too many freakin' pills and he laughed at me and told me it's 'cause I'm an old fart. Course I told him to watch it. He's not far behind me. He'll be sixty-two pretty soon, ya know."

"No, I didn't," she replied. "I got you some grapes. They're full of antioxidants."

"Whatever," he said, curling up his nose. "I like 'em cause they're sweet, not cause they have anything special in 'em."

She opened the freezer door and put the frozen dinners inside. Then she washed the grapes while her father made a pot of coffee. This was their routine. She loved coming to see her dad and spending time with him. He always gave her good advice, or at least now that she was thirty-two it seemed good. She also loved to discuss her cases with him. Erica knew he enjoyed it, too. He had been so lost after her mother's death three years ago and Erica's work gave them something in common.

As a matter of fact, she felt compelled to come see him tonight to talk shop. These cases were driving her crazy and she needed his advice.

"Hey, Pop," she began. "Have you been watching the news about the cases I'm working right now?"

"You bet I have. The news is my favorite TV program. 'Spose you need an opinion from dear old dad, do ya?"

"These are really bad. Freeman and Kendall are working with me, but I'm the lead on these. The women in both cases were murdered in exactly the same way. They were dressed up by the killer; their eyes were sewn open; and the guy wrote *SEE ME* on their foreheads with their own makeup, and of course, that's confidential."

"Don't know what's so hard to figure out about this one—he's nuts! Looney! Psycho!"

They both burst into laughter. Leave it to her Pop to lighten up a horrific situation. She sat down in the chair next to him and he took her hands.

"Kitten," he said, his term of endearment for his only daughter. "These types of cases will tear you up if you let them. You're a magnificent homicide detective, and I'm not just saying that because you're my daughter."

"Thanks, Pop," she sighed, patting his hand. "Unfortunately, we're sure he's not finished. There's absolutely no connection between the victims, except for their physical appearance and age."

"It's a start."

"We may wind up bringing the Feds in on this one." As she said this, she saw his face change as though she'd just put a piece of dung under his nose. She laughed again. "I understand. Believe me I'm not too keen on the idea either, but we don't think these are his first murders. We just can't find any other connections or similar murders in Indiana."

"I'm sure you're right," he confirmed. "Just try to stay focused on the investigation and don't get too attached to your victims. The closer you pay attention to the facts rather than the emotions, the more quickly you'll apprehend this son-of-a-bitch."

"Thanks, Pop. I know...did you eat dinner? I bought you the flaming chicken dinner you like so much."

"I had a peanut butter and jelly sandwich with tomato soup earlier. I'll save the chicken for tomorrow. You best go home and get some rest so you can start fresh tomorrow."

"You sure you don't want me to stay a while longer?"

"You mean you'd rather spend time with your daddy than with that sergeant fella from Missing Persons?"

"*What*?" she said in surprise. Erica hadn't told him about Ben.

"Oh, so you think you can pull one over on your dear old dad, do you?"

"How'd you know?" she asked.

"Remember when you took me to the Christmas party last year? I saw you making those googlie eyes at him across the room. Don't forget, I was a pretty good detective in my time."

"Better than Freeman," she giggled. "He still hasn't figured it out.

"Well, he's not a Barnes."

Chapter 17

Samantha Ritter was shutting down her computer when her boss approached her desk. Tonya Crandall was grinning from ear-to-ear.

"Great work on the Macklin case, Samantha," she said. "You'll be a great lawyer someday."

"Thanks, Tonya."

"I'll see you tomorrow morning."

"See you then," said Samantha. She'd been working for Crandall, Binns and Associates for eight years now. Samantha had started as a legal secretary for the firm while she was going to college. Loving her work, she soon decided to switch to pre-law and then went on to the Indiana University School of Law in Indianapolis, graduating with honors.

Now Samantha worked as a paralegal for the firm and would be taking the Bar Exam in a couple of months. Tonya had promised her a place in the firm if she passed the Bar in two tries. Samantha intended to make it in one.

Still smiling from the compliment, she pushed in her chair, grabbed her jacket and purse, and headed toward the elevator. It was great to be acknowledged. She waved at the cleaning crew and they smiled, waving back at her. Samantha Ritter was feeling good.

In the parking garage, she found her faithful, reliable black VW Beetle waiting. "Someday I'll let you retire and get one of those sporty BMWs," she told it. "Or, maybe I'll keep you as my vintage car and drive the BMW as my everyday car."

This calls for a celebration, she thought. Putting the key in the ignition, she turned it and listened to the motor roar to life. Stopping at the grocery store near her home, she bought herself a big, fresh mixed bouquet of flowers and some Edy's Fudge Tracks ice cream.

Samantha lived in a two-bedroom condominium on Indianapolis' near north side. It had been a foreclosure so she was able to get it at a rock bottom price. With the help of family and friends, she pulled together some comfortable furnishings and several kitchen items. It was the perfect place for a future lawyer.

She unlocked her front door, switched on the foyer light, and dropped her keys into a bowl on the table near the door. Setting her purse on the kitchen counter, she laid the flowers near the sink and put the ice cream in the freezer.

"Sasha," she called, opening a cabinet and extracting a small can of Tuna Delight. "Come on Sasha, time for dinner."

Samantha put the food in a small dish and sat it next to a bowl of water on the floor. "Come on Sasha. Eat this before it spoils."

Retrieving a vase from under the sink, Samantha filled it with water then arranged the flowers in it. She felt a strange chill, like something wasn't quite right.

"What's wrong with me?" she said aloud, shivering. "And where's that darned cat?"

She walked to her dining room by the foyer light holding the vase in one hand so she could flip the next light switch.

"It's about time you got home," he said.

Samantha dropped the vase, which shattered and sent flowers flying. She turned to see a man in the shadows. He had Sasha, holding her tight with one hand, her head in the other.

"Don't scream or I'll snap her neck."

Samantha wasn't sure she could scream, her throat constricted by fear. When she finally found her voice, she asked, "What do you want?"

"I want you out of my life," he said.

"I…I don't understand," she said, confused. She had no idea who the man was.

"Every time I think you're gone, you come back."

"Do I know you?" she asked, squinting, trying to get a better look at him.

"Boy," he said angrily. "Isn't that just like you? When we're in public, I'm the apple of your eye, but when we're alone you act like I don't exist." The cat squealed and wriggled as the intruder tightened his grip on her.

"Please don't hurt her," Samantha pleaded. "Just tell me what you want. I'm sorry if I hurt you." She'd decided she needed to go along with his game or she and Sasha would both be doomed.

"You're sorry for hurting me," he said, sounding more agitated. "That's a new one. I thought hurting me was your deepest pleasure."

"I've changed," she said, desperate to try anything to get him to calm down. "I won't do it anymore, I promise."

"Do you know how many times I've heard those promises from you?" he laughed. "One too many."

He lunged at her, dropping Sasha. Before she could scream he had her. One twist and Samantha Ritter's dreams of becoming a lawyer were over.

Chapter 18

Erica opened the file of photos she'd received from CSI. This victim was a bright thirty-one-year-old woman who'd worked hard for everything. She had such a bright future. Erica's heart sank as she added crime scene photos of Samantha Ritter to the board in the conference room they'd designated for these multiple murders.

Major Stevenson would be there soon to review the cases with her, Freeman, and Kendall. Then there would be a news conference. She dreaded it because as the lead investigator, the major would expect her to accompany him.

"I've got a feeling the major's not going to wait any longer to call in the FBI," said Kendall. "This is getting out of hand. It's like this guy's invisible. Nobody sees him coming or going. None of these women were actively involved with a man."

"Yeah, and no connections so far between the victims except for their looks and age range," said Freeman. "You have any ideas, Barnes?"

Erica pinned up the last crime scene photo, thinking about her father's encouraging words. He'd made her feel better, but this reversed his efforts. She turned. "This guy has to be someone they see as trustworthy. Someone these women might notice fleetingly, but wouldn't think of as a threat. He's inconspicuous to them. That's why he writes *SEE ME* on their foreheads. He wants them to acknowledge him."

"Sounds like a good theory Barnes," said Major Stevenson as he entered the room. "It's beginning to sound more and more like a serial killer. He's probably some psycho who decided to latch on to women with a certain look—like someone who rejected him once upon a time. I've decided to bring in the FBI before the day is out. I doubt this started here."

"I agree, Major," said Erica, although she hated working with the FBI. In her opinion, they would take over. Then they would take the credit when an arrest was made, even though she and her team had already put in the majority of the groundwork. Still, she knew this was big—bigger than anything Indianapolis had ever seen. Serial killers just didn't land in her town.

The three detectives filled Major Stevenson in on all the details of the four murders thus far. Keith Gray was just a victim of circumstance. It looked like the women were the targets—single white females in their thirties with medium length, dark brown hair and eyes. Patel's autopsy had confirmed the COD for Marilyn Novak as predicted by D.I. Spalding. She was sure when the autopsy came back for Samantha Ritter it would be the same.

"Okay, Barnes," said the major. "You're the lead detective, so you'll stand with me during the press conference. I'll make a statement then answer the majority of the questions, which I won't do for long. No details about the women. We don't need any copycats deciding they want to off their girlfriends in a manner that implies it's this killer."

"What do you want me to do if I'm called upon, Sir?" asked Erica.

"You can answer questions about Gray's autopsy, but not about the women's. Like I said, no details about them. Defer any sticky questions to me."

"Yes sir," she said. "They won't get anything out of me."

"Good," he said, giving her a confident smile. "Let's go."

Erica glanced back at her colleagues. Freeman gave her thumbs up, and then she followed Major Stevenson to the press room. It was filled with reporters who looked hungry. Some were so anxious they were wriggling in their seats like they had to pee. She was not looking forward to this, especially when she saw Peter Elliott sitting in the second row. TV news crews switched on lights and camera operators began to record. Many in their seats were poised with open notebooks, electronic notepads, or digital voice recorders in hand.

Erica took her place just behind and to the right of Major Stevenson. She stood with her hands clasped in front of her, a stoic, almost grave facial expression. She was trying desperately to appear professional, despite the horrific nature of these crimes.

There was much rustling of paper and murmuring until Major Stevenson stepped up to the podium. Erica had once thought of him as a heartless bastard. However, her opinion had changed when she was assigned to assist the Missing Person Unit when his wife disappeared. She saw a softer side of him back then. He was actually very human and totally dedicated to his family, doing whatever it took to protect them. Now she admired his ability to lead without showing his personal feelings.

Major Stevenson raised his hands slightly from the podium and the room fell silent. "Good morning. We have called this press conference today to make a statement and answer a few questions about the investigation into the murders of Penny Flanders, Marilyn Novak, Keith Gray, and Samantha Ritter. Please be aware these are on-going investigations and we may not be able to disclose every detail to you today."

He paused and pulled a piece of paper from his jacket pocket. "I want to read this statement and then we will take your questions." The major pulled out his reading glasses, cleared his throat, and read.

"As has been reported, three females and one male have been murdered this past month and may be connected to the same perpetrator. Detective Erica Barnes, to my right, is the lead detective on these cases.

"The male victim, Keith Gray, may have become a victim for simply being in the wrong place at the wrong time. We believe he was killed trying to protect Miss Novak. His cause of death was different than the female victims. He died from injuries sustained from a quick blow to his chest which shattered his sternum and several ribs sending these fragments into his heart and lungs.

"All three of our female victims, however, were not killed in this manner. They all have the same COD, but we are not prepared to share this information with the public at this time. Questions?"

The uproar startled Erica as the crowd went from quiet to mayhem in a split second. She kept hoping Major Stevenson wouldn't have to call on Peter Elliott for a question. Elliott would surely call upon her for the answer.

"Yes, Andrea," he said, pointing to Andrea Atkins of NBC News. She had been a real pain for the major and his daughter during his wife's missing person case, but he continued to treat her with respect.

"Major Stevenson, are you telling us we have a serial killer in Indianapolis?" asked Andrea.

"That has not been determined," he said as his eyes moved to Jerome Porter of Fox News.

"You really didn't answer Andrea's question. Don't you think the women of Indianapolis need to know what they are up against?"

Erica watched her boss, his knuckles turning white as he gripped the podium. She knew he was angered by any implication he wasn't keeping the best interest of the public in mind. She also knew he wouldn't show his anger to them.

"We're very concerned about the safety of our citizens," said Stevenson. "We would advise all females, especially those who live alone, to take extra precautions in their homes. Make sure all windows and doors are locked securely. Install an alarm system if you can. Don't go anywhere alone after dark. Next question."

"My question is for Detective Barnes," shouted Peter Elliott, standing. He obviously didn't care that Major Stevenson hadn't called upon him.

Erica looked at Peter in disbelief. Then she turned to Stevenson who stepped aside to give her the podium. She wasn't happy, but she was the lead on these cases. Besides, this was a vote of confidence from the major and he did say he'd rescue her from any sticky questions.

"Yes, Mr. Elliott," Erica said.

"What is your take on this killer?"

"It appears this perpetrator is targeting women in their thirties. He commits this crime during the dark hours, but not necessarily at the same time of night."

"Yes, but are there other similarities and will the FBI be brought in?" asked Peter.

"I'm not at liberty to answer these questions at this time," said Erica, staring directly into Peter's eyes. She stepped back to signal Major Stevenson to take over.

"That's all we have time for today," he said. "We will update you with information when we can. Thank you all for coming."

Erica turned to her right and waited for the major to take the lead. She followed him out, listening to the din of voices calling to them to answer more questions. A few feet outside of the pressroom, Stevenson turned to her.

"Excellent job of keeping your cool in there," he said smiling. "I know this Elliott character has been giving you headaches. I'm very proud of you." He then turned and walked on.

Erica stood there for a moment absorbing the joy of this rare compliment. Very cool, she thought. Smiling, she made her way back to her desk. It was time to get back to work.

Chapter 19

Brent awoke and reached for Natalie only to find her gone. He sat up and heard her rummaging through her walk-in closet. Getting out of bed, he looked inside and found her dressed in navy blue jogging shorts and sports bra, slipping on a Notre Dame tee shirt.

It had only been two weeks since their first date, but it felt like they'd been together forever.

Natalie turned and saw Brent staring at her, gasping in surprise. "You gave me a start," she said with her right hand over her heart. "Want to go for a run?"

"Can't. I don't have the proper attire with me."

"Hmmm. Did you forget your attire like you forgot your Indiana history?"

"You're not going to let me live that down, are you?"

"Not a chance."

"So I mixed up my monuments and said the monument on the Circle was to honor World War Veterans instead of Civil War Veterans."

"More like you left out the Civil War Veterans."

"Well, you're just so breathtakingly beautiful, you distracted me. I couldn't think straight." Brent winked.

"Freeman, that's got to be the best line I've heard in a long time."

"I didn't *forget* my gear. I have to be in the office early today. Dr. Patel should have the autopsy completed on Samantha Ritter."

"In that case, there's a spare key to the apartment on the counter. It's yours if you want it," she said, her crystal blue eyes sparkling. "When you're ready to leave, just lock up. I don't need to be in court until 10:00 this morning. Closing arguments on the Fuentes case today, you know. Jogging always clears my head."

When he pulled her close, she wrapped her arms around him. "I'm sure you'll be glad to finish this one," he said. "You're brilliant, you know."

"Thanks. Of course, there'll just be another one to take its place," she said, rubbing his back and resting her head on his chest. "Maybe even this sicko you've been chasing."

"Call my cell when you get back from your run and we'll make plans to celebrate your victory."

"And, if by some slim chance the jury acquits Fuentes?"

"Then we'll have a consolation dinner and I'll find a way to cheer you up."

She leaned back slightly so she could look at his face. Brent kissed her full luscious lips like a man whose thirst was unquenchable.

"You are something else, Brent Freeman," she laughed. "I'd better get out of here. I'm going to drive over to Carmel and pick up the Monon Trail. I should be back home by 8:30."

She hugged him tightly one more time. He patted her butt as she walked away, following her out of the bedroom. Looking at him with those twinkling blue eyes, she said, "I'm off to relieve this pre-court stress!"

"Actually, I could help you with that stress relief thing," he said.

"I'm sure you could," she bantered. "Save it for dessert." She gave him one more peck on the cheek, grabbed her running belt and hooded sweatshirt from the bar stool and was on her way.

Brent was dressed and out the door in about fifteen minutes. He looked at the key Natalie had bestowed upon him and smiled. "I wish I'd brought my running gear with me," he said aloud. He looked at the apartment key one more time before pocketing it. Outside, the redbud trees lining the parking lot were in full bloom and the sun was getting warmer as spring progressed.

Once home, a quick shower was followed by fresh clothes, some instant coffee, and two slices of toast. Brent walked back out into the late May sunshine, hopped into his car, and ventured towards the City-County Building. He glanced at the dashboard clock. It was 8:45 and still no call from Natalie. He pulled out his cell phone to check for messages. Nothing. He started to put it back into his pocket when it rang.

"Hello, Major Stevenson," he said, recognizing the caller ID.

"Freeman, you and Barnes talk to Dr. Patel about the Ritter autopsy yet?" asked the major.

"We should be hearing from her this morning."

"I've called in the FBI, since it looks like these cases were perpetrated by the same individual," he said in a commanding voice. "I know nobody likes to work with them, but we're going to need some help so we can solve these cases before the public goes into panic mode. Pass it on to Barnes this morning and let me know when you talk to Dr. Patel."

"Yes, sir," answered Brent.

He pressed the END button and put the phone in his pocket. "Barnes isn't going to like this, not one little bit."

Erica was sitting at her desk intently staring at her computer when Brent arrived. She looked up as he planted himself in the chair beside her desk.

"Well, well—look at you," Erica commented with a glint in her eye. "If I didn't know better..."

"Can it," he interrupted. "Anything new on the Ritter case this morning? Is Dr. Patel done with the autopsy?"

"Touchy, touchy," she said as her eyebrows rose. "Look who wants to get right down to business this morning."

He scowled at her but she chose to ignore him.

"Checked my email and Patel said we should stop by this morning. Barring being called out to the field, she says she'll be available all morning."

"Let's go then," he said with an edge of excitement. "Since our theory about Ritter being another Flanders/Novak is pretty set, Stevenson called the Feds in."

He could tell this didn't please Erica, but what choice did they have? She'd just have to accept it.

"Private calls from the boss. You're such a brown nose," she teased handing him a tissue.

"Shut up," he said, tossing the tissue back at her.

They found Dr. Patel in the autopsy suite when they arrived. The posted schedule said she had an accident victim on the table. Erica and Brent donned lab coats and gloves before entering the suite. Dr. Patel turned when she heard the door open. "Ah, Detective Barnes, Detective Freeman."

"Hey, Doc," said Brent. "I understand you've got something for us."

Dr. Patel gave him a pleasant smile at which Erica raised her eyebrow.

"There is every indication our latest female victim died in the same manner as Penny Flanders and Marilyn Novak. Besides the way she was dressed and positioned at the scene, she had the same type of vertebrae separation in the neck as the first two female victims. She also had the same vaginal and rectal tearing as Flanders. I extracted the tissues from Ritter as I did in the Flanders case and sent them to the Forensics Lab."

"Have you heard anything from Chatham's team regarding the Novak/Gray murders?" asked Brent.

"They're still waiting to do the DNA testing on the tissue, but the bed linens definitely had semen and vaginal fluids on them. DNA is backed up, so it could be another week or two before they get results on this case."

"What about our male victim?" asked Erica.

"Remember the size nine and a half foot print Sofia Parelli found on the carpet at Penny Flanders' house?" asked Dr. Patel.

"Are you telling us Keith Gray had the same foot print on his chest?" asked Erica.

"Precisely, Detective Barnes," she said as she disposed of her gloves and retrieved a file from the counter. "Here's a photo of the print from the carpet. Now look at the photo I took of Keith Gray's chest. It takes several hours to see a bruise like this one. I took this photo before I did his autopsy."

"We definitely have a martial arts expert here," said Erica. "We suspected it in the Flanders case because the shoe was the type used by martial artists. Usually only people who will use it in combat learn this type of kick to the chest. It's meant to kill."

"Again, you are precisely correct," said Dr. Patel. "I've heard of this type of killing, but this is the first time I've seen it."

"Thanks, Doc," said Brent. "At least now there's no doubt all of these cases are linked."

"You are most welcome," Dr. Patel said smiling at Brent.

They left the autopsy suite and were discarding their gloves and lab coats when Erica sniggered, "Dr. Patel has a thing for you."

"No, she doesn't," he said.

"Come on, Brent. You telling me you didn't feel that sexual tension in there?"

"Real romantic," he said sarcastically. "Just where I want a romance to begin—in a refrigerator stuffed full of dead bodies."

"She *is* a doctor. You could be set for life," Erica said.

"Uncle!" he exclaimed, and then looked at his watch.

Chapter 20

"I checked out Lee Sellers and there are several witnesses who corroborate his story of working the morning of the Flanders murder. I really thought he was good for it," said Erica typing her report, pounding the keyboard a little too vigorously. "Besides, I couldn't find a connection between Sellers and our last four victims."

Silence met her. Looking up, she noticed Freeman staring into space. Then he looked at his watch and back to nowhere again.

"If you're worried about her, call her office," Erica suggested, knowing precisely what distracted him. "She was probably running late and forgot to call before she went to court."

"She's not like that."

"You haven't known her very long, Brent," she reminded him. "Besides, nobody's perfect. Maybe this was her one-in-a-million forgetful moment. She did have a lot on her mind this morning."

"I guess," he said, staring at the phone.

Erica knew he must be struggling with the decision of whether or not to make the call so she decided to give him another nudge. "Go ahead. Make the call. What could it hurt?"

Freeman looked at her, and then grabbed the receiver. Erica gave him her undivided attention, watching him for signs of relief. They didn't come.

"Are you sure," he said. "She was supposed to be in court this morning to present her final arguments in the Fuentes case." There was a long pause. "I see," he said his eyes darting from side-to-side. "Thank you…and could you give me a call if you hear from her?" Another pause. "Yes. That's my number. Thanks. Bye."

He looked close to tears. Erica wanted to jump up and hold him, to comfort him, to tell him everything would be all right. She resisted. Instead, she asked, "What's going on?"

"I'm sure you gathered she wasn't in court today."

"Yes. Go on."

"She just didn't show up. She didn't call or text or anything, and she's not answering her phones. It's like she vanished."

"Okay," she said as calmly as she could, hoping her demeanor would sooth his nerves. "I was all for the being late theory, but this doesn't sound like the ambitious young prosecutor you know and love."

"Damn straight it doesn't. Something's happened to her. This case meant too much to her. She wouldn't just blow it off."

"Look. I'm sure you're right, but let's not panic. As Pop always says, we have to focus. What did she say to you this morning before she left?"

She listened as Freeman explained Natalie's planned run on the Monon Trail. He said she usually ran south on it for about a mile and then turned back north to run back to her car.

"Did she do this every morning?"

"I think so," he answered. "She might go further if she had time, or leave earlier if she had an early court date."

"Crap. Anyone watching her would have figured out her routine," she said before she caught herself.

"Oh, God," he said, looking even more distressed, elbows on the desk and his face in his hands. "I should have gone with her. I didn't bring my running clothes with me last night. She shouldn't have been out there alone."

"I know you're not gonna buy this right now, but this wasn't your fault."

He looked at her, his face full of anguish.

"I mean it, Brent. If you'd been with her, you might both be missing."

"Or I might have been able to stop whoever did this."

"Okay. Cut the crap," she said sternly. "We've got to concentrate here. You need to focus like a cop now. Try to set your feelings aside."

"Easier said than done," Brent said, looking close to tears.

"I know," she said. "I think we need to bring in Missing Persons. Let's see if Jacobs or Mayhew are available. You should file a Missing Person Report so they can look into this officially."

"You're right. I need to make this official. I'll go see if I can find them and we'll get the wheels in motion," Freeman said.

"This way we can keep tabs on it while working our own cases," she said. "Don't forget. We've got to get in touch with our pals at the Bureau today."

"I don't suppose you'd be willing to do it without me?" he asked. "You are the lead on these cases. Kendall will help you."

Her mouth fell open and her first selfish impulse was to ask him if he was crazy. However, when she saw his rich hazel eyes heavy with moisture, she backed off. How could she expect him to concentrate on work under these circumstances? He'd be useless to her in his current state of mind.

"I need to get this report out of the way," he said. "Maybe I could go with the guys to Carmel to see if her car is still there."

She knew if she were in a similar situation, he'd have covered for her. She nodded in ascent.

"Thanks, Erica. You're the best."

"I know" she smirked.

"I'd better go find Jacobs and Mayhew. The sooner we get going, the sooner we'll find her."

Erica watched as Brent walked away. She couldn't believe this was happening in the middle of this messy investigation.

She decided there was no point putting off the call. When she reached the FBI, she explained that Major Stevenson had already called asking for their assistance. They told her Federal Agent Spencer Morgan had the case assignment and would head over to IMPD in about an hour to go over the files.

Erica was busy scanning the IMPD databases for hits on similar cases across the U. S. when a stranger approached her desk. He was approximately six foot one, dark skinned with deep brown eyes. Definitely, signs of a six pack under the tight fitting dress shirt he wore along with the arms of a body builder.

"Can I help you?" she asked.

"Are you Detective Barnes?"

"Yes."

"Then it seems I should be the one asking you that question," he responded with a wide toothy grin. "Federal Agent Morgan—Spencer Morgan, at your service."

Erica stood, shaking his hand, peering at him cautiously. "It's nice to meet you, Agent Morgan."

"Same here. I've been briefed on the three female murder victims and understand you believe these may be the work of the same person."

"Yes, and we're afraid these may not be his first. He's too detailed in his rituals."

"Do you have a war room set up so we can go over the evidence you have collected thus far?"

"Sure, follow me."

They spent the next two hours poring over the crime scene photos, autopsy reports and forensic reports. Morgan closed the last file and leaned back in his chair with the tips of his fingers together, a look of contemplation on his face. Then he sat forward suddenly, startling Erica.

"You and your team are correct. This unsub's intricacies in his treatment of women is very organized and deliberate. He's definitely sending a message. We need to do a database search for similar cases."

"I did a state-wide search but found nothing similar. I started a nationwide search just before you arrived," she said.

"You're also correct to assume this unsub has done this before. I think we need to call in someone from the Behavioral Analysis Unit of The National Center for the Analysis of Violent Crime."

"A profiler?" she asked.

"I believe they prefer to be called behavioral analysts, but yes. That's essentially what they do."

She raised an eyebrow eliciting him to say, "You look skeptical, Detective."

"I've never put much stock in this sort of thing," she admitted.

"Trust me, Detective Barnes. You're not the first police officer I've met who has this attitude. I can tell you in cases of serial killers, the BAU has been very successful in creating profiles which have led to arrests. Special Supervisory Agent Trish Zimmer just happens to be wrapping up a case in Chicago. I'll see if she can be here first thing tomorrow morning."

"Just because I have doubts doesn't mean I'm closed-minded," Erica assured him. "Right now we'll do whatever it takes. We want to put this lunatic away before he kills again."

"Then we're on the same page," he said. "How close is your lab team to getting us those DNA test results?"

"Our forensics supervisor said we should have everything on the Flanders and Novak cases by tomorrow morning. If it weren't for the mayor's *concerns*, we probably wouldn't have seen them for at least a month."

"Excellent. This will help give Agent Zimmer and I a place to start our investigation."

"That's what we're hoping for," she said.

"I suspect your DNA lab is pretty backed up. We may be able to get lab results back faster, if you want our help on the Ritter DNA."

"That would be great. Can the two of you be here by 9:00 tomorrow morning?"

"I can't speak for Trish, but I'll be here."

"We'll pick it up from there then," she said. "See you tomorrow."

Chapter 21

"That's where she'd have parked her car," Freeman said frantically as Tyrone pulled into the parking lot. "Let's get out and look around."

Tyrone pulled over. Freeman opened the door and launched himself out of the front seat before the car came to a complete stop.

"Are you tryin' to kill yourself?" shouted Tyrone.

"Give him a break," Jacobs said. "He's just getting to know her and now she's missing. She was supposed to give closing arguments in the Fuentes case today. I wonder if that scumbag had anything to do with this."

"I wouldn't put it past him," Tyrone said as he locked the car. He and Jacobs searched the area for clues. "I'm sure Fuentes has a few *friends* on the outside who owe him a favor or two."

"Think he was trying to intimidate the jury?" Jacobs asked.

"Oh, yeah," Tyrone acknowledged.

"Guys, over here!" yelled Freeman. Jacobs and Tyrone quickened their pace. "Look at this," Freeman said pointing at a sweatshirt in the tall grass. "Natalie was wearing it this morning."

"We should have a CSI team come down here to collect this. They'll need to do a thorough sweep for evidence," said Jacobs. "We should also get a K-9 crew out here as well."

"That's right, man," said Tyrone. "Soon as they get here we're gonna head for the 'hood and look for Miss Ralston's car."

"I'll make the calls," said Jacobs, taking out his cell phone.

"Damn it!" Freeman paced back and forth, running his fingers through his hair. "I should have gone with her this morning!"

"Come on, Brent. They would've had both of you," said Tyrone. "I doubt there was only one person involved or they wouldn't have been able to take her car."

Freeman shot Tyrone a nasty look. "Why doesn't that make me feel any better?"

"This parking lot's just inside Marion County so they're sending a couple of patrol officers over," said Jacobs. "They said Bays and Samuels are about a minute away from here. As soon as they get here, we'll search the neighborhood where Fuentes and his gang normally hang out."

"Thanks, Ben."

The moment Bays and Samuels arrived Tyrone filled them in on what was happening. "It's essential for us to start searchin' for her immediately. Jacobs put out an APB on her car, but Jacobs, Freeman, and I are goin' to search areas Fuentes frequented."

"We'll cordon off the area and wait for CSI to arrive," said Bays. "Since the sweatshirt is over there, I'd bet that's where they grabbed her."

"We need to close off the trail to one mile south of here as well as this whole parking lot. We'll call out another unit to help," Jacobs instructed. "There are a lot of woods around here. We called Indiana K-9 Search and Recovery to bring out a couple of their dogs to search. They can use her sweatshirt to pick up her scent."

"I hear ya," said Bays.

Tyrone noticed Freeman sitting in the car. "You ready to hit the road, Jacobs?" asked Tyrone, pointing at Freeman.

They drove to the near-west side where Fuentes and his gang lived and roamed. Tyrone drove slowly as all three detectives glanced back and forth and down every alley for Natalie's silver Corolla.

"We're going to have to go deeper. Let's take some of these side streets," suggested Freeman. "Shit! What if they're hiding it in a garage? What if they took her out of the county to some remote area?"

"Hey, man. You got to stop thinkin' like that," said Tyrone. "We're gonna find her. I can feel it in my bones."

"And he's got some pretty sensitive bones," quipped Jacobs.

"This isn't the time for jokes, jerk-off," said Tyrone scowling at his partner.

"Oh, you can tell him to lighten up, but I'm not allowed to throw in a little humor?" said Jacobs.

"Shut up. You're gettin' on my nerves."

"You two fight like an old married couple," said Freeman. He knew this was typical banter for the two of them, but he needed them to focus on finding Natalie.

"Oh, no. My Jada don't give me any ways near as much trouble as this jackass."

"*Whatever,*" Jacobs said rolling his eyes and looking out the window.

"Wait a minute. Look there in the pharmacy parkin' lot." Tyrone said, pointing to the southeast corner. "Does the plate number match the number the DMV gave us?"

"Yeah." Freeman bounced on the edge of his seat while Tyrone pulled into the parking lot. Freeman was out of the car in seconds and the first to reach the Corolla. No one was in the front or back seats of the vehicle.

"*Mayhew!* You got a crowbar or something I can pry this trunk open with?" Freeman bellowed.

Mayhew produced the tool. Freeman started to grab it, but Tyrone pulled it out of reach.

"Glove up first," said Tyrone sensibly. "We don't want to lose this case by screwin' up evidence."

Freeman followed Tyrone's advice and took the crowbar from him. He pried open the trunk.

"Holy shit," cried Tyrone. "Jacobs, call the paramedics."

"*Natalie!* Natalie! Can you hear me?" Freeman said, flailing around, afraid to touch her.

Tyrone pushed him aside and checked her neck for a pulse. He could feel her warmth through his glove. "She's still alive, Brent. I've got a pulse."

"Thank, God," said Freeman as tears glistened in his eyes. "Tyrone, look what they've done to her."

Natalie Ralston lay in a pool of blood, battered and bruised. Her mouth was taped shut with duct tape which also bound her hands and feet. Freeman removed the tape from her mouth and gently patted her cheeks, but was unable to arouse her. Then he noticed her swollen jaw looked peculiar.

Jacobs came back with a camera. "We'd better take some photos before the paramedics arrive. They'll be more concerned with helping Natalie than preserving the crime scene."

Tyrone placed his hand on Freeman's shoulder. "Let's walk over here for a minute while he's takin' pictures."

"I wish he didn't have to do that," said Freeman. He bent over at the waist, hands on his knees, breathing deeply.

Tyrone wasn't sure if Freeman was going to pass out or puke. He patted Freeman on the back and walked over to the car where two patrol officers had just arrived.

"Start a log, Bays," said Jacobs. "Samuels, I need for you to tape off an area around the car about six feet out."

A crowd of curious neighbors and shoppers were gathering to see what was happening.

"Okay, folks," Jacobs shouted. "I'm going to have to ask you to back away. We need room for the paramedics. Stay behind the tape the officer is putting out."

From the murmuring crowd came a sweet, soft voice. "That car's been here all day," said a lovely Hispanic woman.

"What's your name, Miss?" asked Tyrone.

"Yolanda Fuentes. I work here. I come to work at 9:00 this morning. The car is here already. I thought some drunk left it here over night."

"So you don't have any idea how it got here, or who it belonged to?" asked Jacobs.

"No, sir."

"You wouldn't happen to be related to Hector Fuentes, would you?" asked Tyrone.

She hesitated looking very uncomfortable. "He's my brother."

Tyrone exchanged a look with Jacobs. What could this mean? Then he heard the sirens and a few seconds later, the paramedics and another patrol car entered the parking lot. As the officers exited their car, Tyrone recognized Angela Sanchez and motioned for her to come over.

"We need for Miss Fuentes to be taken to the station for questioning," said Tyrone.

"What?" cried Yolanda. "But, I've done nothing wrong. I could lose my job."

Her cries caused the crowd to rumble in protest. Tyrone saw Jacobs and the other three patrol officers come running. Tyrone took his partner and Sanchez aside.

"Sanchez, you keep an eye on the girl. As soon as we have more back up, you and Lloyd take her in."

"Sure," she said then went back to where Yolanda was waiting.

"I'll call for more backup before this crowd gets out of hand," said Jacobs.

Tyrone joined Yolanda and Officer Sanchez. "Miss Fuentes, you're not in trouble. We don't believe you had any part in this. However, the victim is someone your brother knows. You may have information important to discoverin' what happened here, even if you don't think you do."

"I see," she said, looking away from him. "I'll tell you now; I haven't spoken to him since...since..." Her voice trailed off as tears formed in her large brown eyes.

"Since he killed Franklin Henderson?"

"Yes."

"Our victim is the woman prosecutin' his case," said Tyrone. "Don't you think it's strange she was left here, where you work?"

"The prosecutor?" she said, making the sign of the cross.

"Yes, Miss Fuentes," Tyrone answered.

"Is...is she dead?" Yolanda asked, tears streaming down her face.

"No, but we think she was left here to die."

"Oh, Holy Mother of God," prayed Yolanda. "Please do not let this be because of me."

"You see now why we need for you to come with us?" asked Sanchez.

Yolanda nodded.

"Oh, and don't worry about your job," said Tyrone. "I'll have a little talk with the manager."

"Thank you."

As Yolanda walked away with Officer Sanchez, shouts of protest filled the air. "It's okay." Yolanda reassured them. "I won't be gone long."

Tyrone went back to the car. The paramedics were checking Natalie's vital signs. He recognized one of them as Derek Winters, but didn't know the other guy.

"Vital signs are stable, except BP slightly elevated. Jaw definitely broken," said Winters. "Let's get a cervical collar on her, Cramer. This is a tight spot. I hope we can get her strapped to the board. Detectives, we need you to stand back and give us room so we can get her on the gurney as quickly as possible."

Tyrone and Freeman stepped aside as Jacobs joined them. They watched as the paramedics did their job.

Once Natalie was on the gurney, Winters checked her vital signs again. "Pulse is 50, but her breathing doesn't seem to be impaired. Good pain response. She twitches when I touch her ribcage on the left. Doesn't seem to be broken, but could be cracked."

"BP is 140 over 90," said Cramer.

"Is that good or bad?" asked Freeman.

"BP's a little high, but not dangerous," answered Cramer. "It usually spikes when you suffer an injury. Our biggest concern right now is this nasty head injury."

"Where are you taking her?" Freeman interjected, wringing his hands and pacing.

"We're taking her to Methodist," said Winters. "It's the closest hospital and they have the best neurology department in the state."

"Can I ride with you?" asked Freeman.

Winters gave Freeman a cross look. "As long as you sit back and let us do our job."

As soon as the paramedics had secured Natalie in the ambulance, Freeman climbed in. He looked at Tyrone and Jacobs with a pained expression on his face just before Cramer closed the doors. Lights flashing, siren blaring, the ambulance headed east towards the hospital.

"Guess we'd better get this investigation underway," said Tyrone. "Good, here come two more patrol cars. This appears to be a rather testy crowd."

"Yeah, well, since we've got sufficient back up, and I see the lab rats are here, we can start questioning a few of these onlookers. Maybe someone saw somebody park the car."

"Doubt anyone's goin' to admit to knowin' anything, but we'll give it a try." Tyrone turned to Jacobs, fierceness in his face. "I'm tellin' you what. Anybody ever does this kind of thing to my Jada, there wouldn't been enough pieces left of them to identify."

Jacobs sighed. "Well let's go shake it up and find out who did this to Natalie."

Chapter 22

Erica received a call from Ben telling her they'd found Natalie Ralston and she wasn't in very good shape. Reluctantly, she joined Brent at Methodist Hospital.

"Hey, Barnes. I thought you hated hospitals," Brent said to her when she came through the waiting room doors.

"Well, some wise ass once told me we're cops and sometimes we have to go to hospitals."

Brent grinned at her, but she could see the pain in his eyes.

"Jacobs and Mayhew are banging on doors trying to find someone who may have seen the bastards who did this," she said. "So far, no luck."

"Nobody in the neighborhood is going to give up these guys. They either hate cops or are afraid these thugs would retaliate if they say anything."

"Did they tell you Fuentes' sister works at the drug store where you found her?" she asked.

"Nobody mentioned it, but I was too busy watching the paramedics work on Natalie," said Brent, looking at her curiously. "Mayhew and Jacobs think it has something to do with this?"

"Maybe. Jacobs had Sanchez take her downtown for questioning. Nearly caused a riot. Anyway, she'd told them the car was there when she came in at 9:00 this morning to start her shift so they decided to interview her to see if there was anything else she might remember."

"What'd they find out?"

"Keep your britches on, partner. I'm getting to it. Since this has turned into an assault case, Mayor Kershner's all fired up about the victim being an officer of the court. Captain Melrose and Lieutenant Terhune stepped in and questioned Miss Fuentes. She told them she hadn't spoken to her brother since he killed Franklin Henderson. Yolanda admitted her brother was really pissed at Natalie for convincing her to testify against him. He blamed Natalie for splitting up his family."

"That mother f..."

"There's more. Yolanda said Henderson's family threatened her several times. Said if it wasn't for her, Henderson would still be alive."

"That's pretty normal, isn't it?" Brent asked.

"I'll excuse your ineptitude since I know you're under a lot of personal stress right now. However, let's not forget we're talking about gang members here. They have a completely different set of rules than the rest of us do. Yolanda suggested they did it to make her brother look bad and to show her what could happen to her some day."

"So what are they going to do now?" Brent asked.

"Captain Melrose plans to ask Strategic Investigations to help. The Criminal Gang Unit would be able to make suggestions on how to deal with the characters in these neighborhoods. They'd also have some snitches who could keep their ears open. Like I said, the mayor's involved now so things will happen." She touched Brent's arm and gazed intently into his eyes. "We'll catch these S.O.B.s."

"That will be little consolation if she doesn't make it through surgery."

"Brent, you can't think this way. She's a fighter," she said. "Did you call her parents?"

"Yes," he said. "They're making arrangements to leave Evansville as soon as possible. I expect them to be here first thing tomorrow morning."

"That's good."

"The great thing is her father gave the medical staff permission to give me details of her condition. Otherwise, all of those HIPAA rules would apply and they wouldn't tell me anything," said Brent. "He hasn't even met me yet. He said Natalie trusts me, so he does, too."

Erica waited, looking into Brent's pale face worried he might pass out from exhaustion. "When was the last time you ate?"

"I don't remember. Maybe a left over donut at around 10:00 this morning."

"Great. This is probably going to take a while. Why don't we go down to the cafeteria and get something to eat?"

"I don't want to leave, you go ahead."

"Then I'm going to go down and get us both something and bring it back. Okay?"

Brent nodded his assent.

She was back in ten minutes with two ham and cheese sandwiches and two iced teas. They sat and ate in silence. Brent's every swallow appeared to pain him. Erica leafed through almost every magazine in the room allowing Brent his quiet thoughts.

The surgery lasted until 11:00 p.m. The neurosurgeon told Erica and Brent that Natalie's injuries were extensive. She had three cracked ribs, which he said should heal well, but could be painful for several weeks. The ulna in her left arm was broken and both arms were severely bruised from what he guessed to be her attempts to fend off the attack. She had apparently been kicked as well as punched. Her left kidney was bruised, but he said the nephrologist felt confident it would heal. She'd also been punched or kicked in the face, breaking her jaw. The concussion was probably the result of hitting her head when she went down from the blow to her face, then being kicked several times.

He explained that when he was confident there were no spinal injuries, he concentrated on his primary concern, the swelling of Natalie's brain. There was excessive intracranial pressure so he inserted an intraventricular catheter into a vacant area called a ventricle. This catheter drains the excess fluid and reduces the pressure. Once Natalie was stable, an orthopedic surgeon set the broken bones in her arm and her jaw, the latter of which he had to wire shut. He admitted her to the intensive care unit for close monitoring of her condition.

"You won't be able to see her before 8:00 tomorrow morning," said the doctor. "Even then, she'll be in a drug induced coma until the brain swelling alleviates. I think you should go home and try to get some sleep. I could prescribe something for you if you like."

"No thanks, Doctor," said Brent. "I want to stay right here."

"Come on, Brent," insisted Erica. "It won't help her if you're a wreck."

"I said no, Erica. I'm staying right here."

"Give it up, Doc. I've known this man for five years and there's no point trying to change his mind once he's made a decision." She turned to Brent. "It's almost midnight and I've got a 9:00 a.m. meeting with our buddies from the FBI."

"Get going then. I'm shocked you stayed this long."

"I'll check in with you tomorrow." She patted his shoulder and left.

Chapter 23

Elizabeth Glenn woke to her "bladder alarm" going off again. "Holy cow," she said aloud. "I must have to get up ten times every night."

She sat on the side of the bed, sliding her feet into her slippers. She glanced at the room across from hers and smiled as she stepped into the hallway. Walking towards the bathroom, she stopped abruptly thinking she'd heard a noise. Glancing towards the living room she stood very still, heart pounding, listening carefully. "I wish your daddy was here instead of thousands of miles away," she whispered, stroking her slightly bulging abdomen.

Hearing nothing more, she proceeded into the bathroom and closed the door. Once she'd relieved herself, she opened the bathroom door and heard it again—just the slightest creak. Her heart raced and her breathing quickened. Could there be someone in the house, or was it only the house settling?

She took a deep breath to calm herself. "I'm being silly," she said as she entered the hallway and walked towards her bedroom. She knew her house so well she hadn't turned on a light. Now she wished she had.

"Hello," he said.

Elizabeth froze in place. This wasn't her husband's voice, but it sounded familiar. Her heart pounded, thumping in her ears. She started to tremble at the terror of what he might do to her.

"P…p…p…please don't hurt us," she begged unable to turn and face him.

He was directly behind her now. She could feel his hot breath on her neck. Chills of horror filled her being when he placed his hands on her shoulders.

"I'm begging you," she said, her voice tight with fear.

"No point in begging is there? You never listened to me when I begged."

"I don't know what you're talking about," she said in a tense whine.

He wrapped his right arm around her, gripping her jaw like a vice. Then he spoke to her in a low husky voice. "You know perfectly well what I'm talking about."

"You don't understand," she cried, barely able to talk through his grip. Panic set in and then disappeared.

***

The next morning at 9:00 sharp, Erica was at her desk when she saw Agent Morgan and a very tall, very pretty female with long, dark red hair walking towards her. The woman was wearing a white cotton blouse and tailored navy blue suit with matching heels. As she came nearer, Erica could see she had icy blue eyes, and a forced smile.

"Ah, Detective Barnes," he said. "I'd like to introduce you to Special Supervisory Agent Trish Zimmer from the Behavioral Analysis Unit or the BAU as we lovingly call it. Trish, this is Homicide Detective Erica Barnes."

Zimmer stretched out a long-fingered, well-manicured hand. "It's a pleasure to meet you. Are the others here so we can get started?"

"I'm afraid Detective Freeman had a personal emergency and won't be joining us. However, Detective Chennelle Kendall is waiting for us in the conference room."

"Excellent. Let's get started," Zimmer said.

Erica led the agents to the conference room and introduced them to Kendall. Morgan went through the forensics files, while Zimmer walked up to the board and took a long look at the photographs from the crime scenes. Erica watched her closely, feeling chills from time-to-time at Zimmer's intensity. She'd seen some pretty fervent investigators in her life, but none quite as focused as this woman. Zimmer tapped her chin with the forefinger of her right hand, left hand on her hip as she paced back and forth looking at each photo several times.

Zimmer abruptly spun, facing the others, causing Erica to flinch. "There is a reason this prompted Agent Morgan to call me in on these cases. There have been similar crimes occurring across the Midwest," she said. "It's exactly the same M.O. as two other murders this year. One was committed in Des Moines, Iowa on January twentieth and one in Springfield, Illinois on March twentieth. The method was the same. Their necks were broken, they were laid out in this same fashion dressed in an older woman's clothing, their eyes were sewn open and they had *SEE ME* written on their foreheads."

"Were they both brunettes?" asked Kendall.

"Yes, Detective Kendall," Zimmer answered. "Agent Morgan, we need photos and reports for the Rachelle Plummer and Noreen Dell cases faxed here immediately. I also want you to ask for the files on Alecia and Wanda Emerson as well."

"Who are they?" asked Erica.

"I believe those cases is where this all started," Zimmer answered.

"Alecia Emerson, a.k.a. Alecia Fox…." said Morgan.

"Alecia Fox, the romance novelist?" asked Kendall before Morgan could finish.

"The same," Morgan continued. "I wasn't sure you'd heard about this one since it happened in Casper, Wyoming."

Erica shook her head. "I'm afraid I'm not familiar with the case."

"They found her in her home just before Christmas last year. Her agent reported to police that he couldn't reach her. Neck broken and the house trashed," Kendall said.

"Yes," said Zimmer. "But there's something they didn't make public. She also had *SEE ME* written on her forehead with a permanent marker. So far we've been able to keep this bit of information out of the press." Zimmer then looked at Erica, one eyebrow raised. "I hope you've been able to do the same."

"We have," Erica said, feeling stung by Zimmer's innuendo. "We've also kept the manner in which our victims were dressed and the fact their eyes were sewn open secret as well."

"Excellent. We think Alecia Emerson was the first victim," continued Zimmer. "It's sloppy. He didn't ransack any of the last four victims' homes. Nor were any of the victims bound, tortured, or *physically* raped before death. That makes this murder personal. Someone she knew."

"Do you have any suspects?" asked Kendall.

"I'll give you my theory in a moment," said Zimmer apparently determined to lay it all out before answering questions. "The second victim, Wanda Emerson, was brutalized in much the same manner as was Alecia Emerson. He murdered Wanda on December twenty-fourth of last year. She's the only victim who was older. We believe her son, Parker Emerson, is the one who murdered her. He is also the prime suspect in his wife, Alecia's, murder."

"I didn't realize she was married," commented Kendall.

"A lot of people didn't. Alecia was one of the most popular romance novelists in the U. S. and she'd sold thousands of copies of her books overseas as well," said Morgan. "People fantasized about her. There wasn't any room to admit to having a husband. Her agent felt it might ruin her image."

"What do you know about Parker Emerson?" asked Erica, hoping to put a face on this guy so they could start the hunt for him.

"Like I said, he was kept out of the spotlight, so there weren't a lot of recent photos of Emerson," said Morgan. "The local police said he was good-looking, dark hair, beard, and mustache, with brown eyes, about five-foot, ten-inches tall. We have a couple of photos from his youth. They aren't great, but we're hoping to work up a computer composite from them."

"Of course, he could have changed his appearance by now," interrupted Zimmer. "He may have shaved and/or dyed his hair. The computer composite will allow us to change these features and age him so we can see him in different ways."

"How did the FBI get involved?" asked Erica.

"When Wanda Emerson was killed in Lincoln, Nebraska," answered Zimmer. "The Lincoln police had heard about Alecia Emerson's death and

Parker's disappearance. The police knew Parker Emerson and his family very well."

"A criminal record?" asked Kendall.

"Parker had done nothing serious," said Zimmer. "A few fights, petty theft, acting out sorts of behavior. However, there are several complaints against his mother for abusing him and his sister, Jordan. Even though the authorities took them from the home on several occasions, they didn't place the children in foster care until Parker was twelve.

"They sent me to Lincoln to check out their concerns about Wanda Emerson's case," continued Zimmer. "Most of the police officers were too young to know the background of Emerson's abuse, but there was an older detective who remembered Parker. His name was Sergeant Aaron Dale.

"Sergeant Dale said he always felt sorry for the kid. Child abuse laws weren't as stringent back then and the court kept sending the kids back to their mother. At age seven, Parker strangled the neighbor's cat because it used his sandbox as a litter box. Two days later, the kid was in Children's Hospital with a broken leg. Said he accidentally fell down the basement stairs. Later, the police discovered they didn't have a basement."

"So, Agent Zimmer, do you think this was the start of his desire to kill?" asked Erica.

"It's not the desire to kill that drives him, Detective. Many times abused children turn to the only means by which they have to vent their anger. They have no control over what's happening to them so they act out inappropriately. Unfortunately, Parker learned to handle anger by using control and abuse against other creatures weaker than he is. Some children who leave abusive situations at an early age and find placement in a nurturing environment can be retrained. His sister, Jordan Collins, for example has no history of violence. Others carry on the *family tradition* into adulthood, or in Parker's case, try to suppress it. If they don't learn to cope, they will eventually explode as we believe he has."

"What about the sister?" asked Kendall. "Was she abused as well?"

"I interviewed her. She claims her mother slapped her a few times, but Parker would intercede taking the brunt of some pretty brutal punishment."

"Jordan lives with her husband and two children in Lincoln," said Morgan as Zimmer began to pace again. "She said her brother came by to see her on Christmas Eve. He seemed calm. Said he wanted to stop by to give his niece and nephew their Christmas gifts personally. When she asked about Alecia, he said she couldn't come because she was preparing for a book tour. Before he left that evening, he told Jordan he loved her and said she was a good momma. She hasn't heard from him since."

Morgan sighed and sat up straighter. "When Jordan's mother didn't call or come by on Christmas Day, she went to check on Wanda and found her nude, bloody body tied to a kitchen chair. She doesn't want to believe Parker would do such a thing.

"When we told her about Alecia, she was shocked. Her husband was on a flight home from a business trip in China on Christmas Eve. Jordan hadn't paid much attention to the news since she was preparing for her husband's and Santa's arrival. Having Parker drop by unexpectedly was distracting as well."

Zimmer stopped pacing and pulled a notepad from her briefcase. She leafed through it. "I spoke to Brenna Copeland of the Child Services Department in Lincoln. She told me only Parker had suffered severe physical injury at the hands of his mother. She thought since Parker was the eldest he probably took most of the punishments to protect Jordan. Another theory, Wanda Emerson may have hated men or hated Parker's father in particular and therefore transferred that hate to Parker. Jordan had a different father."

Zimmer flipped a few more pages. "It gets worse. Apparently, there were signs of Parker's sexual abuse. That's why the authorities removed the children from the home permanently. According to records at Children's Hospital, Parker arrived at the facility on Christmas Eve with a fractured wrist when he was twelve. He told them he'd tripped over some toys. He also had a black eye and several bruises on his arms which looked like he'd been held a little too tightly. After they finished setting his wrist and he got off of the exam table, they noted there was blood on it. A closer look and the doctor saw there was blood on the back of his jeans. The doctor called the police in and Child Services took custody of both children. Turns out she'd used a foreign object to assault him rectally."

"*Christ!*" Erica gritted her teeth and put her head in her hands.

"How could anyone do something like this to their own child?" Kendall exclaimed. "No wonder this guy is so screwed up."

"The judge gave her the maximum sentence, which sadly was only three months in jail and a $500 fine," said Zimmer. "But luckily the children were permanently placed with a foster family in North Platte, Nebraska, approximately 230 miles from Lincoln. Wanda Emerson never fought to regain custody nor did she ask for visitation, which as you can see was probably best for the children."

"His foster parents were good to him, but it may have been too late to heal the damage," said Morgan. "They were strict but kind and he seemed to respect them. They had never been able to have children of their own, so Parker and his sister received a lot of attention. Their foster parents had a lot of money and were willing to help them get into good colleges. Parker met Alecia at the University of Wyoming in Laramie. They were both in the Journalism program. He became a reporter, she became a novelist."

"He finally got a life without abuse, so what triggered him to do this?" asked Erica. "Did his wife do something to piss him off?"

"According to everyone who knew them as a couple, they were perfect together," answered Morgan. "When she was Alecia Emerson, that is. Not sure he liked being in the background when she was Alecia Fox. That could explain the '*SEE ME*' written on the victims' foreheads."

"So what do you think, Agent Zimmer," asked Erica. "What pushed him over the edge?"

"His mother treated him like a parasite. According to what Jordan told Mrs. Copeland, their mother locked Parker in a closet for days without food or water because she said she *didn't want to see him*. I think it was this neglect which put Parker on his present course. He wanted to be seen and loved. Just before Thanksgiving, Alecia's latest novel hit the New York Times Best Seller list and her publisher wanted her to tour and do the TV and radio talk show circuit."

"So he wasn't lying when he mentioned the tour to his sister," said Kendall.

"No he wasn't. Airline tickets had been delivered by Express Mail four days before she was found. We think when he saw she was actually going to leave him, that triggered something and he lost control."

"I guess I don't really understand how this connects with the mother," said Kendall. "Especially if he and his wife got along so well."

Zimmer finally took a seat. Erica wondered if those lovely high-heeled shoes had finally gotten to her. Zimmer clasped her hands together on the table, looking very serious.

"When you see the photos of Alecia Emerson, you will note she looks just like all of the other victims. Dark brown shoulder length hair, brown eyes, approximately five-foot seven-inches tall, and in her thirties. When Wanda Emerson was abusing her son, she was in her thirties, had dark brown eyes and shoulder length brown hair. Jordan was able to provide a few photos of Wanda at this age. I believe in Parker's mind on this particular day, he saw Wanda, not Alecia. The fact she was leaving for months made him feel like he would be shut away in the closet again. I believe he went back to being a little boy who was told he was worthless and shouldn't be seen."

"So where do we go from here?" asked Erica.

Zimmer leaned back in her chair. "I would like to look over all of the files on your cases. As soon as Agent Morgan gets those files on the other four cases, I'd like for you and Detective Kendall to study them. Detective Freeman also, when he's able. Then we can meet back here tomorrow afternoon to give the department a profile."

"Sounds good," said Erica. "I'll see what I can do about..."

Erica didn't have a chance to finish her sentence as Major Stevenson burst into the room.

"Kendall, Barnes. We've got another one."

Chapter 24

"Victim is Elizabeth Glenn, age 34," reported Patrol Officer Bays. "Same M.O. as the Flanders woman except this one has a rose *and* a teddy bear. We called the Coroner's office. Dr. Patel should be here soon. Mark Chatham's already in there taking photos."

"Thanks, Bays," Erica said as she signed the log, and then handed it to Kendall. "A couple of FBI agents, Agent Spencer Morgan and Supervisory Special Agent Trish Zimmer, will be here soon. Make sure they're given access."

"The rest of the Forensics Team should be here any minute," Bays said. "Samuels is securing the perimeter. I feel bad for her, only on the job eleven months and already first responder on two gross murders."

"You said she had aspirations of becoming a homicide detective," interjected Kendall handing him the log. "She'll be looking at this sort of thing, or worse, almost every day. Wait until she has her first decomp."

"I've been on the force for eight years. So far, I haven't had the misfortune of going out on a decomp," he said. He wrinkled his nose as though he could smell it through his thoughts.

"Be glad," said Erica. "Who called it in?"

"Her supervisor at Golden Rule Insurance. Name's Madalyn Harrison. She said Mrs. Glenn would never take time off without calling in. She got worried when she couldn't reach her on her home or cell phone."

"You said *Mrs*. Glenn. Where is her husband?" asked Erica.

"According to Mrs. Harrison, he's in the Army and is on his second tour in Afghanistan," answered Bays.

"F'ing great." Erica walked in a circle then kicked the air wishing it was Emerson's face. "Glenn's over there risking his life for his country and now we have to send him this news."

"It's not fair," said Kendall.

"Which room's she in?" Erica bellowed in frustration.

Bays indicated the bedroom at the end of the hallway on the right. Erica took the lead, but stopped abruptly after glancing into the small bedroom on the left across from the master bedroom. "Hang on, Kendall."

She walked into the tiny room and turned in place taking in every detail. There she saw a baby crib and changing table. It was a baby nursery in progress. Winnie the Pooh characters waited to be hung on the walls and an unopened stroller box sat in the corner. Erica's heart sank as she realized Elizabeth Glenn must have been pregnant.

"Oh my God," Kendall said as she walked in behind her. "Do you think the bastard knew?"

"I don't believe so." They turned abruptly to see Zimmer standing in the doorway. "Sorry. I didn't mean to startle you."

"What makes you think he didn't know?" asked Kendall.

"I took a quick look in the master bedroom. She doesn't look pregnant yet so she's probably less than six months along. Besides, he's looking for a particular type," Zimmer stated. "He's choosing women who resemble his mother during the period when she abused him so he can try to rid himself of her. He finds those who are alone because his mother lived alone. It was just a fluke Marilyn Novak had company the night she was murdered."

"But he murdered his mother already," Erica spat. She couldn't understand how he could keep killing innocent women when he had already tortured and killed the woman who had caused him so much pain.

"True, Detective Barnes; however, Parker Emerson has had a psychotic break and is convinced she keeps reappearing," said Zimmer. "The interesting thing is the remorse he shows after he's finished."

"Remorse?" said Kendall scowling. "Where's the remorse?"

"Every victim who has been killed since he murdered his mother has been killed swiftly. He does this so they will not suffer through the more tortuous obscenities he commits upon their bodies. At some point, he must realize the woman isn't his mother. After this realization, he dresses them neatly, tries to put on makeup so they will look nice, and gives them a rose."

"So, does he feel guilty or something?" asked Erica, not sure she believed any of this.

"I know for those of us who think rationally, it's hard to understand how someone could feel guilty after committing such heinous crimes. But yes, I believe this guilt is now playing a part in all of this."

"Hey, did you guys take a good look in here yet?" asked Agent Morgan.

Erica entered the room first and looked at the body of Elizabeth Glenn all laid out on her funeral bed. Eyes sewn open. Frumpy dress. Too much makeup. Rose and teddy bear in hand.

"Over there," Morgan said, pointing to the dresser mirror.

On the mirror, in what appeared to be lipstick, were the words *PLEASE STOP ME DETECTIVE BARNES. I NEED YOU TO STOP ME!*

"What the hell?" exclaimed Kendall, turning to look at Erica.

"What does this mean?" Erica directed to Zimmer.

"It could mean any number of things," Zimmer began. "I assume your name is in the paper or on the news as one of the detectives in charge of these cases."

"Yeah," said Erica, feeling uncomfortable.

"With the remorse he's feeling, he may be reaching out to you to stop him from killing again. Of course, there is something else," Zimmer said rubbing her chin.

"What?" demanded Erica, an inexplicable tingling sensation running down her spine.

"You're a professional, so I may as well be blunt," Zimmer responded. "He may have become fixated on you."

Erica looked at her and could feel her mouth open in shock. She blinked a couple of times then started pacing up and down the room.

"Detective Barnes, you *are* in your mid-thirties. You have dark brown, medium length hair and brown eyes. I'm guessing you are approximately five-foot, seven-inches tall. You *are* his type."

"Are you saying he's going to come after me?" Erica asked.

"Not necessarily," answered Zimmer.

"That's it? Not necessarily?" said Erica trying to keep from becoming hysterical. "*Great!* I'll sleep loads better now."

"I understand your concern..."

Erica lost it and got right into Zimmer's face. "I really don't think you do understand. I live alone and I'm his type. Now he's leaving me messages. I'm a little more than concerned right now."

Zimmer took a step back from Erica and didn't blink an eye, but raised a condescending eyebrow as she had the day before. Erica was pissed. She wondered if this bitch was a human or a robot. She abruptly headed down the hall. "I'm going outside for some air."

She met Dr. Patel on her way out. "Victim's in the back bedroom, all the way down the hall and to the right." She didn't pause to see if Patel had any questions.

As she made her way outside and stopped, she realized Kendall was right on her heels. "Why are you following me?"

"I wanted to make sure you're okay." Erica could see the concern in her eyes. Kendall was a great cop and friend.

"Sorry, Kendall. That bitch pisses me off. She's so stiff. She tells me her theories without batting an eye, as if it's some fact out of a book instead of my life on the line. Holy crap. Why did he latch onto *me*?"

"Maybe it's like Zimmer said, he's seen your name in the paper or maybe he saw the news conference."

"Shit! The news conference. Then he does know what I look like. This is really freaking me out."

"Oh, sweet Jesus," said Kendall. "We'd better move back inside."

Erica turned to see a flurry of reporters coming their way. She and Kendall headed for the front door. She instructed Officer Samuels to stop them from coming any closer and to tell them they needed to talk to Major Stevenson if they wanted a statement.

"Detective Barnes," shouted the reporters in various volumes and tones. "Can we have a statement? Is this the same killer as the other three cases? Do we have a serial killer in Indianapolis? We heard this one was pregnant."

"No comment!" Erica shouted as she slammed the door. "How the hell did they find out she was pregnant already?" She could still hear their muted voices as she went further into the house. Bastards, she thought.

Erica stopped and took a deep breath before entering the master bedroom. Zimmer was walking around the room looking at everything. Morgan was talking to Dr. Patel, so Erica decided to join them.

"Dr. Patel," said Erica. "Does this one match our other three victims?"

"My preliminary exam would indicate it is the same as the Flanders, Novak, and Ritter murders," stated Dr. Patel. "However, as in the Novak case, I do not see any signs of sexual assault and he left her this extra gift." Dr. Patel pointed at the teddy bear.

"I wonder why he'd switch his M. O.," said Kendall.

"Come over to this side of the bed," instructed Morgan. "Let's say he's standing here and has just laid her on the bed. He looks up and what does he see?"

"The nursery," said Erica. "The crib can be seen from here."

"Precisely. He'd already killed Mrs. Glenn, but apparently couldn't bring himself to complete the sexual act," stated Zimmer as she joined the group. "The teddy bear is for the baby. The baby could be why he's asking Detective Barnes to stop him. He didn't know Mrs. Glenn was pregnant when he killed her. Then he saw what was across the hall. When he stripped her of her clothing to redress her he saw the proof of her slightly bulging stomach."

"So this is all part of his remorse thing?" asked Kendall.

"Yes. His killing has escalated. He's killed five people in less than two weeks. The four killings he committed before settling here were spread over five months."

"We should probably give your profile today," Morgan said to Zimmer. "We're going to need to get several sketches out showing how he might look if he changed his hair length or color, shaved, gained or lost weight, etcetera."

"You're right," said Zimmer. "Let's go back to the conference room at the police station and prepare our statement. Barnes' team has everything well in hand here."

"Detective Barnes," said Morgan. "Can you meet us back at the station in a couple of hours?"

Erica nodded. She watched as Zimmer and Morgan left the scene. Time to go back to work.

***

Two hours later, they were in the IMPD Homicide Department ready for SSA Zimmer to give the profile. She distributed several reports which included photos of how Parker Emerson might look today.

"Good afternoon, Detectives. I'm Supervisory Special Agent Zimmer from the FBI's Behavioral Analysis Unit. I'm here to tell you that we believe the man you are seeking in the murders of Penny Flanders, Marilyn Novak, Keith Gray, Samantha Ritter, and Elizabeth Glenn has murdered at least four other people. Alecia Emerson in Casper, Wyoming; Wanda Emerson in Lincoln, Nebraska; Rachelle Plummer in Des Moines, Iowa; and Noreen Dell in Springfield, Illinois.

"He has a history of being physically and sexually abused by his mother, Wanda Emerson. He has issues with abandonment which we feel was the trigger for his psychotic break. He murdered his wife, Alecia, after he realized she was serious about going on a lengthy book tour without him. Although his mother was his second victim, the anger he has been internalizing has manifested itself into a need to rid his self of her. His psychosis and the guilt he feels for killing his mother is causing him to see her over and over again in women who resemble her at the height of the abuse. He is seeing her everywhere.

"Parker Emerson is Caucasian, thirty-five-years old, five foot, ten inches tall. He has brown eyes and did have short dark brown hair, a beard, and mustache. However, he may have changed his looks in some way. He's certainly had time to make changes. I've had photos of what he may look like today created and we'll post them in the conference room. We discovered he was a Karate combat expert trained by one of the militia groups in Wyoming. So remember, expertise in this area makes him armed and dangerous. He was a journalist, so he could be working for a newspaper—most likely a smaller one so he isn't noticed. On the other hand, he may have taken on some sort of labor position to keep himself out of the lime light.

"The unsub left a message for Detective Barnes at the crime scene this morning. It asked her to stop him. His mental status is deteriorating. He's going to become more careless and may reveal himself to her. I would urge all of you to look carefully at anyone you see approaching her. Her safety during this investigation is a top priority. Thank you."

Erica was flabbergasted. She'd seen a hint of humanity in the stoic one. Maybe Zimmer wasn't so bad after all. Time would tell. For now, she needed to type up her report and go check on her partner.

Chapter 25

Brent walked into the Intensive Care Unit with its walls of soothing pastel blue. Each room had windows facing the hallways instead of solid walls for medical personnel to keep watch. There were three other patients besides Natalie. Two were in serious car accidents and one had just come into the unit after open-heart surgery.

Natalie's room was in the center of the unit. Brent approached Room 103 with quiet reverence. There she was. Bruised and swollen. Not looking anything like the beautiful woman he'd kissed goodbye a little more than 36 hours ago. At least it wasn't the last time he'd get to kiss her.

Mayhew had called to let Brent know the canvass of the neighborhood got them nowhere. The *Code of Silence* was in full force. People were either scared they'd be next, or didn't trust cops. Of course, Mayhew had said, "We're not givin' up, Freeman. We're gonna keep pounded on doors till we find out what happened to your lady."

Just after Mayhew's call, a lab tech came by and took Natalie for another MRI to see if the swelling in her brain was subsiding. When Natalie returned, Brent asked the nurse how it went. She said the doctor would be in for rounds in about a half an hour and would give him an official report. Then she gave him a toothy smile, which he took as a sign that things were looking better. This had given him a sense of relief, but he was worried about the induced coma.

When the neurosurgeon came in, he told Brent the swelling had subsided. They had started weaning her off of the pentobarbital at 2:00 a.m. The doctor expected her to start responding by mid-morning.

Brent slowly approached the bed. When he reached her side, he stroked her hair gently. There were tubes in her right arm and her left arm was in a cast so he decided not to hold her hand. He watched her monitors—pulse 60, blood pressure 125 over 80, oxygen concentration 98. A low moan interrupted his thoughts.

Looking down, he saw Natalie's eyes flicker like someone trying to wake up from a long deep sleep. He pressed the nurse's button.

"Natalie. Natalie, it's Brent. I'm here. Open your eyes."

She moaned again.

The nurse came into the room. "How's our girl?"

"I think she's trying to wake up."

"Her blood pressure is a few points higher than it has been," she said looking at Natalie's chart. "That's a good sign. It means she's starting to respond to other stimuli, like your touch. She can probably hear our voices."

The nurse said her name while stroking her leg. Natalie's eyes finally opened, but she looked confused and frightened. She tried to speak, but couldn't open her mouth.

"Now, now honey. It's okay," said the nurse sweetly. "You're in a hospital and we're taking very good care of you. This gentleman's been right here in this hospital since they brought you in. You just lie still now and try to relax. You can't open your mouth right now because your jaw was broken and the only way it could heal properly was to wire it shut."

"Uh, mmm," Natalie said trying desperately to communicate.

"You'll be able to figure out how to talk through those immobile teeth soon enough. Right now you need to listen calmly and I'll explain what we are doing." The nurse touched her arm and stroked her cheek in a nurturing manner, and then continued. "You'll be getting nourishment through an IV for a couple more days. Then you'll gradually be drinking liquefied sustenance through a straw. I know it's uncomfortable, but you'll be fine."

Brent was impressed with how the nurse could calm Natalie with her soothing voice and gentle touch.

"Somebody hurt you, honey," said the nurse. "Do you remember? Blink once for yes and twice for no."

Natalie blinked twice.

"It's okay, Natalie. Sometimes we get a little forgetful right after an injury like this."

Brent looked into Natalie's frightened blue eyes. "Natalie, sweetheart, don't worry. I'll be here. I won't let anyone hurt you ever again."

Natalie stared at him, then back at the nurse.

The nurse walked over to Brent then touched his arm and whispered, "Natalie may not know who you are. Amnesia and confusion often accompany this type of head injury, especially when a patient has been in a drug-induced coma. You need to be patient. She'll come around."

Brent's expression bore his disappointment, but he managed to put on a smile. "I've called your parents, Natalie. They should be here soon."

Tears welled in Natalie's eyes. She glanced at Brent and then looked imploringly at the nurse.

"Are you in pain, honey?" the nurse asked.

Natalie blinked once.

"I'll go call the doctor and ask what pain meds you can have, okay?" said the nurse smiling. "We have to be very careful what we give you right now. Do you want Detective Freeman to stay with you for a while?"

Natalie blinked twice.

Brent's eyes filled with tears, but he'd quickly turned away from her. He walked out with the nurse.

"Don't take it too hard, Detective. She barely knows who *she* is right now. Give it a couple of days. Hopefully seeing her folks will help."

Brent and the nurse parted company. Walking towards the waiting area, he spotted a couple who appeared to be in their 50's. The man had salt and pepper, neatly cut hair and was wearing blue jeans and a blue Polo shirt. His companion was beautiful with white blonde hair and the same frightened crystal blue eyes he'd just seen in the hospital bed staring up at him in confusion.

"Mr. and Mrs. Ralston?"

"Yes," said Christopher Ralston. "Are you Brent?"

"Yes sir, I am."

"This is my wife, Linda. Where is our daughter? How is she?"

"Actually, I just saw her. She just regained consciousness. She's still a little disoriented, so don't be upset if she doesn't recognize you right away."

"Where is she? I want to see my daughter," Linda demanded.

"I'm sorry," Brent said as he blushed. "Right this way." He led them to the Intensive Care Unit, introduced them to Natalie's nurse, and then left them to their privacy.

Slowly, Brent walked down the hall, head down, and hands in his pockets.

"Hey, Freeman. How's she doing?" asked Erica.

He looked up to see his partner standing a few feet away. "Better. She's awake and her parents are with her," his voice cracked and he turned away from Erica. "Kendall stopped by for a few minutes. She said there was another one."

"You've got enough to worry about here. Kendall and I can handle everything. Besides, we got two hot shot Feds helping us now."

Brent turned to face her grabbing her shoulders. He wanted to shake her. "Kendall told me about the message this asshole left for you."

Erica tried to push his hands away, but he wouldn't let go.

"Stop it Brent. Kendall worries too much. He just said he wanted me to stop him and that's what I intend to do."

"Don't take this so lightly. I don't want to have to break in a new partner when I get back." He couldn't help himself. He pulled her to him hugging her, hanging on; afraid he'd lose her, too.

"You're such a sentimental fool," she said, patting his back.

He squeezed her one more time, and then released her. He decided to change the subject because he knew Erica wouldn't listen to him and he didn't have the strength to argue with her.

"Let's get back to your original question," he said. "Natalie is doing remarkably well. She has some amnesia, but the nurse said it was normal with the head injury she sustained and the drugs they used to put her in a coma. Her memory should come back gradually."

"How long could it take?"

"Don't know. Right now, it's hard for her to communicate with her jaw wired shut," he said. "With the memory problem, I'm not sure when she'll be able to tell us who did this to her. She's going to need a lot of therapy before she can walk, or even write down anything."

"I'm so sorry, Brent. I know I've given you a hard time about her, but I just wanted you to slow down a little and get to know her first."

"I realize that, Erica. You're family—family watches out for one another. That's why I'm worried about this guy focusing on you," said Brent ready to try to get her to see reason despite his weariness. "You do realize you fit his profile—dark brown hair and eyes, right height and age?"

"Yeah, believe me; Supervisory Special Agent Zimmer already pointed out that little tidbit to me. But you don't have to worry. Kendall will have my back until you return; then you can watch out for me."

He frowned at her, but she grinned at him in response.

"Please don't worry. You know I can handle myself. This Saturday I'm ready for Shodan, and by afternoon I will have my first black belt."

"I hope you're as good as you think you are," he said as he squinted at her in an attempt to look intimidating.

"I am," said Erica. "Now that Natalie's parents are here, you should get some rest. I'll talk to you tomorrow."

Brent saw Erica look over her shoulder as she left the waiting room. He plopped down in a chair feeling exhausted. She was right; he should go home for a while. He only hoped Erica would be careful. Black belt or not, this killer had similar skills. Underestimating him could get her killed.

***

Down in the lobby of the hospital, Erica encountered Ben Jacobs and Tyrone Mayhew. They were smiling as if they'd just won the lottery. She couldn't imagine why they might be so happy. "What's up with the two of you?"

"We got good news for Miss Ralston," said Mayhew. "Jury's in and they threw the book at Fuentes."

"I take it the judge brought in the second chair to finish up then?" asked Erica.

"That's right. That brother-in-law of mine doesn't mess around," said Mayhew. "He had that second prosecutor give his arguments two days after Miss Natalie was hurt. I'm sure Norman didn't want these jack offs thinking they could intimidate the court."

"Judge Jackson is a good man," said Erica.

"I take it you just came from seeing her," said Ben.

"No, I only saw Brent. Her parents are with her now. She's regained consciousness but she's very confused. Besides, Freeman wanted to hassle me about the love note Emerson left me at the last crime scene."

"He left you a note?" exclaimed Ben.

She could see the panic in Ben's eyes as he made the statement and it sparked her anger.

"You've got to take this seriously," he said.

"I am taking it seriously. Besides, Freeman just gave me the lecture so I really don't need to hear it again from you. I'm a big girl and I'm perfectly capable of taking care of myself."

"Whoa, little lady," said Mayhew. "No need to get so ticked off. We care about you. Freeman can't function without *you*."

"Sweet talker," she said sarcastically.

Mayhew laughed. "We know you can take care of yourself. However, even the best cop can be caught off guard—male or female. We got your back, sister. Always."

"Thanks, Tyrone."

She turned and smiled at Ben apologetically before the elevator doors closed. She hoped it would convey how sorry she was for jumping on him. The only reason she was so short with everyone came from a deep fear that this maniac would be around the next corner. He just might catch her unawares. Moreover, as much as she hated to admit it, SSA Zimmer and Brent were right. She did fit the victim profile.

Erica started toward the exit door and nearly ran into Peter Elliott.

"Well, well. Detective Barnes. Imagine running into you here."

"I was visiting a sick friend, Mr. Elliott."

Elliott gave her a sly look. "How *is* our lady prosecutor, anyway? I was hoping she was awake and ready to give us a statement."

Erica glared at him. She would have loved to put him on the receiving end of *Hiji Ate*. A quick elbow to the chin might just take that irritating smirk off his face.

"Unless *you'd* like to give me a comment for the record."

"Nope," she said doing her best to keep her temper in check. "I've told you before, any statements for the press come from Major Stevenson or Deputy Chief Lewis. I've got nothing to say about this case, or any other case you may be curious about."

"Okay, Detective. You know you really should allow me to make up for my obvious insolence. I wouldn't ask any questions about your cases if you'd let me take you out to dinner."

"No thanks." She started to walk away, but he grabbed her arm and turned her around to face him.

"I'm just trying to be friendly. Why are you being such a bitch?"

"If I were you," she said through gritted teeth, "I would release me before you get arrested for assaulting a police officer."

He aggressively let go of her arm, pushing her away. "Well, you can turn me down, but you can't stop me from doing my job. See ya around, Ms. Barnes."

She felt a cold rush make every hair on her body stand on end. Something about his quick temper and the flaming of his dark brown eyes made her feel uneasy. She'd never let men intimidate her, but this one was an exception—popping up every time she was alone. Was he following her? Was he waiting for the opportune moment to strike?

"Erica, wait up." Ben was running towards her. "Mayhew's going to stay with Freeman for a while and he drove. Want to give me a lift to my car and maybe have some dinner?"

"Sounds great."

"What's wrong? You look a little pale."

"Nothing, Ben. I think I'm just a little tired and a lot frustrated about everything. And, you know I don't like hospitals. It takes a lot for me to step through those doors."

"I know, but it shows how strong you really are. I'm sure Freeman appreciates it."

"Let's get out of here before my head swells up so big I can't fit through the front doors."

Ben put his arm across her shoulders and they walked together. She felt safe now. His simple touch reeled in her fears, both past and present. She was not alone.

Chapter 26

Ben left early to go to his apartment for some fresh clothes before heading for IMPD. At dinner the night before, Erica told Ben about the strange feeling she had every time Peter Elliott approached her. They discussed the idea of Ben moving in for a while, but in the end, she decided against it for now. She could see he was disappointed, but she'd just given him a key. She wasn't quite ready for the next step.

While drinking her second cup of coffee, she heard the familiar thump of the newspaper against her door. She retrieved it and waved at elderly Mrs. Yates across the hall as she watched her slowly bend over to pick up her copy.

Tossing the newspaper on the table, she went to the kitchen to retrieve her bagel and coffee. Unfurling the paper, she took a look at the front page. Something she wished she hadn't done. Right there in huge letters: SERIAL KILLER STRIKES AGAIN with Peter Elliott in the byline.

"Holy crap!" she said, and then read the article.

Although the Homicide Detective in charge, Erica Barnes, has been avoiding this reporter's questions, it has come to my attention that these killings are all similar in nature and have probably been committed by the same individual. Each of the victims has been a female in her thirties with shoulder length brown hair and brown eyes. However, the last victim, Mrs. Elizabeth Glenn was the only victim who was married and pregnant.

"How did he know she was pregnant?" She continued reading.

A reliable source has also confided that each victim was laid out as though prepared for her own funeral. Major Robert Stevenson, head of the Robbery and Homicide Division at IMPD, refused to confirm or deny any details of the shape these bodies were in at the time of discovery. He also would not confirm whether the FBI has been called in. However, two FBI agents were on the scene of this last horrendous murder—Supervisory Special Agent Trish Zimmer from the Behavioral Analysis Unit at Quantico, Virginia and Agent Spencer Morgan from the Indianapolis field office.

All I can say is any woman in her thirties who fits the description of these victims should be cautious. Don't go anywhere late at night by yourself, make sure your doors and windows are securely locked, and report any suspicious behavior in your neighborhood to the police immediately.

"Oh, great! Now we're going to have phone calls out the whazoo. That son-of-a-bitch is getting on my last nerve."

She threw down her paper, grabbed her purse, and went out the door without finishing her coffee or bagel. Her cheeks were so inflamed with anger she could barely feel the warmth of the sun on this beautiful, spring day. Storming off towards her car, she crashed into a man who was walking down the sidewalk, nearly knocking him over.

"Oh my gosh! I'm so sorry Joe. Are you okay?"

"I'm alright. What you in such a hurry for, Erica?"

"I've got a couple of big cases weighing on my mind, Joe. How's the landscaping business been treating you?"

"It's okay. We're getting busy again, but I'm thinking about a change."

"That's nice," she said, not really listening due to all the distractions of this latest slap in the face from Peter Elliott. "Aren't you usually at work by now?"

"I have an appointment this morning, but I'm going to catch up with them later. You have a nice day, Erica."

She watched as Joe Davidson walked toward his vehicle. Short but muscular, with brown eyes and long blonde hair pulled back in a ponytail, he had a square jaw and high cheekbones. She thought Joe was probably in his late thirties. They always spoke when they saw one another. Joe recently divorced and had moved here a couple of months ago from Arizona. He'd heard Indiana was a nice place to live and decided this would be a good place to get a fresh start. Erica was glad to have him as a neighbor.

At least her encounter with Joe had softened her mood a bit.

By the time she reached the station, she wasn't quite so enraged. Entering the Homicide Unit, she saw Kendall standing near her desk.

"Stevenson's been looking for you," said Kendall. "Did you see the paper?"

"Yeah. I can't believe this guy. He confronted me at the hospital last night. I'm pretty sure it's why I got *honorable mention* in his article."

"Well, the switchboard's been lighting up like a Christmas tree and Stevenson's been pacing in his office. I suspect he's already heard from the mayor..."

"*Barnes*!" Major Stevenson was standing in the doorway to his office. "In my office! Now!"

She gave Kendall a quick look before heading for Stevenson's office. When she entered, she saw Agent Morgan sitting in the corner. She assumed this was what Kendall wanted to tell her before Stevenson interrupted them.

"Agent Morgan," she said nodding politely in his direction.

"Good morning, Detective Barnes," Morgan replied.

"Barnes. As you've probably already guessed, Mayor Kershner called me this morning. He's very unhappy about the publicity we're getting from this Elliott character. What do you know about him?"

"He works for the *Indianapolis Star*," said Erica. "He has shown up at each of the crime scenes, and I feel like he's been stalking me."

Stevenson glared at her. "What do you mean, 'stalking you'? I thought he was just giving you a hard time at the crime scenes."

"I mean, I've been alone on several occasions when Elliott just seems to appear out of nowhere. He even showed up at Methodist Hospital last night after I left Freeman. He was ticked because I wouldn't disclose any details about Natalie Ralston." She decided not to tell him about the dinner invitation from Peter.

"You didn't indicate to him in any way that we were considering these serial murders, did you?" Stevenson gave her a confident look.

"No, absolutely not. I told him if he had questions he should talk to you or the deputy chief."

"Major Stevenson," said Morgan. "If I could just interject, I'm sure this reporter didn't get this information from anyone working directly on this case. We've specifically instructed all involved to keep the details of the way the corpses were treated a secret. Elliott may be guessing, or maybe he overheard a conversation, or he may have talked to a civilian witness. I think we should bring him in and question him."

Panic shot through Erica like an icy arrow. "I'd rather not be in on the interview, if that's all right with you sir."

Stevenson gave her a stern, disapproving look to which she quickly responded.

"Like I said, he and I have had several confrontations. I've also discovered recently, he lives in my apartment building. I feel you'd get better results if Agent Morgan and Detective Kendall spoke with him."

"I agree, Major," said Agent Morgan, smiling at Erica. "Detective Barnes could watch from the observation room."

Stevenson raised an eyebrow looking from Morgan to Erica and back. "I see your point. He might just clam up as soon as he sees her. He'll probably start screaming about freedom of the press, claiming he can't reveal his sources, and all that shit."

"Thank you sir," said Erica.

"Agent. Let's have you make the call to Mr. Elliott. If nothing else, he'll be thrilled the FBI wants to talk to him."

"I'll be glad to make the call," said Morgan. He looked at Erica. "Shall we adjourn to the war room?"

Morgan and Erica walked toward the conference room. Erica signaled for Kendall to join them. After Morgan made the call to Elliott, the three of them strategized about what questions he might ask the annoying reporter.

Major Stevenson was correct when he said Elliott wouldn't be able to resist the invitation to speak with Agent Morgan. Elliott agreed to be there within the hour.

Mark Chatham made sure the photos from the Glenn crime scene were in the war room for them to post. Erica busied herself tacking up the photos while Kendall and Morgan discussed their approach to the Elliott interview. Then Erica picked up the file SSA Zimmer left behind to see if there was anything she'd missed.

"So where is Zimmer today?" asked Kendall.

"She had to go back to Quantico for a few days," said Morgan. "She'll check in tomorrow. Worst case, she'll fly back here immediately if we have another murder."

"Well, then, I hope I don't see her for a long, long time," said Kendall.

"Agent Morgan," said Erica as she approached them with the file. "Do you have these photo enhancements of the suspect on your laptop?"

"Yes. What are you thinking?"

"I'd like to try something. Do you know how to use the facial reconstruction software?"

He looked at her apprehensively. "Yes."

"Pull up this one and save it under another name so we can make changes."

Morgan did as she asked.

"Now, let's give him a clean cut look. Dark hair, neatly trimmed around the ears, short sideburns. That's it. Now make sure the hair on his forehead is trimmed back and add a little wave to it right about here." She pointed to the area opposite the part. "Perfect. Now let's take a few pounds off him. There, right there."

"Did you see someone who looks like this, Detective?" Morgan asked.

"I'll let you know in a minute. Now, let me see the choices for eyeglasses. Something up-to-date, those thick frames. Try those." She pointed at the screen.

She looked at the composite and couldn't believe what she was seeing. "Take a good look at this, Kendall. Does this guy look familiar to you?"

Kendall took a good hard look at the photo, and then her mouth dropped. Her eyes grew two sizes larger. "Put a suit on him and he'd look just like Peter Elliott."

"That's what I thought," said Erica triumphantly. "This could be why he knew things about the murders no one else does."

"Wait a minute," said Morgan. "There are a lot of people who look alike and the samples are just derived from Emerson's photo. We don't have a photo of Elliott to compare it with via facial recognition software. We have to be damn sure it's Elliott before we start accusing him of murdering these women. This could really blow up in our faces."

"Yes, but don't forget our suspect has a degree in journalism," Erica reminded him.

"I'm not saying it isn't him," said Morgan. "I'm just saying we have to take this slow and not tip our hand. I know Zimmer said the killer might have a job in journalism; however, she also said it would be something behind the scenes—someone who doesn't want to bring a lot of attention to himself. Elliott creates front page headlines."

"Well, maybe he's hiding in plain sight," Erica countered, beginning to feel frustrated at Morgan's lack of enthusiasm.

"Don't worry, Detective. If it's him, we'll put him away. However, we need concrete evidence, like the facial analysis or DNA. We need to work him so he doesn't spook and take off again. If it isn't him, we don't want to give him the ammunition to put us through the media ringer."

"I see what you're saying," said Kendall.

"So do I," said Erica, "but I don't have to like it. Let's save this sketch so we can print it."

"Let's see where we get with this interview," said Morgan. "Then we'll decide how to proceed."

Chapter 27

Once Agent Morgan and Detective Kendall had joined Peter Elliott in the small interrogation room. Erica took her place in the dimly lit room behind the two-way glass. She watched as her colleagues scrutinized Elliott. Then she saw Morgan open his file, rub his chin, close the file, and then lean back in his chair.

"Mr. Elliott," Morgan began. "I'm FBI Agent Spencer Morgan and this is Detective Chennelle Kendall. But of course, you two may already know one another."

"I don't think I've had the pleasure of meeting Detective Kendall, but I've seen her around." Elliott sneered as he looked from Kendall to Morgan. "By the way, where is Detective Barnes?"

Erica had wondered how long it would take for that question to pop up.

"I thought she'd want in on this. You behind the glass, Detective Barnes?" he shouted, waving and unnerving her.

"Bastard," she muttered under her breath.

"Detective Barnes had more important things to deal with today," Kendall replied.

"Get him, Chennelle," Erica said softly although there was no need to do so since they couldn't hear her.

"Mr. Elliott," continued Morgan ignoring the off subject remarks. "You seem to be a little too familiar with several recent murder cases, specifically the murders of Penny Flanders, Marilyn Novak, Samantha Ritter, and Elizabeth Glenn. I note you didn't include Keith Gray in your article in this morning's *Indianapolis Star*."

"I'm a good investigative reporter. It would seem the women of this city are the ones in danger. I believe Keith Gray was collateral damage."

Erica watched Morgan jot down some notes while Kendall stared at Elliott. She heard the door open behind her and Major Stevenson joined her in the observation room.

"So, Morgan's interviewing Elliott?"

"Yes, sir. They're just getting started." She and Stevenson stepped closer to the glass and watched the interview intently.

"I should have known he was up to no good when he called me last night for comments," said the major. "I cut him off pretty quick. He never got the chance to ask me about any of the details he put in the *Star*."

Erica nodded.

"What makes you believe you have acquired accurate information in regard to these murders?" asked Morgan. "The police department hasn't disclosed any details to the press."

"I have my sources."

"What sources?" blurted Kendall.

Erica's heart thumped with anticipation. Would Elliott give up his source? She doubted it. Was he in contact with the killer, or did he have first-hand knowledge?

"Now, now, Detective Kendall," said Elliott smugly. "You know as a reporter I can't reveal my sources."

Morgan resumed the interview. "Mr. Elliott, you must realize what you've written under the pretense of making women think about their safety will only put them in more danger."

"No, I don't believe they're in more danger," he snapped.

"Well, they are!" countered Morgan. "You've not only given this killer reason to do it again, but have set the stage for copycats and false reporting."

"Agent Morgan, I know you're with the FBI and all, but how could you know my little article could have such an impact?"

"In reference to our killer, you've given him exactly what he wants. Attention. Your article makes him feel like people are seeing him for the first time...and...he likes it." Morgan had shown a hint of emotion for the first time, recovering so quickly Erica wasn't sure she'd actually seen it.

"In reference to copycats," Morgan continued, "there are a lot of people out there just waiting to have their own psychotic break. They think if they mimic someone else, they won't be caught. Oh, and there's another group I almost forgot. Those who love to confess to murders they didn't commit."

"Why would anybody do such a thing?" Elliott sneered.

"Is he out of his fucking mind?" snorted Stevenson.

"I think so," Erica replied.

Morgan must have agreed. He continued to explain. "Again—attention. Pure and simple. They want the attention."

"I can think of better ways to get attention," said Elliott.

"That's obvious," said Kendall, eyes flaring. "It seems strange to us that you've been the first reporter at each of these crime scenes."

"All of us have police scanners, you know. Sometimes we get there close to when the cops do. The local NBC News reporter got to the Flanders' crime scene at the same time I did."

"We know, since the two of you and her cameraman tromped all over the footprint evidence." Morgan leaned in towards Elliott, intimidation flexing in his upper arms. "However, Mr. Elliott, we spoke with Andrea Atkins and she said you called her with a tip about the murder scene."

"I *got* a tip, so I shared it with my *ex-friend*, Andrea."

"A tip from other than the scanner?" asked Kendall.

"Yes."

"Okay, Mr. Elliott, let's cut through the bullshit," Morgan said gruffly.

Erica wondered if this shift to a harsher tone was a further attempt to intimidate Elliott or just Morgan getting frustrated. It could be a little of both.

"What I want to know is, are you *serious* about keeping the women in this city safe or not?" Morgan's voice had increased in volume with each word. He stared at Elliott in silence, keeping Erica on the edge with anticipation.

Elliott couldn't stare Morgan down. He started to look all around the room, first to Kendall, then the wall to his left, then back to Morgan. He shifted in his seat, apparently unable to find a comfortable position. Finally, he spoke.

"Of course I want them safe. I'm not an asshole."

"Could've fooled me," said Kendall.

Morgan stood suddenly slamming his fist on the table. "Then how are you getting your information, Mr. Elliott? Has this guy been contacting you?"

"*What?*" Elliott said, rearing back in his chair as though Morgan had tried to punch him.

"Mr. Elliott, it's not a difficult question." Morgan leaned in even closer.

Elliott looked at him frowning. "Okay, Agent Morgan. The day Flanders was killed I found a phone message on my desk in the afternoon. It told me to go to the Flanders' house for a big story. I asked the clerk why no name was listed on the message and she said he wanted to be anonymous."

"You're sure she said '*he*'?" Morgan sat down again, still glaring at Elliott.

"Yes. She said *his* voice was raspy, like he had a cold or something. So, being the dedicated newsman I am, I went. I owed Andrea a favor, so I called her."

Morgan and Kendall looked at one another, shook their heads, and turned their gazes back to Elliott.

"I'll need your clerk's contact information so I can confirm your story," Kendall stared at him with her pen at the ready. He gave her the name and number and Kendall left the room.

"Great idea, Kendall," Erica said aloud. "Leave him alone with Morgan for a while and make him sweat what you're up to."

"So what happened when you got to the Flanders' home?" asked Morgan more calmly, leaning back in his chair.

"Like I said, I gave Andrea a call and we both got there at the same time, just after the cops arrived."

Erica noticed Elliott wipe his brow. He was beginning to sweat. She had to admit to herself that Morgan knew what he was doing after all. If he'd jumped up at her with those flaming eyes, she'd confess to whatever he asked.

"How do we know you didn't make the call to your office yourself?"

"*What?*"

"Now we're getting to it," Stevenson said to Erica.

"People who try to disguise their voices often sound raspy," noted Morgan. "You know, like when they call in sick. They want to fool somebody."

"Whoa, wait a minute. You're not saying you think…oh, *hell no!*"

"Say I believe you," continued Morgan, his voice escalating again. "Then where the fuck did you get the idea these women were laid out in any particular fashion? What made you think Mrs. Glenn was pregnant? Where did your version of the details come from, Mr. Elliott? *Where?*" Morgan slammed his fist on the table making everyone jump, including Major Stevenson.

"I'm not saying another word. Are you about to arrest me? If so, get my boss on the phone and have him send our attorney down here."

Morgan stood again, leaning on the table like a great cat about to pounce on his prey. "Look you son-of-a-bitch, I don't like you. I don't think what you're telling us rings true and I sure as hell don't like it when somebody deliberately lies to me. Maybe I will have a little talk with your boss. See what he or she thinks about all this."

"I don't have anything else to say." Elliott looked away, pursing his lips and crossing his arms in front of his chest.

"Are you willing to give us your fingerprints and a DNA sample today, Mr. Elliott?" Kendall asked, upon re-entering the room.

"Why would I want to do that?"

Erica saw Morgan pull a page from his file and slap it on down on the table. "Because of this," he said.

"That looks like me," said Elliott.

Morgan simply raised an eyebrow affirming Elliott's assessment with his expression.

"Is this *him*? Do you know who you're looking for?"

Morgan didn't answer. His stare caused Elliott to lick his lips and run his fingers through his hair nervously.

"We're not going to divulge who this person might be," continued Kendall. "However, giving us a DNA sample and fingerprints would go a long way in eliminating you as a suspect. I would think you'd want to comply in lieu of the fact this composite looks so much like you."

"Fine," he said. "Where do I go?"

"I'll have an officer escort you to the lab," Kendall answered.

"You're free to go as soon as you're finished giving your samples, Mr. Elliott," Morgan told him. "Please make sure you're available for further questioning. And, call us immediately if you're contacted again."

Peter Elliott rose slowly, scowling at Agent Morgan. Kendall opened the door and escorted him to one of the patrol officers on the floor.

Erica looked at Major Stevenson who returned a tense glance. "So, what do you think, Barnes?"

"I don't trust him. He's as good a suspect as we have right now. Of course the FBI does have DNA from our suspect to compare to Elliott's, so we'll see."

Kendall and Morgan joined them in the observation room.

Morgan spoke first. "Kendall confirmed the clerk received the call and left Elliott the message. I don't think he's our killer."

Erica shot him a look of disbelief.

Morgan continued with his explanation. "Even though he resembles the composite, I believe his responses were those of a cocky reporter, not a murderer. However, I do believe he is hiding something else. I think he's communicating with the killer. He couldn't possibly have known this much about the murder scenes if he hadn't. Unless you think he has someone at IMPD in his pocket."

"We can talk to our patrol officers and forensics team, but I doubt they'd blab to this guy. He hasn't been around that long," said Stevenson. "So, what's your proposal for the next steps, Agent Morgan?"

"We put a tail on him. He won't make a move without our knowing it."

"Sounds good." Major Stevenson shifted his attention to his detectives. "Kendall, you write this one up. Barnes, I want you to figure out where you're going with this investigation. Freeman will be on leave for a few more days. You and Kendall need to get some more interviews underway. Try to find some connection between our victims. He had to have met them at some point. There has to be a common thread."

"Yes, Major," Erica and Kendall said at the same time then left Major Stevenson and Agent Morgan to their discussion. Approaching her desk, she noticed a bouquet of red sweetheart roses sitting on it.

"Look there. Seems you have an admirer," Kendall commented.

"It would seem so." Erica wondered why Ben would do this at work. She looked for a card, but didn't see one. Her cell phone rang. It was Ben.

"Hey there," she said, smiling widely. "Thanks for the roses, they're beautiful."

"What roses? I wouldn't send roses to you at work."

Her smile faded. "Well, if you didn't send them, who did?"

"Look there, on the floor." Kendall was pointing to a place near Erica's desk. It looked like a card had fallen from the flowers.

Erica picked it up, telling Ben to hold on while she opened it. Inside was an eerie message: *STOP ME—YOU DON'T HAVE MUCH TIME*. She dropped the card on the desk and backed away.

Kendall looked at it without picking it up, and then went for Morgan and Stevenson.

"It's him," she said to Ben. "He wants me to stop him. Stevenson's coming, I've got to go."

She hung up the phone, sank into her chair, and glared at the roses. "Don't worry you psycho bastard. I *will* stop you."

Chapter 28

Detectives Mayhew and Jacobs were cruising down Washington Street. They'd just come from Yolanda Fuentes' apartment. Her landlord said Yolanda had moved out and left no forwarding address. They were now on their way to Lucinda Morales' home. Lucinda was Hector Fuentes' girlfriend and the only other person who might know where Yolanda was staying. They'd decided another talk with Yolanda was in order. She had to be the key to finding out who ordered the attack on Natalie Ralston.

Mayhew glanced over at his partner. "Jacobs, what are you lookin' so down in the mouth about?"

"Nothing," he replied.

"Don't give me that bull," Mayhew retorted. "I can see you're worked up about somethin'. Spit it out."

"Can you keep a secret?" asked Jacobs.

"Say *what?* I'm a cop. Of course I know how to keep my mouth shut."

"Okay, but you can't tell anyone about this yet—especially not Freeman."

"Oh, I got ya. You don't want me to tell him how you been gettin' it on with his partner?"

"How did you find out?"

Tyrone chuckled. "I have my ways. So what's goin' on? She break up with your sorry ass already?"

"No," Jacobs said, rolling his eyes. "It's this serial killer case she's on. This psycho is communicating with her."

"I know you said he left a message in the last victim's place."

"Tyrone, I called her while you ran into the convenient. He sent her roses and a note. Major Stevenson was headed her direction so she couldn't give me the details, but her reaction didn't sound good."

"Sorry, man." Tyrone immediately took on a more sympathetic tone. "I know if this was happenin' to my Jada I'd be ready to bust some heads."

"I wish she'd let me stay with her at her place," said Jacobs. "Or, at the very least consider staying with her dad for a while."

"I know where you're comin' from." Tyrone shook his head, smiling. "It's hard to deal with those strong-willed, independent types. I know. I've been married to one for ten years."

"Looks like the Morales house up ahead," said Jacobs.

When they pulled up to the Morales residence, there were several people congregated on the front porch. There were three young men wearing the colors of Fuentes' gang, a plump elderly woman, and a gorgeous tall, thin woman with long, flowing black hair.

The detectives approached the group. Jacobs started to introduce himself. "Sorry for the interruption...."

"Then don't interrupt," shouted one of the young men, and the others laughed.

Mayhew raised an eyebrow. "What my partner here was tryin' to say before he was interrupted was we are here to speak to Miss Lucinda Morales. Is she here?"

The tall young woman turned to look Mayhew in the eye, her gaze cutting. "I'm Lucinda. You come to arrest *me* now?"

"No Miss," said Mayhew. "Is there a place we could speak to you privately?"

"Well, Mr. Policeman, I don't think it would be possible," she said batting her long eyelashes. "There is nothing I need to say my friends and grandmother cannot hear. Go ahead. Ask your questions."

Jacobs and Mayhew looked at one another. What could they do? "We're looking for Yolanda Fuentes," said Jacobs. "Do you have any idea where we can find her?"

Lucinda's eyes suddenly flared with anger and she pointed her finger at Jacobs. "If I could find her, she'd be dead. She betrayed her brother and now he is in jail. If she is wise, she has fled this city."

"I guess we'll take that as a no," said Mayhew. "Best be hopin' we don't find her dead or you might just be joinin' old Fuentes in the slammer."

"It's your kind who got him into this mess, so fuck off!" she said, directing her rage at Mayhew.

"Just 'cause she wanted to be with a black man didn't mean Fuentes needed to go killin' the guy," Mayhew countered.

"You know nothing about family honor, *pinchero*." She spat on the ground in front of them and turned away.

"I got a feelin' that wasn't very nice," said Mayhew. "Let's go Jacobs; this was a real waste of time."

"Yeah, Jacobs. Go away. You're not wanted here," said one of the young men.

Jacobs and Mayhew left, walking sideways keeping their eyes on the group. You never knew when one of them would decide it would be cool to shoot a cop.

Lucinda walked towards the house while the young men laughed. Her grandmother simply shook her head and followed Lucinda into the house.

Once in the car, Mayhew turned to Jacobs. "Next time we need to come to this neighborhood, we're bringing Garcia with us."

"What for? They probably look at him as a traitor. No wonder we can't find Yolanda Fuentes. If they threatened to kill her, she could be hiding or out of the state by now."

"Or, out of the country," said Tyrone. "And it's for sure nobody in Henderson's 'hood will be protectin' her. They think it's her fault Henderson's dead."

"We need to get Special Investigations involved," said Jacobs. "If anyone understands how these guys think, it's them."

"Do you ever think we're goin' to figure out what happened to Miss Natalie?"

Jacobs ran his fingers through his hair as though the action would spark some new and brilliant answer. "If she gets her memory back and can give us a good description, then yes. I just hope she's pissed and not so scared she doesn't want to give us the info."

"Couldn't blame her if she was, bro. Couldn't blame her if she was."

Chapter 29

"So this maniac sent you flowers now?" shouted Brent. Erica pulled the phone away from her ear to keep her eardrum intact.

"Calm down so I can update you. Morgan and Kendall had just finished interviewing Peter Elliott. I was observing because of our recent history. When Elliott left, Kendall spotted the flowers on my desk. If you ask me, Elliott probably sent them."

"No one saw him bring them in, did they?"

"Apparently they were left at the information counter by a delivery man from the flower shop. Morgan went down to the flower shop and questioned the owner. She told him she'd found an envelope on the counter with $50 cash, a note with instructions and the sealed card she was to attach. She just thought it was a secret admirer or something. Morgan took the CDs from her security cameras. He planned to look at them before he comes back."

"Lab got the flowers?"

"They're checking for prints and toxins. Major Stevenson wants them to make sure the flowers weren't sprayed with some sort of poison."

"I don't like this bastard focusing in on you," said Brent, that big brother tone in his voice.

"Really? I'm not too keen on it myself," Erica said, oozing with sarcasm. "Zimmer seems to think this guy feels guilty over killing Elizabeth Glenn's unborn baby. She believes hurting a child, even an unborn child, was something he hadn't planned."

"So does she think he'll start making mistakes because of it?"

Erica thought for a moment. "This guy says he wants me to stop him. He wants to get caught, but he won't quit until he does. The note indicated I don't have long. His pattern of killing seems to be coming every three days, which could mean I have less than 48 hours before he kills again. I think putting the responsibility of catching him on me provides him with an excuse. He wants to make it my fault when he kills again."

"So will Special Agent Zimmer be there today?"

"She arrived in Indy early this afternoon. Morgan called her and they should both be here in about twenty minutes." She paused staring at the wall. Then she started to think about Peter Elliott and her anger began to flare. "I still think Elliott's a good suspect, even though Morgan doesn't seem to think so."

"He's sure been around a lot. He knows where you work and where you live. Has he been bothering you at home?"

"Not lately. I just find it odd he's always just around the corner when something's going down. It's very coincidental those flowers showed up the very day he comes in here to be interviewed."

"So what's Agent Morgan doing about it?"

"He put a tail on the guy, but we'll see how long it lasts. Enough business, how's Natalie doing?"

"Natalie's doing better. Brain swelling is gone. They'll probably take out the catheter tomorrow morning. She's starting to remember a few things, just not me."

"I'm sure it will come with time."

"Probably will. Anyway, her parents are staying in her apartment. They have photos of her as a kid and that's helping jog her memory. The doc is very optimistic about a full recovery."

"That's good news. Be patient, Freeman. It takes time to recover from this type of trauma. Not just the physical either. She's probably going to be terrified to go anywhere by herself for a while."

"She won't have to if I've got anything to say about it," declared Brent.

"Barnes, we're ready for you," said Kendall.

"Be right there, Kendall. I've got to go. Call me at home tonight. Say hello to Natalie for me."

"Sure, if she'll see me."

Erica heard the phone click as he hung up on his end. With a heavy heart, she put down the receiver. She hoped today would be the day Natalie would start remembering, if not for Brent's sake for her own. They needed to get the bastards who did this to her off the street and send a message that intimidation of this sort would not be tolerated.

"Agent Morgan," Erica said as she entered the conference room. "I thought Special Agent Zimmer would be with you today."

"When Trish heard you received a second message from Emerson, she took the next flight to Lincoln. She's decided we needed to have another chat with Emerson's sister, Jordan Collins."

"Does she think Mrs. Collins knows more than she's telling us?" asked Kendall.

"Trish doesn't think Mrs. Collins is intentionally hiding information regarding Emerson's whereabouts, if that's what you're asking. She's going to try to profile Emerson through the one person who knows him best. What was he like as a child? Has he ever displayed any psychotic behaviors? What are some of his skills, besides journalism? These things could help us locate her brother."

"What's Agent Zimmer's strategy?" asked Erica.

"She's hoping to get Jordan to agree to a press conference to be broadcast tomorrow morning. We want her to try to convince her brother to turn himself in."

"Problem is, he's fixated on Barnes catching him before he kills again," Kendall pointed out. "Even if his sister does this, how can we be sure he'll see it?"

"We can't, Detective." Morgan looked defeated. Erica saw every line in his dark handsome face. "It's a long shot, but it's worth a try."

There was a knock at the door, and then the face of Mark Chatham peered around it. "May I interrupt?"

"Come in." Erica rolled her eyes at him. "Agent Morgan, have you met our Crime Scene Supervisor, Mark Chatham?"

"No, but I've read his crime scene reports. Can we assume you have some news for us?"

"First of all, the fingerprints on the vase Detective Barnes received yesterday belonged to our information desk clerk, the florist, and her delivery man. Sorry Barnes, none of them matched your news reporter buddy nor do his prints match those of Parker Emerson. Peter Elliott is not your perpetrator. I did, however, pull a great thumbprint off of the card. *It* belongs to Parker Emerson."

Erica's heart sank like a heavy weight, beating hard. She had to take deep breaths to bring it back to normal. It was fear—pure and simple. This killer was getting way too close.

"That confirms Parker is here and is the most viable suspect in the killings," said Morgan. "He's getting a little distracted though. Handling the card without gloves was a huge mistake."

"Or he wants me to know it's him," said Erica. "He said he wants me to catch him."

"The lab tested the flowers and water for toxins and found none," Chatham continued. "I didn't expect Tox would find anything since the flowers were arranged by the florist and then delivered without anyone else handling them."

"What else you got for me?" asked Erica.

"We've got the DNA on the Gray-Novak murders. They'd definitely had intercourse. No other sperm donor was found."

Erica figured this would be the case. "What about the hair found on the dress Novak was wearing?"

"As was the case in the Flanders' murder, they belong to Wanda Emerson."

"That's why all these damn clothes don't fit the victims. Emerson must have taken some of his mother's clothes after he killed her," Morgan concluded.

"I know you and Agent Zimmer think he's had some sort of breakdown," said Erica, now feeling skeptical about Emerson's intentions. "Sounds like he decided he liked killing women and wanted to play dress up."

"I'm not so sure he took them because he planned to start killing women across the U. S.," Morgan stated. "I'll have to consult Trish on this one. He may have taken his mother's clothes because it symbolized something to him. He finally felt like he had some sort of power over her. Now he could take things away from her instead of the reverse."

Erica still wasn't convinced this guy wasn't just some nut job who liked getting off on the kill. She focused her attention on Mark, giving him a nod so he would continue with his report.

"We also found similar hairs at the Glen crime scene along with some blond hairs with dark roots. Those shorter hairs were a familial match to Wanda Emerson, thus another link to Parker Emerson. Obviously these hairs were dyed."

"Could you tell what color they were originally," asked Kendall.

"A dark brown. Tests showed the use of a bleaching solution and then blond hair color. Wasn't Emerson's natural hair color dark brown?"

"Yep," said Morgan. "He's obviously disguising himself. He could have gotten a nose job, an eye lift, any number of minor surgeries which could alter his appearance just enough so we wouldn't recognize him even if he were standing right in front of us."

"If he had surgery, do you think the doc is still alive?" asked Erica.

"Not likely," answered Morgan. "I'll get our agents in the field offices along Emerson's path of destruction to check out plastic surgeons in those areas. I'll have them pay special attention to those who are known for doing illegal surgeries and/or have died recently of unnatural causes."

"Sounds like we need to let women who fit our victims' description know we definitely have a serial killer out there and to be extremely cautious," said Kendall. "We'll need to put his photo out there with his latest hair color and hair length. Of course by now, he could have changed it again."

"They'll have to be reminded he targets women who live alone," added Erica. "They may want to stay with relatives or friends until we catch this creep. So, are you moving in with me, Kendall?"

"With my warm dark skin and this five-foot, nine body? He's not interested in me."

"But, he's definitely interested in me," said Erica.

"Okay, girl," exclaimed Kendall. "That does it. I'm sleeping on your couch."

"The hell you are. I was just pulling your leg." Even as Erica said it, she wasn't convinced herself. Deep down she was terrified.

"Don't be so stubborn," Kendall fired back. "He's communicating with you. How long before he decides to go after you?"

"Don't be ridiculous," Erica retorted, slamming back in her chair and crossing her arms over her chest.

Kendall jerked her head towards Agent Morgan. "He probably will come after her eventually, won't he?"

"Detective Kendall is correct," said Morgan. "It has been my experience that people who send these types of messages do eventually go after their obsession."

Erica sighed, closing her eyes then turned to look at Agent Morgan. "That's only if we don't catch the psycho first, right?"

"Look, Detective Barnes," said Morgan leaning towards her. "I think you know as well as I do that no matter how skilled you are in your job or in the martial arts, this murderer is bigger and stronger than you. Unless you get in the first substantially debilitating blow, he will win."

"I think my Glock is a pretty good equalizer," she said.

"Come on, Barnes," Chatham chimed in. "Listen to them. You don't have to go it alone. I wouldn't want to meet this guy in a dark alley."

"Okay, okay. I see I'm outnumbered." She surrendered reluctantly but was grateful for all of the support. "I'll think about making arrangements so I'm not alone."

"Well," said Kendall rolling her eyes. "That's progress. At least she's *thinking* about it."

"So I guess it's time for us to pull something together for the news media," said Morgan, bringing the focus back on the case. "I can make the statement of warning. I will try to make it sound like I'm giving out more information than you and Major Stevenson did last week. It's just too bad Elliott reported those few details in the paper before we had a chance to do it."

"He's got all of the women in this city terrified," said Kendall. "Of course, maybe it's not such a bad thing. Maybe they'll be more alert."

"As long as we don't get a lot of crank calls or too many mistaken identities," said Erica.

The door swung open and in walked Major Stevenson. He was wearing latex gloves and holding an envelope the size of a note card. "You've had another delivery, Barnes. I just received it. Glove up and let's open it."

"Here you go," Chatham said as he reached into his pocket and pulled out a pair. "Always keep some with me."

Erica pulled the gloves on and took the envelope from the major. She dreaded what could be in there. Pulling out the small note card, she saw its cover was the painting *The Scream* by Edvard Munch. She opened it carefully and then read it aloud.

"Erica,

Did you like the flowers I sent yesterday? I bet you thought they were from your boyfriend. I've seen him leaving your place. He a cop, too? Is this why you're so distracted that you haven't stopped me yet? Don't you care if someone else dies? If you don't stop me, then it's all your fault. I've seen her again. It won't be long. STOP ME!!!!!"

Everyone fell silent. Erica gently folded the letter looking around at all of the solemn faces in the room. Was it going to be on her head if someone else lost her life tonight? How could she stop him? He was like a phantom.

"I know what you're thinking, Barnes," said the major gruffly. "You're a good cop, one of my best. This jerk is playing head games with you. He says he wants you to catch him, but I doubt it. He's baiting you, trying to make you vulnerable. Don't let him get away with it."

"Yes, sir." She said it with conviction, because she knew he was right. Letting Emerson screw with her mind and emotions was the worst thing she could do.

"I don't agree, Major Stevenson," said Agent Morgan rising abruptly. "He's using her first name now, which makes it personal. This type of serial killer has a compulsion. Agent Zimmer and I agree Parker's guilt in killing Elizabeth Glenn's unborn child took a toll on him. Emerson wants to be stopped because he knows he won't be able to stop himself. He's probably been researching Detective Barnes and feels she's most capable of doing this."

"I see what you're saying, Agent Morgan," said Major Stevenson. "However, whether he wants to be stopped or not, he's trying to make my detective think it will be her doing. I want to make it perfectly clear, whether compulsion or not, Emerson is making a choice, however irrational it may be."

"On that we agree. I'm going back to my office. This latest note makes it imperative we get a press release ready for the 5:00 news," stated Morgan. "I'll also have one of our staff start the search for plastic surgeons. Major, would you like to stand with me during the news conference?"

"Yes, Agent Morgan. I would like for the women of this city to know the police are doing everything possible to protect them."

Morgan looked at Erica, his deep brown eyes very serious. "Let me know if anything happens tonight. I can probably have one of our agents watch your place, if it would make you feel better."

"That won't be necessary," she replied. "Thank you for your concern. I do appreciate it."

Agent Morgan nodded. Once he and Major Stevenson left the room, Erica turned to Kendall.

"Kendall, there has to be something we're overlooking. Let's cross-reference our female victims' phone and bank records. We need to find out if they used the same repair guys; did they just have the cable company out; did they go to the same dentist—anything to link them."

"I started to do just that," Kendall responded. "There is a number on their phone records for a landscaping company and bank records which show our first three victims all wrote checks to this same company." She paused while she pulled out the files. "Here it is. Meadow and Dale Landscaping, LLC."

Erica thought for a moment. Where had she heard the name before? She got up and walked the length of the room concentrating. Then it hit her.

"Holy crap! I knew I'd heard it before."

"What?" said Kendall, confusion in her eyes.

"The name of the landscaping company; it sounded familiar and I know where I've heard it before." She tapped her chin contemplating what she felt would be impossible.

"What are you thinking, Barnes?"

"Chennelle, one of my neighbors works for that landscaping company. We need to find out if he was assigned to the crew working for these women."

"Why would you suspect your neighbor in particular?" asked Kendall.

"Physically he is the right height and he's very muscular. He also has blond hair with dark roots."

Kendall rolled her eyes. "A good defense attorney would say he's muscular because of his job."

"Wait 'til you see him. When you see his face, you'll see he looks enough like our guy to be him, with some surgery, of course. He has brown eyes and short hair with dark roots and blond tips. Now that I'm thinking about it, he's very backward. He says hello to me when he sees me, but he pretty much keeps to himself. I don't want to believe it's him, but he'd be just the type no one would notice."

"We should probably check out the rest of the crew as well. There could be others who bear a resemblance to our killer."

"You're right, Kendall. Although Joe would definitely know where I live; he could have been talking about the cases and bragged about being my neighbor."

"I'll make some calls and we'll see if we can get these guys in here tomorrow morning," Kendall volunteered.

"Excellent," said Erica. "I'm going to keep looking at our records. If we find more of a connection between this landscaping company and our other victims, we just may be on our way to catching this son-of-a-bitch."

Chapter 30

"Hi. Is Natalie Ralston still in Intensive Care this morning? I know they were planning to take out her catheter early today." Brent waited for the hospital information clerk as he watched her pecking away at the keyboard.

"Yes, dear, she's still in ICU. There's a notation she will be moved this afternoon. You can check with the people in the waiting room up there."

"Thank you," he said.

Brent walked slowly down the hall towards the elevators—a path which was becoming much too familiar. Reaching his floor, he took the trek to the waiting area to find Natalie's mother sitting there. The Intensive Care Unit personnel were very strict about visitation and they wouldn't be able to see her for about fifteen more minutes.

"Mrs. Ralston," he said, getting her attention.

She laid down her magazine and removed her reading glasses. She didn't stand, so Brent sat next to her on the couch. "Please dear, call me Linda. Mrs. Ralston sounds so formal."

"I'll try. How is she this morning?"

"She's doing much better, Brent. The doctor successfully took the catheter out this morning. They plan to move her this afternoon after he comes back to check the area where the catheter was inserted. It will be nice to be able to visit her whenever we want, won't it?"

He smiled at her and nodded, watching her facial expression. It was much softer than on the first day they met.

"Brent, I want to apologize for snapping at you when we arrived. I'm sure you can understand how stressful it was for me."

"Of course I can," he said.

"She's our only child. We had a very difficult time getting pregnant. We'd pretty much given up by the time I was 32. Of course, they say the minute you give up is when it will happen."

"So I've heard." Brent tilted his head to look at her and saw tears glistening in her eyes.

"Chris and I couldn't be prouder of her. Back in high school, she told us she wanted to be a lawyer. She wanted to put the bad guys away. We thought, oh well, at least she'll be in a courtroom not out on the street."

"We're going to catch the people who did this to her," said Brent, a slight crack in his voice. "We won't let the bad guys win."

She nodded. "I know the two of you just started seeing one another, but I've never heard Natalie so excited about a man before. She's always so focused on getting her career started. You must be quite impressive to snatch up her heart so quickly." She gave Brent a wink and a smile.

"Do you believe in love at first sight, Mrs.…I mean Linda?"

"It didn't happen that way for Christopher and me, but I'm sure there are those who experience it. Just be careful to make sure it isn't *lust* at first sight. Sex is a beast who catapults us into thinking we are in love, but what we must do is figure out what will be left when the beast relaxes."

Brent blushed and Linda looked away.

She continued. "The marriages I've seen last the longest have been those where friendship comes first. Having things in common—religious beliefs, similar political views, and child-rearing beliefs—is very important. When there's a friendship and the heat of passion fades, which it will, then there's a good foundation for a long and relatively happy marriage."

"Is that what you and your husband have?"

"I think so. I'm not saying there weren't some rough times and some nasty disagreements. Nothing is perfect. But we've seen each other through some pretty rough times."

She paused, sighing. Pulling her purse close, she retrieved a handkerchief from it and wiped her eyes. "Natalie gave this to me for Mothers' Day when she was ten. She was so proud of herself. She had talked an elderly neighbor into letting her help her clean up the leaves and debris winter had left in her yard. She only took $20 even though it took her about six hours to complete. Her father took her to the department store and she bought me a set of hankies and a small music box. These are the things a mother treasures." Linda dabbed at her eyes again and took a deep breath.

"Sounds like she was a great kid," said Brent, patting her shoulder.

"Natalie was never any trouble as a child. Smart as a whip. I'm just so grateful you and your colleagues found her in time." She was tearing up again. Brent put his arm around her this time.

Christopher Ralston entered the room with two cups of coffee in hand. "What's going on here? You're not trying to steal my bride are you young man?" he quipped.

"Oh, Chris," Linda laughed. "Good news. Right after you left to get the coffee; they told me they'll be moving Natalie to a regular room today."

"She's starting to remember more, son," said Chris. "Oh, and it's time for her to have a visitor. Why don't you go ahead? Okay with you, Linda?" Linda nodded her ascent.

Brent thanked them and checked in with the volunteer before heading back to Natalie's room. He walked with eyes to the floor. He looked up when the nurse said hello, smiled and waved. When he reached Natalie's room, she was sitting up. Her face was in the latter stages of healing bruises—shades of strange greens and yellows. Her eyes no longer swollen and the bandages removed from her head, he could see some blonde stubble beginning to grow where they'd shaved her hair.

He stopped just inside the door and she smiled at him. Natalie motioned for him to come in.

"Did you hear?" she said through her teeth. It would be a few more weeks before they could unwire her jaw. "They're moving me to a regular room today. Isn't it great?"

"That's fantastic."

"I know it was hard on Mom and Dad to just visit for fifteen minutes every couple of hours," she said. "So how's it going? Have you found out who did this? I wish I could remember more."

"You will," he said, his heart swelling with love. "To answer your question, we have our suspicions, but we don't have evidence strong enough to make an arrest. We want to make sure it sticks."

"You rope 'em, I'll tie 'em."

Brent laughed. "Cowboy analogies now?"

"I'm in a good mood. I have some more good news."

"I love good news. Let's hear it."

She smiled at him with an impish glow greatly exaggerated by her clenched teeth. "I remembered something about us."

His eyes widened with joy and surprise. "You mean us, like you and me?"

"That's precisely what I mean. Well. At least I hope it's real and not some dream."

"Go ahead," he said anxiously. "Tell me what you remember and I'll confirm if it's real."

"Actually, I had a couple of recollections. Yesterday afternoon I was napping between visits from Mom and Dad. I saw us walking around the Circle. You kept talking about the Soldiers' and Sailors' Monument. I let you go on and on, and then I informed you I already knew all about it from my Indiana History class back in high school."

Brent blushed. "That happened about three weeks ago. I guess you didn't want me getting too cocky."

"Then, last night I was flipping through the TV channels and found a documentary on twins. Then it hit me. You have a twin sister, right?"

"*Yes!*" Unable to contain his excitement, he started to grab her into a hug but stopped short.

"Oh, good Lord," she said. "Hug me."

Brent took her into an embrace, but not too tight. No telling how sore she still might be. "Oh, Natalie, this is great news." He stood back and looked into her glowing face. Even through the bruising, he could see her beauty.

"It's the best news. The psychologist told me this means my memory is starting to return. Often times the long-term memory, especially pleasant memories come back first. He also told me it could take months before I remember everything. In our last session, I did remember falling to the ground and losing my sweatshirt. I just can't remember anything about who attacked me."

"Don't worry. Jacobs and Mayhew are two of the best detectives around. Between the three of us, we'll find these guys."

"I'm not worried," she said taking his face in her hands, pulling it towards hers. Unable to pucker, she gently pressed her mouth to his cheek. "I may not be able to remember everything right now, but I feel a connection with you that is strong and resilient. We're going to be okay, I just know it."

"Time's up," chimed the nurse. Brent kissed Natalie on the forehead then told her he'd be gone for a while. He wanted to check in with Major Stevenson.

She nodded, and smiled the best she could manage.

Brent stopped and spoke with Natalie's parents before heading to the elevator. They were thrilled to hear she was remembering more. Linda promised to call him when Natalie moved to her new room.

Chapter 31

Erica saw Brent leaving Major Stevenson's office. He walked towards her smiling.

"What's up, Freeman?"

"Just checkin' in," he replied. "Natalie's doing a lot better. They're moving her to a regular room today. She should be going home in a couple of days."

"Great," Erica exclaimed. "So when are you coming back to work?"

"Beginning of next week. Last night was the first night I've slept straight through since Natalie was attacked."

"Sorry I haven't been in to see her. This killer has Kendall and me hopping." She knew he wasn't going to buy her excuses.

"I understand. I know the hospital reminds you of what happened to your mom."

"Yeah, well that too, but we really have been busy with these cases," said Erica. "This maniac is killing every three days now, like clockwork."

"Is he still contacting you?"

Erica had no desire to go through this conversation again. However, she knew he'd pester her until she caved. She filled him in on the cases to-date, including the most recent note.

"You do realize he may come after you, don't you?"

Erica hated the big brother stance Freeman was taking, even though she knew his intentions were good. She was sick of everyone harping on her situation.

"Believe me, I'm very well aware. Kendall, Stevenson, Chatham, and our esteemed Agent Morgan, have hassled me for days." She purposely left out Ben, not ready to share the nature of their relationship with him.

"Okay." He smiled at her. "I'll back off as long as I know somebody's keeping an eye on you in my absence."

"Shut up," she said, trying not to smile. She missed working with Brent. She had nothing against Kendall; but she'd worked with Brent so long they could practically read one another's thoughts.

"I've got to get going," he said. "Want to walk me down?"

"Sure. Why not?"

As they waited for the elevator, Detective Pitts from Robbery approached with a handcuffed suspect. He said hello but didn't engage in conversation, keeping his eyes on his charge. They all got in and Brent pushed the button for the first floor.

"I expect you're headed for the basement so you can load this one up?" Brent asked Pitts. Pitts nodded and Brent pushed the button for the basement floor.

"So is Natalie starting to remember more?" Erica asked, keeping the conversation off of her own circumstances.

"Yes, she remembered our conversation from three weeks ago when we went downtown. Then she told me she remembered bits and pieces of the attack during her session with her shrink."

"Hey, stand still," Pitts commanded and jerked his prisoner into line.

Erica noticed the guy was shifting nervously. "What's he in for Pitts?"

"Car jacking," said Pitts.

"I told you them assholes was lying. They jus' wanna see me in jail," spouted the suspect.

"Nobody asked you, Darnell. Best you keep your mouth shut until you talk to the lawyer you wanted so badly."

Something about Darnell's glare turned Erica's blood to ice. She never wanted to meet up with him in a dark alley. The door opened on the first floor. Erica and Brent walked towards the building entrance.

"When you see Natalie, tell her we all wish her well," said Erica. "I'll come by after she gets back home."

"You bet. I'll see you Monday."

Her heart lifted as she watched him leave knowing he'd be back in a few of days. For now, however, it was time to go back upstairs and try to figure out Parker's next move.

***

It was almost 6:00 in the evening. Natalie had finally convinced her parents to go downstairs to get a bite to eat. In her new room for three hours now, she wanted some alone time. Although her mother meant well, the memory exercises she'd created were driving Natalie crazy. Her father was excellent at sensing Natalie's frustration and would keep her mom away for at least an hour. She pulled out her new novel and started to read. Within ten minutes, Natalie was napping peacefully.

She heard the door to her room open slowly. Her eyes fluttered open and she saw someone approximately six-foot tall wearing scrubs, gloves, and a surgeon's mask come into the room. She thought this was odd since the room was not under quarantine.

"I think you have the wrong room," she said, still groggy from her nap.

The figure moved slowly towards Natalie's bedside. "Natalie Ralston?"

"Yes, I'm Natalie Ralston."

He pulled down his mask and she knew immediately that she'd seen him somewhere before. She just couldn't remember where. Then he grabbed the extra pillow that was sitting in the guest chair.

Natalie had no chance to yell before the man plunged the pillow down over her face. She struggled, kicking, trying to scream through her locked jaw, flailing her arms. She finally made contact with the intruder's face, scratching him.

The intruder pressed the pillow tighter over her face. Then her arms fell and she lay still.

Chapter 32

Erica met with Kendall and Morgan in the war room at 7:00 p.m. ready for the conference call with Parker Emerson's sister, Jordan Collins. Erica tapped her pen on the table nervously, waiting for the phone to ring. The call was already five minutes late. Erica hated it when people weren't on time.

"Barnes, please," Kendall exclaimed.

"What?" she replied, confused by Kendall's discontent.

"The tapping. It's getting on my nerves," she said. "I noticed you do that every time you're losing patience."

"Sorry, I didn't realize..."

"No problem," Kendall said as the phone began to ring.

Morgan reached for the phone, hitting the speaker button. "Federal Agent Morgan here with Detectives Kendall and Barnes."

"Special Supervisory Agent Zimmer and Mrs. Jordan Collins here."

"Hello, Mrs. Collins," said Morgan. "Thank you for speaking with us today."

"It's okay." Erica heard the sweet timid voice of Jordan Collins for the first time. "I'm not sure how I can help, but I'll try."

"As we understand it, Mrs. Collins, you last saw your brother, Parker, just before Christmas," stated Morgan.

"Yes."

"How did he seem to you?" asked Erica.

"What do you mean?"

"Was he nervous? Calm? Secretive?" Erica could hear Jordan sigh deeply before she answered.

"He seemed calm, but distracted. He usually didn't visit without Alecia and he never just *dropped in*."

Erica glanced at Morgan before she asked her next question. He nodded slightly, a signal she took as approval. "So this was unusual behavior for him?"

"Yes," she answered, voice cracking. After a few moments of silence, she continued. "I just can't believe he had anything to do with Alecia's murder. He loved her so much."

Zimmer said, "It's alright, Jordan. Please, tell the others what you told me about his visit."

Erica imagined the agent patting Jordan Collin's shoulder in sympathy, though she wasn't sure if the woman was compassionate enough to do so.

"Okay," Jordan replied, breathing deeply.

The silence weighed heavily on Erica, but she knew this was the FBI's show. If not, she'd be pressing the woman. At this rate, it could be midnight before they finished.

"The thing is," Jordan began, "it doesn't surprise me to hear Parker might have killed our mother. She treated him like vermin, worse than vermin. Growing up, I was terrified she'd kill him and then she'd kill me, too."

"Did he ever try to defend himself?" asked Erica.

"I don't recall ever seeing him try. He probably would have gotten it ten times worse had he struck back. He'd thought about running away, but didn't want to leave me behind."

Agent Morgan stepped in. "Did you and he ever have any private conversations about your mother's behavior?"

"Not really. He's five years older than I am and I guess we just kept this knowing silence. The only thing he ever told me was to stay out of her way." She choked up, but pushed herself to continue. "He'd protect me from her. He'd take the blame for things I'd done. One time I tried to get the cookie jar by pulling a chair up to the counter. I accidentally knocked it off and it broke to pieces." Jordan's voice shook.

"He'd just come inside from playing baseball with the neighbor kids. He saw what I'd done and heard Mama screaming, *'what the hell's goin' on in there'*. He told me to get down and go to my room. I did what he said. Next thing I know he's screaming. I snuck down the hall and saw her taking pieces of the broken cookie jar, cutting his back with them. Then she took a couple and plunged them into his buttocks. It was horrible!" Jordan was sobbing now. "She shook him and screamed at him. Then she shut him up in the closet for three days. I'd have given him some food or water, but she had the key and I was only five."

Silence prevailed at this stunning revelation. How could a mother do this to her own child? If she didn't want her children why not put them up for adoption rather than inflict such cruelty? Erica almost felt sorry for Parker Emerson.

"This sort of thing went on and on," stated Jordan, sounding like she had pulled herself together. "My mother was the cruelest person I've ever known, but somewhere deep inside I couldn't hate her. But I didn't have to be one bit like her. Parker seemed to admire me as a mother. He and Alecia never had any kids. Maybe he was afraid he might be like Mama. Maybe Alecia was too wrapped up in her career. I don't know the reason; all I know is he was always good to me and my family."

"I've explained the profile to Jordan," said Zimmer. "She understands a plea to him from her through a news broadcast might just bring him out."

"I love my brother," Jordan stated. "But if he's doing this, I have to try to stop him. It's my turn to protect him—even if I'm protecting him from himself."

"Thank you, Mrs. Collins," said Erica. She couldn't help but feel the deepest sympathy for Jordan. She'd lost her childhood to cruelty, she'd lost her brother to madness, and now she might lose her confidence. How many times had Erica heard family members ask if she thought they'd take the same path as their murderous sibling or parent? Too many to count.

"We're going to record something tonight," said Zimmer. "Tomorrow, we will broadcast it in Indianapolis, Fort Wayne, Chicago, Cincinnati, Louisville, and Dayton. We want to get the message out to surrounding areas in case he's decided to move on."

"In the meantime, Mrs. Collins," said Erica, "please call our office or the FBI if Parker contacts you."

"I will," she said quietly. "This has to stop."

The call over, Erica scanned the room. Agent Morgan was writing notes and Kendall was staring at the crime scene photos. Erica froze with disgust and disbelief. They'd wait until morning, watch the first broadcast and hope it would produce results.

Engrossed in her thoughts, she jerked as someone knocked on the door. She could have sworn she saw Kendall jump as well. The door opened slightly and Major Stevenson's assistant peeked around it.

"Detective Barnes, your father is here to see you."

"My *father*?" Surprised he would come into the city to see her she headed for the door.

"Yes, I had him sit by your desk," said the assistant.

"Tell him I'll be right out," said Erica. "What on earth does he want? Why didn't he just make a call?"

"Only one way to find out," said Kendall with a toothy smile.

When she approached her desk, she could see him leaning forward, elbows on his knees, wringing his hands. She hadn't seen this body language since the day her mother went into the hospital for the last time. Her thoughts immediately shot to her brother and his family. Could something have happened to one of them?

"Hey, Pop," she said as she reached him, laying her hand on his shoulder. "Is something wrong? Is Rick okay?"

"Your brother is fine," he said in a tone she hadn't heard since she was a teen and had violated curfew.

She stepped back as he rose and looked her in the eye. "Erica. Why didn't ya tell me the psycho you're huntin' has been leavin' ya messages?"

His eyes bored through her and she felt just as guilty as she had that night as a teen. She'd gotten out of it pretty easily back then. She'd had a flat tire and had changed it herself. The proof was all over her since she was filthy from head to toe and the flat was in her trunk. She wasn't sure how she'd explain her way out of this one.

"Pop, it's all part of the investigation. I knew you'd worry about it, but I can't let him scare me off, can I?"

"Don't forget, I was a cop, too. I've had to deal with many a nut case in my day," he replied, voice shaking.

"You don't have to worry. Really," she said, but could see he wasn't reassured. "I'm taking every precaution and I've got lots of people, including the FBI, looking out for me."

"I'm the one who should be protectin' you," he said. For the first time she realized what was driving this conversation. Her father felt guilty all these years because he was working the day her mother died. By the time he showed up at the hospital, she'd already slipped into a coma and he didn't get to say goodbye.

"Sit down, Pop," she said, taking her own seat at the desk. "This guy is attacking women who live in houses, not apartments. Our best guess is he chooses women in houses because the neighbors are less likely to hear what's going on."

"I hope ya don't think this makes me feel any better." He frowned at her, his bloodshot brown eyes close to tears.

"No. I'm sure the only thing that's going to make any of us feel better is to catch this guy," Erica said patting her father on the knee. "I'll tell you though, after talking to his sister today I almost feel sorry for him."

"What!"

"I said *almost*," she whispered, hoping he'd lower his voice, too. "He was brutalized as a kid. I don't know how he got this far in life without going off the deep end." She could see his expression and knew he thought she was caving. "Believe me, Pop, I don't feel sorry enough for him to let my guard down. He's killed five people—six if you count Elizabeth Glenn's unborn child."

"Well, you're an adult and I guess I'll just have to take your word you'll be careful." When he looked at her, she felt a deep sensation of love and concern on his part. "No matter what, I'm your dad first. I love you Kitten."

"Ditto, Pop," she said stroking his cheek with affection. Then she realized something. "Wait a minute, you rascal. How'd you find out about the notes and the flowers?"

"I've still got connections," he said puffing out his chest.

"Shall I come by tonight with some grub?"

"Yeah. Bring me something good. I'm tired of all the healthy crap you keep putting in the fridge. How about some Kentucky Fried Chicken and all the fixin's—mashed taters with gravy and coleslaw?" He got up and started to leave, but turned back to her instead. "And make sure you get the original recipe. All them new fangled ways they're cookin' these days ain't near as good as the original."

"You've got it," she said with a grin. She was sure it wouldn't hurt to go off the diet for one meal.

He winked at her and turned limping toward the exit. She saw him wave at some of the detectives and wondered if they were the ones who'd ratted her out.

Her mind wandered to the Emerson children again. At least her parents had loved and cared for her. They'd made her feel like she could accomplish anything and that she and her brother were special. It was hard to imagine the hell Jordan and Parker went through. Did Parker sacrifice his sanity to make sure his sister came through it without the same emotional scars he was suffering? Did the system fail him one too many times?

Whatever the cause, she couldn't let it cloud her judgment at this point. Like her father told her when this all started, she had to focus on the facts and keep her emotions in check.

Chapter 33

The door closed softly. Natalie lay as still as she could in case he'd decided to come back. She wasn't sure what gave her the presence of mind to pretend she was dead. It was too hard to struggle with the pain in her face and one arm in a cast. The man was definitely not a medical person. He didn't even take her pulse to make sure he'd finished her off. She heard the door open again and still lay frozen in fear with the pillow over her face. She was too terrified to remove it for fear he'd see she wasn't dead.

"Oh my God! No! No!" she heard Brent shout. She heard him open the door again and scream for help.

She flung the pillow to the floor. "Brent," she said as loud as possible, pain throbbing through her wired jaw from the strain. Her bruises felt fresh again.

Brent turned and ran to her. "Oh God, Natalie. I thought you…I mean, the pillow…."

"Someone tried to kill me. I pretended I was dead." She began to shake violently. "I scratched him though." She showed him her hand. He could see skin and blood on the fingertips of her right hand.

"I've got to get the crime lab over here to process you." He looked at her with imploring eyes. "Can you ever forgive me?"

"For what?" she asked, confused by the question.

"This is the second time I should have been here to protect you, and…."

"Stop right there," she demanded. "Seems to me the mayor was all hyped up when this happened, but he doesn't assign someone to sit outside my door. This one's on him."

"I've got to call this in. Don't wipe or wash your hands. This DNA evidence will be the first break we've had," he smiled at her, stroking her cheek. "You're one tough cookie."

"Wait until the adrenaline wears off."

Brent called headquarters and they dispatched two patrol officers to seal off the crime scene. Mark Chatham personally came out to collect the fingernail scrapings. He had two other team members collect her gown, the pillow, sheets, vacuum the floor, and dust for prints. Sergeant Jacobs and Detective Mayhew also came to the scene.

After Mark collected the samples and she'd changed to another hospital gown, Natalie moved to another room. Brent had gone to the cafeteria to let Mr. and Mrs. Ralston know what happened. Mrs. Ralston immediately started blaming herself for leaving Natalie alone. They were in her new room when she arrived.

"Natalie," her mother cried as the nurse wheeled Natalie into the room.

"I'm okay, Mom. Really." She wanted to reassure her, but knew her mothering would be worse than ever now. "Where's Dad?"

"He's talking to that nice Sergeant Jacobs."

"Where's Brent?"

"He's with your father and Sergeant Jacobs. Detective Mayhew told me he'd be in shortly."

Just as she finished her sentence, Detective Mayhew entered the room. His tall, dark presence was intimidating yet reassuring. "Hello again Miss Ralston," he said to Linda. "How are you doin' Miss Natalie?"

"As well as can be expected, I guess. I suspect I'll shed a tear or two once the shock wears off. Right now all I want is justice."

"Precisely what I had in mind," he said, smiling. "Were you able to see him at all?"

"I was sleeping. I woke just as he was about to put the pillow over my face." She heard her mother wince. "Mom, you don't have to stay and listen to this."

"It's okay, dear," said Linda. "I want to stay."

Natalie turned her attention back to Mayhew. "He wore surgical gear—the hat, mask, long sleeved gown and gloves. What skin I saw was brown and he had dark brown eyes. I couldn't say whether he was Hispanic or African American."

"It gives us a place to start. I'm sure our distinguished mayor will push for this DNA to be top priority when he realizes he screwed up royally by not providin' protection for you. Seems he got a little lax when the trial was over," Mayhew said, pacing. "You should know we aren't so sure the reason for all this was Fuentes tryin' to intimidate the jury."

"Why not?" asked Natalie.

"Because, we found you in the parkin' lot of the store where his sister, Yolanda, works. It could have been a message to her from Henderson's gang of thugs. Maybe they decided to use you to make it look like Fuentes ordered it."

"She must be scared," said Natalie.

"I hope so," he said. Natalie looked at him, confused by such a statement. "What I mean is she's disappeared. I hope she left of her own free will."

Natalie sighed deeply as she heard her mother's sympathetic moan. She certainly didn't want to see this girl harmed. Maybe she returned to her family home in Mexico. Until she heard otherwise, she would cling to this thought.

Brent, Sergeant Jacobs and her father entered the room.

"Hello, Sergeant Jacobs," said Natalie. "I wish we could have met under better circumstances."

"So do I. My partner here treating you okay?"

"Now you know I am the epitome of decorum, Sergeant," Mayhew quipped.

"I'd tell you what I think," Jacobs responded, "but we are in the presence of two ladies."

Natalie's father came to her side. He broke down. She held him, and then began to cry as she felt his pain. All her defenses had shattered and the fact that someone wanted to kill her became a vivid reality. The only thing keeping her from falling apart right now was the fact she'd survived both attempts. Maybe she had been a cat in a former life.

Mayhew spoke first. "We should go talk to the staff and see if anyone saw this *doctor* roamin' the halls. I hope that our search team can find those scrubs the guy wore. In the meantime, there will be a police officer posted outside your door while you're here."

"Thanks, Detective Mayhew." Natalie wiped her tears. Then she looked to her right and saw her mother wiping her face with the handkerchief she'd given her so long ago.

"Brent, could you give me a few minutes with my parents?"

"Sure," he said. "I'll just check out what's going on and find out who's got first shift outside the room."

"Come back in about fifteen minutes, okay?" said Natalie.

He nodded and smiled at her.

"Mom, Dad, I want you to go back to Evansville."

"What?" shouted her mother. "How can you ask such a thing?"

"I'm not asking. I love you both, but you can't protect me. We're very close to finding out who did this and the police will be more diligent in watching over me now."

"Please don't make us go home." Her mother burst into tears again. "I want to be close by."

"Let's make a deal," said Natalie. "If I let you stay until I get out of the hospital, you won't come for visits until 1:00 in the afternoon and you'll leave by 3:00."

"Only two hours," Linda whined.

"Mom, I need to get my strength back. I don't think you realize how much energy it takes to *entertain* you. You understand, don't you Dad?"

"Yes, sweetheart," he said. "Linda, she's right. She's an adult. There will be more people looking out for her now. It's time for us to let her be."

"Okay," Linda said reluctantly. "I'm outvoted again, as usual."

"I want you to go to the apartment now and get some rest. When you get up tomorrow, go to the art museum, or go downtown and tour the city. Circle Center Mall is fantastic and I bet you haven't seen it yet."

"Alright," Linda conceded. "But we will be here at 1:00 sharp. And call us if you need anything before then."

"I will. Thanks, Mom."

Her parents departed as Brent entered. He looked tired and much older than his twenty-eight years. She held out her hand for him, signaling him to come to her.

"I remember something," she said holding his hand.

He sat on the bed. "What is it?"

"I remember how much I love you," she said, pulling him closer to her. They embraced and she held onto him, feeling safe and wishing it would last forever.

Chapter 34

Erica hadn't even known Joe's last name until it came up on the employee list from Meadow and Dale Landscaping, LLC. Davidson, Joseph Ray Davidson. She found a Joseph Ray Davidson from Tempe, Arizona who had recently divorced one Sharon Joy Davidson. Erica decided she and Kendall would talk to him, even though records hadn't come up with photo ID from Arizona yet. This might not be the real Joe. This guy could have killed him and stolen his identity.

"Hey, Joe," said Erica as the two detectives entered the room. "They tell you why you're here?"

"Something about our workgroup doing the landscaping for all those ladies who was killed."

"That's correct," said Erica. "This is Detective Kendall. She's been working this case with me."

"Pleasure to meet you, Detective Kendall. So what do you need from me, Erica…or should I be calling you Detective Barnes?"

Ignoring his question, Erica plunged on. "Joe, it turns out you're the only worker who has been to all of the houses where these women lived."

"That's just a coincidence, Erica. I'd never hurt a lady. I'm always polite, ain't I?"

"Yes, Joe. You've always been really nice," said Erica looking into his frightened face and hoping this was a coincidence. "But hiring your company is the only link we've found between these victims. Right now, it doesn't look good for you to be the only employee assigned to each of them. However, if you can give me solid alibis for your whereabouts on the nights in question and a DNA sample, we'll get this cleared up."

"*Damn!* I don't know about any way to give you one of them alibis. You know I live by myself. Wife divorced me and we never had no kids. If this happened in the middle of the night, I was probably sound asleep in my own bed 'cause I gotta get up real early."

Kendall finally spoke. "Then give us a DNA sample and your fingerprints. We can compare it to the killer's and take care of things."

"I want a lawyer," he said, pursing his lips. Erica knew he was making his intentions very clear. He had no intention of cooperating further. She recited his Miranda rights and told him he was being held on suspicion of murder.

"As soon as you are processed then you'll be able to call your attorney," Erica said.

"So you're really arresting me for those murders?" he said, looking as though he might cry. "I thought we was friends."

Erica turned away. She liked Joe and couldn't believe he had anything to do with this, but he had no alibi and refused to cooperate. He was the only person of interest so far who was connected to all of the victims *and* had similar features to Emerson. What else could she do?

Kendall spoke up. "I'm sorry Mr. Davidson, but you've left us no choice. Once your attorney arrives, he'll explain everything."

"Thanks a lot, *Detective Barnes*."

Kendall gave Erica a tap on the arm and they left the interrogation room. "I'll have someone come up to process him," said Kendall.

"I've known Joe ever since he came here," said Erica. "I don't think it's him. He may have the build and the hair, but his reactions don't fit Zimmer's profile."

"What do you mean?" asked Kendall.

"In his notes to me, Parker Emerson declares himself. He wants me to catch him. Why wouldn't he be cockier or grateful or something?"

"Maybe we should ask Agent Morgan to question him," suggested Kendall. "He's had a lot more experience with this type of killer than we have."

"Probably a good idea."

Erica put in a call to Spencer Morgan. She explained the situation with Joe and his lack of cooperation. That had made him appear guilty, but she needed a more objective person to try to get Joe to talk.

Morgan agreed and arrived by 1:00 in the afternoon.

"Where's our suspect?" he asked.

"We put him in interrogation room three and his lawyer is with him, of course," said Erica. "I think he asked for a lawyer because he's scared. However, since I know him personally, I felt having you come in with a less biased set of eyes might help us gain a better perspective."

"You're a very wise woman, Detective," said Morgan. "I'll take your vote of confidence in me as a compliment."

"Well," she said, taking in the warmth of his eyes. "You're not so bad for a Fed."

"Thanks—I think."

She led him to the conference room and told him she would observe from the other side of the glass. The idea of the FBI questioning him just might make him realize that cooperating would be beneficial.

"Hello, Mr. Davidson," said Morgan. "I'm Agent Spencer Morgan from the FBI field office here in Indianapolis."

"I'm Stanton West," said the attorney.

"Mr. West, we asked your client to come in this morning to answer a few questions the police had in regards to several murders in the area. We believe these murders were committed by the same person."

"I understand," said Mr. West. "However, I don't see how this has anything to do with my client. He just happens to work for a landscaping company which services thousands of homes in the area."

"Yes, but it has come to our attention that your client is the only worker who was assigned to all of the victims' homes," said Morgan. "The FBI has a DNA match for our suspect. The officers asked if Mr. Davidson would give a sample and he refused, instead asking for you. The seriousness of these crimes is such they couldn't put him back out on the streets without being sure he's telling the truth. Also, no judge in this town—county, state, or federal—will let him out on bail for less than a million."

"Is this true, Joe? Did they ask for a DNA sample? If they did, it could clear this up."

Joe spoke for the first time. "I was upset. I volunteer to come in here and the next thing I know they're saying I might of done this. People ask for a lawyer all the time on TV. I thought it was the best thing to do at the time."

"Freakin' TV shows," Erica said from behind the glass. "The man simply panicked."

"So you think I should go ahead and give them this sample?" asked Joe.

"Yes, Joe. Most definitely," said Mr. West.

"Okay, then," said Joe. "Anything to get out of here."

"It's my understanding they've asked the lab to compare your fingerprints to the one we believe belongs to our suspect," said Morgan. "The DNA will be conclusive because only identical twins share the same DNA profile. You're not a twin are you, Mr. Davidson?"

"No, sir, I'm not."

"We should be able to get you out of here late tonight," said Morgan, "as long as your fingerprints aren't a match."

"*They won't be!* I told those detectives I never hurt any ladies in my entire life. Just ask my ex-wife."

"We intend to look at everything," said Morgan. "I'll leave the two of you now. An officer will be here soon to escort you back to the county jail. I'm sure they'll arrange for the testing as soon as possible."

When Morgan exited, Erica was waiting for him. She talked as they walked toward her desk. "You certainly made it look easy," she said.

"He may have been caught off guard by you and Kendall. You said the two of you are friendly, he lives in your apartment complex?" Morgan stared at her momentarily, his deep brown eyes boring into her soul. "He may have even been feeling like you betrayed him in some way. He probably couldn't believe you'd think him capable of something so horrendous."

"You mean he got his feelings hurt?"

"Precisely," he said. "The more I work with people like Trish Zimmer, the more I understand the delicate nature of the human psyche. How we take something someone says to us could depend upon whether we're already in a sour mood or extremely happy. In one situation we'd take it as a personal slight, in the other we'd just let it roll off our backs."

"I see your point," she said.

"If you want my opinion, this isn't our man. His communication process is too orderly. Parker Emerson's mind is so fragmented at this point; he couldn't have made it through two interrogations without revealing himself in some way."

"I agree with your assessment. I just hope Joe forgives me for putting him through this."

"He seems like a nice enough person," said Morgan. "Once his lawyer gets through telling him how much trouble he could have saved himself by cooperating to begin with, he'll be asking you for forgiveness."

Erica rolled her eyes. She wouldn't be so quick to forgive if she'd been hauled in for something she didn't do.

"So," said Morgan. "Did you eat lunch yet?"

"Actually, no," she answered. "After eating all that KFC with Pop last night, I was thinking about skipping lunch."

"Bad idea," he said. "Skipping meals doesn't help burn calories from the previous day. A nice salad gives your body a boost and burns those extra calories. Do they have salads in the cafeteria?"

"Yes, would you like to go down and check it out?"

"Let's do, then we can finish our conversation on your Mr. Davidson."

"Okay, deal."

Chapter 35

Dominik Michalski placed her key in the door lock, turning it easily. She pushed the door and propped it open with her carrier full of cleaning supplies. Picking up her favorite vacuum sweeper from the porch, she placed it just inside the door. Entering, she felt a chill run down her spine. Something seemed off. Light spilled into the hallway just beyond the living area. Miss Haag never left her lights on and criticized those who did.

Ignoring her things, Dominik ventured into the hallway to investigate the source of the light. It came from Miss Haag's bedroom. She slowly walked in that direction. Peering through the bedroom doorway, she could see feet with shoes, then legs, a flowery skirt, and pale hands resting on the abdomen holding a single red rose.

She screamed.

***

"Housekeeper found her when she came to do her weekly cleaning this morning," explained Patrol Officer Bays. "Housekeeper's name is Dominik Michalski. Works through a cleaning service called Housekeeping Experts.

"You have any info on the victim?" Erica fought off a feeling of sickness and tried not to feel responsible.

"Name's Gina Haag, age 34. Same general looks as our other victims. Miss Michalski had never met Miss Haag. Said the cleaning arrangements are made through the company. The homeowner provides a key to the main office and the cleaning service sends out whoever is available. So basically, we don't know much about Miss Haag."

"Hey, Kendall," said Erica. Kendall walked towards her. "I need for you to search for an address book, computer, refrigerator notes; something that might give us a clue as to next-of-kin. I'll go see how Dr. Patel is doing with our victim."

Kendall nodded and headed for the kitchen. Erica took the long walk down the hall, a feeling of dread, like ice water in her veins. She wanted to avoid making this personal. Somehow, she needed to keep this psycho's words out of her head. Logic dictated this wasn't her fault. Why wouldn't her emotional side follow suit?

Dr. Patel stood next to the bed looking down on Gina Haag, shaking her head. She turned and Erica locked eyes with her.

"Detective Barnes, this is definitely the same killer. Initial examination shows signs of broken neck vertebrae. As you can see, he used the same method of sewing the eyes open and wrote *SEE ME* across her forehead with lipstick."

"Can you determine time of death?"

"There is some decomposition. Rigor mortis has come and gone. These facts, plus her body temperature, would put her time of death sometime between 4:00 p.m. and 11:00 pm on Friday night.

That was three days ago. Erica's gut wrenched and she feared she might throw up. After taking a couple of deep breaths, she nodded and walked away. Air, she needed air and she needed it quick. As she opened the front door, Erica practically ran into Agent Morgan.

"I heard," he said. "Can I help?"

"It's the same guy. Too much detail not to be. He said he'd do it again and he did."

"Wait a minute," Morgan grabbed her arm and frowned. "I know what you're thinking and you'd better get it right out of your head."

"The FBI train you guys to read minds now," she fired back, irritation mounting.

"No, but experience does count for something. You're a great cop, Detective Barnes. Don't let this monster burn you out."

"I'm not going to! It would be nice if everyone would give me some credit here. I'm human. Logically, I know he's full of shit and I can't control him. Even if he hadn't sent the flowers and the letters, I would still feel some responsibility for not having caught him by now. *Okay?*"

"I hear ya," Morgan said and threw up his hands. He turned abruptly, making his way around her to enter the house.

"Crap," she snarled. Now she'd alienated her FBI buddy. She'd apologize later, because she liked him and did need his help. She would even take whatever assistance the stiff Agent Zimmer was willing to provide. Parker Emerson was here and had now committed six murders in Indianapolis. "I've got to get this guy, before he moves on to start fresh somewhere else," she murmured.

As she sucked in the fresh spring air, she noticed a group of reporters at the end of the driveway. There again stood Peter Elliott. How did he always manage to be first on the scene? She wanted to go over and punch him, but no point being arrested for assault. He definitely wasn't worth it. She decided to avoid the jackass and go apologize to Morgan.

Turning on her heel, Erica reentered the house. She walked down the hall to find Agent Morgan in conversation with Dr. Patel. She decided not to interrupt them, and walked around the room, looking for clues and something to help her get to know Gina Haag.

A carved mahogany box sat on the dresser. Lovely and carved like the type found in most import stores. Opening it, she found a pearl necklace. It must have been special as it was the only piece of jewelry in the box. A key underneath it looked like it fit a safety deposit box. They'd have to look for her bank records. The rest of its contents looked like memorabilia—some Girl Scout patches, a tassel from a graduation cap, and a ticket stub from a Broadway show.

Other items on the dresser were pretty standard. A couple of fancy cologne bottles, a fake plant, a silver brush and comb set, possibly antique, and a photo of what looked to be Gina and a Labrador Retriever. She wondered what had happened to the dog.

"Barnes," said Kendall from behind her, which caused Erica to jump.

"I didn't hear you come in. You find anything we can use?"

"Found this list of names and phone numbers on the fridge. I called the one which said *the school* and found out she's employed as a third grade teacher at James Whitcomb Riley. She didn't report in this morning. School personnel called her parents about an hour ago to let them know of their concern. Parents haven't arrived yet because they live in Columbus, Indiana. They're probably going to show up here any minute."

"Let's have Officer Samuels keep an eye out for her parents. We don't want them coming in here, not until the body is moved."

"I'll go give her the heads up," said Kendall.

"Oh, Kendall, before you go, did you find anything in the kitchen to indicate Miss Haag had a dog?"

"No, why?"

"There's a photo of her on the dresser with a Lab. Could be a previous pet, I guess. You better go talk to Samuels." Kendall nodded and left the room.

Erica continued her search of the dresser, opening each drawer and investigating its contents. Gina Haag was very organized. Every panty folded neatly, all of her socks paired up and placed in perfect rows; her bras folded neatly. This young lady was a bit too obsessive-compulsive for Erica's taste. She didn't find anything out of the ordinary and moved on around the room.

She turned as she heard the morgue attendants bring in the gurney. They unzipped the body bag spreading it over the gurney. They carefully wrapped the whole coverlet around Gina to preserve any evidence on or around the body. Dr. Patel had come back and was helping with the transfer.

Erica noticed Agent Morgan looking around the room and decided it was time to render her apology.

"Agent Morgan." She watched him turn at the sound of her voice. "I'm sorry for my behavior earlier. This has been a bitch of a case. I shouldn't be taking my frustrations out on you."

"No sweat," he said. "I'll try to show a little more respect and stop being so protective."

"It's not that I don't appreciate everyone's concern..."

"Honestly, Detective," he interrupted. "I do understand. It would drive me crazy if everyone was hovering." He paused, turning away from her.

He'd called her Detective. He must be too polite to say what he really thinks. She walked around the room looking for clues, and then tried talking to him again—business this time.

"Do you think he saw the news conference this morning?" she asked. "I mean, it appears he did this a couple of days ago, before Jordan's plea was recorded."

"Hard to tell," he responded, his tone of voice softening. "I guess it would depend on how often he watches the news or how early he needs to be at work. Hopefully, he'll watch sometime today. I'm hoping Trish has been able to convince the news stations to air it more than once and not just during the regular newscast hours."

"Let's just hope it works," said Erica.

Chapter 36

Parker Emerson was picking up a few groceries after work. Bread, bologna, sodas, and chips—his meal of choice. He thought he'd buy some apples for a change of pace, but stopped short. There she was again. How could this be? She keeps coming back. He put her down and she rises from the dead.

Parker saw his mother walking down the produce aisle. He knew she hadn't noticed him, but when had she ever? He knew if she had seen him, she would have come after him. She'd think nothing of embarrassing him in front of everyone. Then the headache came, fire burning his gray matter, blinding pain piercing his temples, the nausea overwhelming. He left his shopping cart, moving quickly towards the exit. He made it around the corner of the building before he started regurgitating.

"I have to do it right this time," he whispered, spitting vile fluids from his mouth. "I can't let her take over my life again. I hate her! I hate her!" He started pacing, holding the sides of his throbbing head.

"No, no, no. I love her. She's my mother. You can't hate your mother. It's a sin. I'll go to Hell. No, no, no, no," he continued in an angry, but low voice so no one else could hear. Barely able to open his eyes to the light, Parker peered through slits, hoping no one saw him. He breathed deeply, needing to pull himself out of this terrorized state. He must destroy the enemy.

Determined, he came back to the front of the store just in time to see her leaving with two bags of groceries. He watched her as she walked to her car before he dared get into his vehicle. His engine ground to a start and he waited for her to pull out of her parking space. Parker followed his mother, staying two car lengths back. He didn't want her to know he was coming.

He watched as she pulled into the driveway of a small brick ranch home.

"This is how she does it," he said to himself, driving past. "She's constantly moving."

Parker watched as she took her bags to the house. While he slumped in his front seat of his vehicle, hate filled his heart. Confusion filled his head. How was she able to keep getting a new house? Was she tricking people into letting her use their houses? Did she know he was on her trail?

Once she was inside, he drove on. He'd come back one night after dark. Stealth was the best way to deal with her. His panic and excitement merged into frenzied thoughts. He'd get rid of her finally, but he had to be prepared. He had to make it permanent. He couldn't stand these headaches. He wanted to live in peace and it would never happen as long as she lived.

Parker arrived at his apartment fifteen minutes later. He'd forgotten all about needing groceries. Actually, he wasn't hungry any more. In his bedroom, he found his backpack in the closet. He unzipped it and checked its contents. Sewing kit, comb, shoes, *nunchaku*—but he needed a dress. Looking through his closet, he chose the white one with purple rosebuds on it. He folded it neatly and placed it on top of the other contents.

"There now," he said, starting to calm somewhat. "All ready. I just need to keep this with me and when the time is right…."

"*No Parker!* What are you doing? It doesn't work because it's wrong. Let that nice Detective Barnes catch you."

"No, no, no," he told himself. "She's not very good or she'd have caught me by now. Maybe she doesn't care or she thinks some other case is more important."

He looked in his dresser mirror. "But you messed up really bad. You killed a *baby!*"

"It wasn't my fault, it wasn't my fault," he whined. "She should have told me. I never would hurt a baby."

"But you did. You killed a baby!"

"Not listening to you anymore." Parker clamped his hands over his ears and paced. "Not listening, not listening, not listening."

He spotted the television. Turning it on, he increased the volume. This would drown out the voices. He knew what he had to do. He didn't want to hear about the baby anymore.

"This is Andrea Atkins and we have a special news report. We recently received confirmation from the FBI and IMPD that there is a serial killer amongst us. The suspect's name is Parker Emerson." An old photo of him flashed on the screen. "He is suspected of killing his wife, author Alecia Fox, and his mother Wanda Emerson as well as two others across the Midwest before settling in Indianapolis. He is now being sought for questioning in the murders of Penny Flanders, Marilyn Novak, Keith Gray, Samantha Ritter, Elizabeth Glenn and her unborn child, and most recently Gina Haag."

"What is she talking about?" said Parker angrily, turning away from the television. "She's wrong, she's wrong. I only killed her. Just Mama."

"Today, we have a taped plea from Mr. Emerson's sister, Mrs. Jordan Collins of Lincoln, Nebraska. Parker, if you are out there, please listen to what your sister has to say."

"Jordan?" He turned to see his sister on the screen. She looked nervous. He knew she was very shy and had a hard time talking to a group of people. He knelt in front of the television touching her image. He loved her so. Why were they doing this to her? She must be so scared.

"Parker, sweetie, please, please stop what you're doing. Mama is dead. You're safe now. Honey, are you taking your headache medication." She started to cry.

"Oh, no. Don't cry, Jordan. Are they hurting you? I can't let them hurt you."

"Parker," she said between sobs. "I love you. You always protected me. You're the best big brother anyone could ever want." She paused, wiping away her tears. "Please, Parker. Please turn yourself in. Let *me* protect *you* now. I can get you a real good lawyer. I miss you. I love you. Please call Detective Barnes or the FBI and turn yourself in."

Parker sat with tears streaming down his face. Jordan was still crying, too. He hated seeing her cry. She was too sweet to understand what he had to do. Too innocent. Someone was telling her lies. Then it came to him. Detective Barnes must have told Jordan their mama was dead. It's part of her plan to get him to give himself up. Then she doesn't have to work so hard.

He stood up and pushed the television off of the stand. It came down with a crash, splintering its casing and breaking essential parts.

He paced angrily.

First, he'd take care of Mama. Then he'd take care of Detective Erica Barnes.

Chapter 37

Erica's day started out with a nasty surprise. When she opened her door to retrieve her morning paper, she discovered a note taped to it. She recognized the handwriting. Parker Emerson left her another message and this time, it was much too close for comfort. Shaking, she left the door open and went back into the apartment for a pair of gloves. Blowing out a deep puff of air, she realized she'd been holding her breath. Careful not to tug too hard and tear it, Erica pulled the letter from the door.

Placing the unopened envelope into an evidence bags—a paper lunch bag was the best she could do—she decided to go in early and take this straight to Mark Chatham. It had been three days since they'd discovered Gina Haag's body and now this. Although she hadn't read it yet, she was sure it was yet another unfriendly reminder of his intent.

Erica's heart was still pounding when she reached the forensics lab where she found Mark Chatham hard at work. He logged in the evidence, and then Erica watched as he carefully slit open the envelope with a scalpel.

Leaning over the worktable to read the letter, Erica's breath quickened with every word. When she finished, she swayed a little.

"Barnes, you okay?" asked Chatham.

"Yeah, I just stood up too quickly," she said, trying to hide her fear. "How soon can we get this processed for prints and DNA?"

"I'll do the best I can," Chatham promised. "Prints shouldn't take too long, but DNA is another thing. I'll do what I can to push it through."

"Thanks," said Erica, on her way to the door. She pulled off her gloves and disposed of them before exiting.

Arriving at her desk, she sat down and found a message from Detective James Pitts from the Robbery Division. Since he'd recently started working the night shift, he'd asked her to call him at home before 11:00 a.m. She knew she'd have to wait for a short while to give him time to reach his south side residence. The urgency of the message piqued her curiosity.

"Hey, Barnes," said Kendall. "I just saw Mark Chatham. He said you got another message from our nut case. What this time?"

"He taped a note to my apartment door."

"He knows where you live? You need somebody to stay with you."

"I'm fine, Kendall. Why do you think I'm taking all those Karate lessons?" Erica tried her best to lighten things up, despite the roiling in her gut, but it didn't work.

Kendall frowned at her. "This isn't funny, Barnes. You know as well as I do, the odds are against you winning a physical confrontation with him, no matter how much combat training you've had."

"Yeah, but as long as I've got my Glock nearby, I'm sure I can deal with him."

"It's good to have an equalizer on hand, but he's sneaking in after dark. He has the element of surprise on his side. People don't always have their wits about them when they're awakened in the middle of the night, or if they've just arrived home from work."

"Thanks for your concern, Chennelle," said Erica, her temper rising. "Don't forget how he took out Keith Gray. Gray didn't do Marilyn Novak any good. Besides, he's attacking women in houses, not apartments. There's less chance of a neighbor hearing and calling 9-1-1 before he's done with the victim."

"*Okay!*" Kendall threw up her hands in surrender. "Let's get back to the note. What did he have to say this time?"

"Basically it was my fault Gina Haag died. He said I should have stopped him."

"So, Wonder Woman, why haven't you arrested him?" she said, voice dripping with sarcasm.

"That's the good news."

"Let me guess," Kendall huffed, starting to pace. "He's going to do it again if you don't stop him."

Erica nodded, feeling the weight of the situation despite the fact she had no real control over this mad man. Logically, she knew he played mind games with her to throw her off balance. Even though he claimed he wanted her to stop him, he wasn't going to make it easy.

"He saw Jordan's broadcast," said Erica. "Looks like it backfired. He's really pissed about the fact I *made her cry*."

"Have you talked to Agent Morgan about this latest communication?"

"I called him on my way in. I told him I was taking the envelope to the lab so Chatham could dust for prints and check for DNA."

"Do you know if Morgan's going to talk to Zimmer about it?"

"I'm sure he will." Erica leaned back in her chair and let go of a huge sigh. "I wish he didn't have to tell her, but I guess she needs it for the profile."

"What's up with you and Zimmer?"

"I don't know, Chennelle. Something about her rubs me the wrong way." Erica shook her head trying to put her thoughts into words. "She's too…too…."

"Stiff?" said Kendall with a grin.

"Right. She doesn't smile or crack a joke. She's way too serious and stuffy."

Kendall laughed. "Barnes, you crack me up. You know how many people have said that about you?"

"*Really?*" Erica frowned at how much this observation stung.

"Thing is, if you really watch me when I'm working, you'd probably say the same about me. Women are too often looked upon as weak. If we show any emotion, we're not only weak but also hysterical. Don't know about you, but I feel like I have to be straight-faced and stoic when I'm working a case. *Just the facts, please*. Otherwise, I'm not taken seriously."

Erica nodded. She understood exactly what Kendall meant, but wasn't sure she'd change her mind about Supervisory Special Agent Zimmer any time soon.

Kendall continued. "I'm just saying she may be a completely different person away from work."

Erica decided to steer this discussion in another direction by telling Kendall about the message from Detective Pitts. Looking at her watch, she decided she'd waited an adequate amount of time to make the call.

"Pitts here," answered the gruff, scratchy voice on the other end.

"Well, you're precisely who I'm looking for." Erica tried to sound more light-hearted in an effort to dispel any *stiffness* rumors.

"Detective Barnes, I've got someone you and Kendall should talk to. Her name's Ranae North. We were called in on a robbery attempt last night. We're not so sure it was one."

"Hang on a minute, James; let me put you on speaker so Kendall can hear." She pushed the speaker button and urged him to go on.

"After listening to her story, I thought this guy sounded like your serial killer."

"You've definitely got our attention," said Erica, a chill of excitement coursing through her. "How'd she get away?"

"The lady had a gun."

After the conversation with Detective Pitts ended, Erica looked up the attempted robbery report on the computer. She found it and wrote down the victim's contact information.

Ranae North matched Emerson's type, five-foot, six-inches tall with dark brown hair and eyes. The timing went along with his schedule as well. She called Ranae's cell phone, taking the chance that Ranae had not gone back to work following her ordeal. Erica guessed correctly. Ranae stayed with her mother on the south side after the attack. She agreed to allow the detectives to come by and discuss what happened.

Kendall drove and Erica quietly stared out the passenger window. She hoped Ranae North remembered something more now that she'd had time to get past the initial shock. In the report, the description of the perpetrator seemed rather vague.

"You know what worries me," Kendall said, breaking the silence.

"What?"

"If this is our man, people are going to find out she survived because she had a gun. Lordy, we'll have a mess on our hands."

"I hear ya. Every woman in this city will be buying a handgun."

"Damn right," agreed Kendall. "Next thing you know we'll be getting all kinds of accidental shooting calls. Some poor slob gets home early from a business trip and the wife shoots him. One of the kids sneaks back into the house after curfew. It'll be a nightmare."

"Hopefully, we can keep a lid on it," said Erica. "The news media would have a field day with this one."

Pulling into the driveway, Erica turned to take a good look at a car parked across the street. "Holy crap!" Her exclamation made Kendall jump. "This cannot be happening."

"What's wrong?" Kendall asked glancing around.

"Peter *f'ing* Elliott, that's what's wrong."

Kendall looked in the rearview mirror. "The black sedan across the street?"

"Yep." Erica gritted her teeth, unable to keep the anger out of her voice. She could feel her pulse quicken at what Peter could already know and why he was here. "Let's hurry up and get in there before he realizes it's us."

"He probably already knows," said Kendall. "It's like he's freaking psychic or something."

They exited the car and moved swiftly towards the front door. They didn't get a chance to knock because a short, thin woman, who Erica guessed to be in her mid-fifties, greeted them.

"You must be the detectives Ranae is expecting. I'm her mother, Jessica North. Please do come in."

They followed Mrs. North into the small two-story home, through a short foyer and into a great room. It was tastefully decorated with a tan leather couch, matching loveseat and chair. There were two dark wood end tables and coffee table. She'd arranged her furnishings to make the huge HDTV the center of attention.

"Please have a seat and I'll let Ranae know you're here."

"No need, Mother," said the soft, sweet voice of Ranae North.

"This is Ranae," her mother began. "Oh dear. I introduced myself to you, but didn't get your names."

"I'm Detective Erica Barnes and this is Detective Chennelle Kendall. We're from the Homicide Department."

"Homicide?" Mrs. North looked at her daughter in confusion. "Ranae, I thought this was about the attempted robbery? Did you find the robber dead?"

"To our knowledge, he isn't dead," Erica assured her. "Detective Pitts called us in because he thinks this intruder fits the description of the man who's been breaking into women's homes in the middle of the night and killing them."

"Oh, Ranae!" Mrs. North's hand leapt to her mouth. She looked at her daughter with an expression of horror.

"Now do you understand why I have a gun, Mom?" Ranae turned her attention to Erica. "She's been upset with me for buying it. I don't like it myself, but I live alone and felt I needed protection. Apparently, I was right."

Erica just smiled at her and asked her if she'd mind answering a few questions. Ranae agreed and they all sat down. Kendall pulled out a notepad while Erica started the interview.

"Miss North…."

"Please call me Ranae."

"Ranae. The description you gave the detectives last night was rather vague. Do you remember any more about the intruder, other than he was short and wearing dark clothing?"

"It was very dark. I didn't get a chance to see him up close. I shot at him when he kicked down my door. It all happened so fast."

"I understand. Could you tell if he was Caucasian, Hispanic, African American?"

"The only part of him I could see was his face and he was definitely white."

"Did you see his hair color or length of his hair?"

"No. He had on a dark hooded sweatshirt. The hood was up and tied tight. I don't remember seeing any hair coming out from under the hood. I also don't remember any facial hair—no mustache, no beard. I just didn't get a good look at anything. At least not anything that wants to stick in my mind."

"Anything more stand out about his clothing?"

"Not really. Sweatshirt was dark, probably navy, or black. He may have been wearing blue jeans. I know he was wearing white shoes, running shoes maybe. Like I said before, the room was really dark. After I shot at him the first time and missed, he didn't wait around for the second one. There was a blood trail and I heard one of the cops say they found a bloody bullet in the wall, so I must have hit him."

"So you don't know where he was hit?"

"No, Detective Barnes." Ranae paused for a moment and then her face lit up with realization.

"What is it?" asked Kendall.

"This just popped into my head. I've told this story a dozen times but I just realized something. He had a backpack with him."

"A backpack?" Erica sat forward brimming with curiosity.

"Yeah. The type hikers use to keep hunters from shooting them. When he turned to run, I saw a flash of orange in the moonlight. I've seen those types of backpacks online."

"This could be a big mistake on his part," said Kendall.

"Is there anything else he did or said?" asked Erica.

"Oh! He called out to me in a sort of singsong way. Kind of like a kid might. He said, *'So you think you're so clever, moving around all the time. I'm going to get rid of you this time.'* I didn't say a word. I was too scared. I just sat there with the gun until he kicked in the door and then I started shooting."

"A good choice to be quiet. No reason to let him know exactly where you were." Of course, Erica knew if Ranae hadn't had the weapon, it wouldn't have mattered. He would have found Ranae in seconds and murdered her. "So, you didn't recognize the voice?"

"No. I have no idea who this man was," said Ranae. "But from what he said, it sounded like he knew me."

"Do you have any questions you want to ask Ranae, Kendall?"

Kendall shook her head.

"Then I think that's all for today." Erica reached in her pocket and pulled out a business card. "If you think of anything else, give me a call."

"Do you think he'll come after me again?" asked Ranae, looking concerned.

Erica had no idea how to predict what this lunatic would do next. "Since he knows you have a gun and aren't afraid to use it, I don't think so, but I can't guarantee it. The profiler from the FBI who's working with us seems to think he's seeing someone else when he sees these women—someone who physically harmed him during his childhood. He's most likely psychotic and may still think you're this person. You may want to stay with your mother for a while."

The Norths escorted the detectives to the door.

"By the way," Erica added. "Please don't talk to any reporters about this. There's one in the black Ford across the street. We want to keep this quiet for a while until we can actually prove he's the same person who's killing our victims."

"No problem. I understand completely," said Ranae as she opened the door. "Thank you, Detectives."

"Our pleasure," said Erica.

They moved swiftly to their vehicle as Erica heard Ranae shut the front door. She couldn't help looking. Elliott had his window down smiling smugly. He gave her a little wave and she flipped him the bird as Kendall drove past his vehicle. She'd pay for that one in tomorrow morning's edition, but at this point, she didn't care.

Chapter 38

Brent decided to stop by the Missing Person Department to get an update on Natalie's case. He found Tyrone Mayhew at his desk.

"Freeman!" said Mayhew, extending his hand. "How's it goin'?"

"Much better," said Brent as he shook Mayhew's hand heartily. "Did the lab techs find anything when they processed Natalie's room?"

"Nah. The bastard was all suited up like a doctor. The only evidence we've got right now is the skin and blood from under Natalie's fingernails." Mayhew breathed a heavy sigh. "Of course, with lab backups it could be weeks before we get the DNA profile. By then, he could be long gone."

"Whoever is responsible must be afraid she's getting her memory back."

"That's what me and Jacobs figure." Mayhew shook his head. "Problem is, even Special Investigations hasn't been able to tap into this one. They're afraid there might be a gang war over it all."

"Maybe I should talk to Fuentes while he's still in county lockup," said Brent. "Maybe I can get something out of him you didn't."

"I doubt he'll tell you anything, but it's worth a try. Today would be a good day to do it," said Mayhew. "I hear they're transferrin' him to Michigan City in a couple of days."

"Guess I'd better get my ass over there today then."

"Yeah. Tomorrow he could be tied up with all the preliminary transfer shit. By the way, is Natalie gettin' close to goin' home?"

"They should spring her day after tomorrow. Her parents plan to stay for a couple of days after she's out to get her settled."

Mayhew gave Brent a big smile. "It's all goin' to work out."

***

Brent walked into the county jail determined to get answers from Fuentes. It would be a lot harder to get to him once he transferred to the penitentiary. Brent needed to know who nearly killed Natalie—twice. The likelihood of Fuentes giving up one of his own seemed pretty slim, but he had to try.

After going through the jailhouse rituals of giving up his weapon and being searched, Brent found himself in a ten-by-ten interrogation room. The small table and four chairs bolted to the floor prevented any smashing of skulls.

Five minutes later, a guard escorted Hector Fuentes into the room. Shackled around his ankles and wrists, the chains attached to a heavy canvas belt around his waist, he slowly shuffled into the room. Smirking, he took the seat across from Brent.

"You look pleased about something,"

"I'm always happy to see you Mr. Detective, sir," Fuentes said, voice dripping with sarcasm.

"Yeah?"

"So you come to say bye-bye?" Fuentes gave a baby-like wave. "You gonna miss me when I take off for my new luxury suite in paradise?"

"I need to ask you some questions regarding another matter." Brent did his best to keep his tone of voice professional.

"Ah! Is this about the lady prosecutor?"

"As a matter of fact, it is."

"Mmm. I thought so. I saw you eyeballin' her in court. You two...?" Fuentes made a crude hand gesture.

"I'm investigating her kidnapping and beating, and the recent attempt on her life."

"From what I heard, *amigo*," Fuentes said leaning back in his chair, "you're a homicide cop. Why you on this one?"

"We cover attempted murder as well as actual homicides."

"So, you came as a cop, not a boyfriend?"

Brent ignored Fuentes' remark and got straight to the point. "Rumor has it, you ordered the hit." He stared deep into Fuentes' eyes.

Fuentes opened them wide in faux surprise. "You know is not good to listen to rumors, *Puerco*."

It wasn't the first time nor would it be the last time he was called a pig, so he let it go. Stone-faced, he stared at Fuentes and waited for him to continue. It didn't take long.

"I got no reason to hurt the lady."

"Really?" Now Brent's tone turned to sarcasm. "The fact she prosecuted you wasn't reason enough?"

His nose curled in anger as he spat out each word. "Hey, man. If I wanted her fuckin' dead, she'd be dead. And, I sure as hell wouldn't have waited until the bitch presented her case. Los Hombres didn't have nothing to do with it. *Comprende*?"

Brent squinted at him. He'd had enough. He leaned menacingly towards Fuentes. "Look you mother fucker, I ain't playing games here. If you and your *compadres* didn't do this, then who did?"

"Maybe you lookin' in the wrong 'hood, *pinchero*."

Brent sat back in his seat again, eyeing Fuentes.

"Think about it, Detective. Who benefits more from this? Not me. Most of the jury already decided I was guilty by then. If you were a juror who wasn't sure, would you want to put me back out on the street or put me in jail?"

Brent hadn't thought about it this way. "How do I know this wasn't your way of getting a new trial?"

"You don't," Fuentes said calmly. "Thing is, looks to me like someone was leaving my sister a message. If it was a Los Hombres, he'd be dead. I wouldn't be in here if I didn't love Yolanda. She made a mistake. I protected her. Los Hombres are family. They would not have done this."

Eyes widening, Brent turned to Fuentes. "Are the Los Hombres seeking retaliation?"

Fuentes stared at Brent, a grin slowly developing on his face. "*Yo no se, pipucho.*"

He didn't know? Brent didn't buy it. Fuentes knew something. Los Hombres must have gone after Henderson's gang. He motioned for the guard to indicate he was ready to leave.

"*Adios, pipucho!*" Fuentes laughed and smiled.

"By the way," Brent said from the doorway, "your sister has vanished. I hope she's okay."

"Don't worry—she is."

The serious look on Fuentes' face was reassuring. At least Yolanda was safe. Brent left the room and picked up his belongings.

"With his freakin' connections, he'll have them before we get a chance to get started. I've got to get back to Missing Persons and warn Mayhew." The look on the jail attendant's face made Brent realize he'd mumbled his words aloud. Brent exited the building and practically ran back to the City-County Building. He headed straight for the Missing Person Unit.

Brent caught sight of Jacobs and shouted his name.

"I was just getting ready to call you," said Jacobs. "Mayhew said you'd gone to the jail to talk to Fuentes."

"Yeah, I just finished." Brent wrinkled his brow and breathed heavily from his jaunt. "I've got something important to tell you."

"Me first. Clearwater from Criminal Gangs called about ten minutes ago. He thinks he found the guys who beat up Natalie."

"Alive?"

Jacobs looked startled. "Why would you ask if they were alive?"

"Are they?"

"No," Jacobs said eyeing Brent. "They found them in an alley off Illinois Street early this morning. They were part of Henderson's crew. Shot execution style, base of the head. Nobody could have survived it."

"Then I'm too late." Brent ran his fingers through his hair and paced back and forth. "Fuentes is being sent upstate soon. I wanted to see if he'd confess to putting the hit out on Natalie." Brent told Jacobs the rest of what Fuentes said.

"Now I know why you thought they were dead," said Jacobs.

"No point in looking for Yolanda. Fuentes made it clear to me his sister was safely hidden away."

"So she's alive?"

"According to Fuentes, he's forgiven her. She's family and that's all he cares about. When he realized Natalie had been dumped where his sister works, I'm sure he let his goons know to get her out of town and *to send them a message*."

"God, I hope this doesn't start a war."

"If it does, Clearwater and I will be very busy." Brent stopped his pacing and sat down in the nearest chair. "By the way, how do they know these are the guys who actually hurt Natalie?"

"We received an anonymous tip this morning telling us where to find *the bastards who beat up the prosecutor.* One of the deceased has some pretty nasty scratches on his face. Forensics will compare his DNA with the DNA from the scrapings collected from Natalie's fingernails. I'll bet he's the asshole who tried to kill her in the hospital."

"A DNA match would be good because she didn't get a good look the guy's face. Of course, she may have seen the faces of the guys who kidnapped and beat her in the first place."

"Do you think she could identify them if I put them in a photo lineup? We've got mug shots of them since it appears they'd all been in a little trouble before," said Jacobs.

"I'm sure she'll be willing to try. Her memory's coming back a little every day, but she still doesn't remember a lot about the attack."

Jacobs leaned back in his chair. "I'll go see her in the morning. Hopefully this will make her feel safer."

"I hope so, Ben. I hope so."

Chapter 39

Erica saw Sensei Nakamura smile at her as she approached her opponent and bowed. She'd worked hard for this moment—this chance to obtain her first black belt in Karate. She took her stance and focused her full attention on her opponent, moving gracefully. She executed each move perfectly and when it was over she knew she had accomplished Shodan.

Sensei Nakamura announced the names of each student who had passed the test. When he called Erica's name, she glanced at the spectators catching a glimpse of her father's proud face. It made her feel like a child again. A wisp of sadness overtook her as she wished her mother was here to share this moment with them.

She stepped forward, she and Nakamura bowed to one another, then he presented her with a black belt. Having a difficult time keeping a solemn expression, she knew she had to quell her excitement. Otherwise, Sensei Nakamura might snatch it away from her for being disrespectful. They bowed to one another again and she took her place in the line of students.

The ceremony complete, she heard the chattering of excited parents and other family members so proud of their thirteen-year-olds for their accomplishments. She felt a little strange being the only adult in the class, but then again she hadn't been interested in Karate as a child.

"Look at you!" Her father was standing behind her grinning from ear-to-ear. "I'm very proud of you, Kitten."

"Thanks, Pop," she said, barely able to contain herself.

"Hopefully this will come in handy if you meet the loony dude face-to-face."

She put her arm around him and gave him a quick peck on the cheek. She knew he wasn't very familiar with the martial arts. He probably didn't realize how in a real combat situation nobody plays fair like they're required to during lessons. Explaining it to him now would only cause him to worry more.

She waited until the crowd dissipated and then approached Sensei Nakamura.

"Sensei," she said with a bow. "I would like to introduce you to my father, Michael Barnes."

"Ah, you must be very proud of your daughter, Mr. Barnes."

"I most definitely am," he said, beaming. "Well, Kitten, it's getting close to my bed time. Call me tomorrow."

"Sure thing, Pop," she said. She watched as he limped toward the door. He'd taken a bullet in his left hip a few years ago. Of course, the fellows at the station teased him until the day he retired about getting shot in the ass.

"May I talk to you about the case I'm working?" she asked as she turned her attention to Sensei Nakamura.

"Most certainly, young one. I'm not expecting anyone else this evening. Let us wait until the others have left. I'll make us some tea and we can speak freely."

She slowly gathered her things, wiping her face and neck with a towel. She knew she smelled like a sweaty gym. Not much she could do about it now though. Martial arts studios rarely had shower rooms.

The workout had been good for her. It kept her mind off of Parker Emerson for a time, but it was only temporary. The image of his notes and the anxiety of knowing he hunted another victim as she stood there in her prideful glory made her cringe. She had no doubt he would continue as long as he thought his mother was still alive.

Of course, Ranae North had injured him. The blood type in her house matched Parker's. The DNA tests would give them 100% confirmation. She'd left the office while Kendall was calling the hospitals in the area to find out if he'd sought medical attention. Erica wondered if she'd been successful.

"So, Erica. What would you like to ask of me?" Nakamura inquired, offering her a cup of aromatic tea.

"Sensei, I'm pretty sure I know the answer to my question, but would like your input," she answered.

"You still do not trust your inner voice, young one." He shook his head. "Please, go ahead with your questions and I will do my best to answer."

"This case I've been working, the one I consulted you on a few weeks ago."

"The serial killer who knows martial arts."

"Yes, Sensei. He has been communicating with me and everyone is worried he will come after me."

"And you want to know if you will be able to defend yourself," he said. "Again I must say to you, young one, listen to your inner voice. It tells you much. You've taken self defense classes as part of your training, yes?"

"Yes," she answered. "But I'm feeling very vulnerable right now. This man knows where I live, and of course, where I work. He's angry with me now for upsetting his sister by having her do a recorded plea on television."

"He is very protective of her. She must mean a great deal to him."

"They were both abused as children, but according to his sister, he was brutalized more severely," said Erica. "Apparently he has had a psychotic break and thinks he keeps seeing his mother in every brunette he comes across."

"I see." Nakamura's eyes darkened with sadness. "The only thing you can do is play dirty. In class, we must have respect. When there is a real threat, we must survive. Kick, scratch, gouge, whatever it takes to win. Use your intellect. It will aid you in escaping this monster."

"Thank you, Sensei. I'd better make my way home to a nice hot shower. I need to be up bright and early tomorrow."

"Take care, young one. Trust your instincts."

Erica bowed to the master, gathered her things, and headed for the parking lot.

***

Erica pulled into the parking lot of her apartment building contemplating what Sensei Nakamura had said. He was right. Whenever she followed her instincts, they served her well. When she ignored them, she usually found herself in trouble. Right now, she felt anxious. She checked to her left and then to her right. She peered out the back window. Satisfied she was alone; she opened her door, got out of the car and locked it. Just as she reached her building, Joe walked out.

Erica smiled, but could feel the blushing of her cheeks at this awkward situation. "Hi, Joe, how are you?"

"I'm doin' alright," he said, lowering his eyes.

"I'm glad to hear it," she said, glancing to the right.

"Well, some things are good, some's not," he said.

"What do you mean?"

"Well, I got fired from my landscaping job."

"That's awful!" Whatever guilt Erica felt before at detaining him just increased ten-fold. "I'm so sorry. Is there anything I can do? I could talk to them for you."

"Don't you never mind, Erica. I got me another one." He looked up, smiling at her. "They needed a maintenance attendant here at the apartments. I started today."

"That's great!" At least now her guilt assuaged and she came back down to a tolerable level of embarrassment. "I really am sorry about suspecting you."

"I admit I was pretty pissed off at first, but I can understand how it must have looked. Besides, I'm a firm believer everything happens for a reason. The hourly rate I'm making is less, but with the break they give me on the rent I'm actually making more money."

"Can't beat more money."

He winked at her. "It's all good."

"You've got a great attitude, Joe. I'm not sure I'd have been so forgiving."

"I don't know, I bet you would have. You have a good night now. I sure hope you find this guy soon."

"Me too, Joe."

Chapter 40

The sun was shining on this beautiful late May morning. Brent had visited Natalie the evening before and told her about his visit with Fuentes, the two dead men, and how Ben Jacobs hoped she could identify her attackers from a photo lineup. He smiled as he remembered the tears of joy and relief on her face. Jacobs would be there early because today Natalie was going home.

"Hey, gorgeous," Brent said as he entered her room.

Already dressed in a pink sundress, tan sandals, and the chic blonde wig her mother bought for her, she gave him her warmest smile and ran her fingers along one side of the wig. "What do you think?"

"You look great," he said, smiling at how beautiful she looked in spite of her injuries. Only four more weeks to contend with her wired jaw and arm cast, and most of the bruising had faded away.

"Are you sure? You're not just saying that to make me feel good, are you?"

"I'll confess, it's a little short, but I'll get used to it."

"Hopefully, when I get back on my regiment of vitamins, my real hair will grow faster and I won't have to wear this thing when it starts warming up out there. I heard it'll get up to 65 degrees today."

The love he felt for her was the only warmth he wanted. No matter what she wore or how many bruises, she was the most beautiful person he knew. Her inner beauty meant more to him than he could put into words.

A knock on the door brought him out of his revelry. Ben Jacobs stood just outside the door.

"Hello," Jacobs said, approaching Natalie with his hand extended.

"Hello, Sergeant Jacobs."

"I assume Brent told you why I wanted to see you today?"

"Yes. He said you had some photos for me to look through."

"I know you've had some problems remembering exactly what happened, so if you don't recognize any of the men in these photos, don't worry." Jacobs took a page out of the folder he was carrying. "I've created this sheet of photos. If you see someone you recognize, please point him or them out to me. Take your time. There's no reason to hurry."

"Of course," she said. "I'm ready whenever you are."

Brent could not help but admire Natalie's strength. Nothing seemed to get her down. He watched as she looked intently at each photo, seeming to take in each one with due consideration. He hoped against hope she would identify the two dead men so they could rest assured no one else would come after her.

"These two," she said with conviction. "These are the men who attacked me."

"You're sure?" asked Jacobs.

"Absolutely, I'm totally confident. I guess I've been blocking things, but seeing their faces brings it back. This one grabbed me as I headed back to my car. The other one took my keys and they threw me in the trunk of my car."

She'd started shaking. Brent held her and asked her if she wanted to stop. She shook her head.

"I have to get this out, Brent." She turned, facing Jacobs again. "They took me to a building somewhere. They pulled me out of the trunk and started taking turns hitting me. When I fell, I hit my head on something and was too dizzy to get up. They started kicking me, yelling things I don't remember. I was sure I was going to die. The next thing I remember is waking up in the hospital."

"This is great, Natalie." Jacobs looked at Brent. "She ID'ed our two corpses. Seems the Los Hombres took care of them for us. Since they did it to frame Fuentes and scare his sister, I doubt they'll send anyone else after you."

"You know, one of these guys looks familiar to me, too," said Brent.

"He was busted for a carjacking not too long ago," said Jacobs. "Turns out he made a call from jail to his pal the day Natalie was attacked in the hospital. He was out on bail the next day."

"Now I remember him! Barnes and I saw him at the station. Pitts was taking him to booking. The four of us got on the elevator together. Barnes asked me about Natalie and I told her Natalie remembered some things." He looked at Natalie, terrified she'd scream at him to leave once she realized he'd more or less told one of her attackers she might be remembering his involvement.

"Brent, it's okay," she said sweetly. "How could you have known? Everyone thought Fuentes ordered it. His skin was so light; I mistook him for Hispanic when he tried to attack me here in the hospital."

"Time to let go of what happened and start living your lives again," said Jacobs. "Thanks for taking the time to do the identification."

"Thank you, Sergeant," said Natalie. "Thanks for all the hard work."

"I'll leave you two alone now. See you at work, Freeman."

"Sure thing," said Brent.

"Where's the danged doctor," she spouted. "I want to get out of here."

"I invited your parents over for dinner tonight. They changed their plans and decided to go back to Evansville tomorrow. I'm making my famous lasagna."

He saw a strange look on Natalie's face, and then realized what he'd said.

"Oh, don't worry. I spoke to the dietician to find out what you can eat and how to prepare it. She told me it would be weird for you at first, but I can puree the lasagna and you can drink it through a straw. Like the stuff they've been making for you this past week."

"Really?" Her face brightened a little. "Did she say it would taste the same?"

"Yes, she said it will taste the same, but it will feel weird because it's liquefied. The part people have a hard time with is the difference in texture."

"I'm game for whatever. If I don't like it, you can fix me some chicken soup."

"Deal."

Natalie's doctor entered the room smiling. He made one more quick exam, and then the nurse came in with the discharge paperwork and instructions. After all of the signatures were completed, Natalie reluctantly sat down in the wheelchair. She wanted to walk, but hospital rules forbade it. Brent left with her baggage to take out to the car and meet her by the main entrance. He pulled up just as the nurse wheeled Natalie outside.

Once securely seated, Natalie turned to Brent. "Can we go downtown and walk around the Circle? I've been cooped up in there so long, I just want to get out and walk."

"Sure, as long as you don't tire yourself out. We don't want your parents thinking I'm a crappy caretaker, do we?"

Natalie laughed. Brent could see lightness in her manner he hadn't seen in a long time. They found parking off of Washington Street and walked the block to the Circle. Arm-in-arm, they crossed to the Soldiers' and Sailors' Monument. Natalie looked up to the clear blue sky, closed her eyes, and breathed deeply while the sun illuminated her face.

"I'm so lucky to be alive." She opened her eyes and looked into his. "I'm even luckier to have you in my life, Brent Freeman. I love you."

"I love you too, my angel," he said. They walked to the fountain area and sat on the edge. She squeezed his arm tightly and laid her head on his shoulder. He closed his eyes and thanked God for bringing this wonderful woman into his life.

Chapter 41

Parker woke from a sound sleep. The clock on the wall came into focus and he saw it was 11:30. He rubbed his eyes and got out of bed. Walking to the kitchen, he picked up the remote for his new twenty-inch television and turned it on. Someone had broken in and vandalized his apartment. He came home one day and found his old television broken into pieces. It confused him because nothing else was touched. He couldn't call the police for obvious reasons, so he installed a deadbolt lock on the door to keep out future intruders.

He could hear the fussing of some reality show which preceded the news at noon. He started a pot of coffee and turned back toward the bathroom for a shower.

They'd scheduled him to work night shift this week, but he'd have to call in sick. Unfortunately, the bitch had a gun this time so he had to lay low for a couple of days. Luckily, the bullet had only grazed his left thigh, but it had bled a lot and it still hurt like hell. He'd bought hydrogen peroxide, anti-bacterial cream, gauze and tape along with extra strength pain relief tablets. He carefully removed the bandage and looked at the wound.

So far, there was no apparent infection. He knew the cops would be checking every hospital and health care facility looking for him. He couldn't take the chance. His work wasn't complete.

After a nice hot shower, Parker treated the wound and bandaged it. He slipped on his boxer shorts and went to the kitchen for a cup of coffee and a stale donut from yesterday. Then he heard it.

"In what seemed to be an attempted robbery two days ago, police say the victim, Ranae North, shot her assailant. The bullet was recovered at the scene and they are not sure how badly wounded her assailant was. A search of area hospitals and clinics has been unfruitful. We now go to our correspondent, Andrea Atkins, who is covering the news conference at IMPD headquarters."

Parker walked into the living room transfixed with his coffee in one hand and donut in the other. He watched as *she* walked up to the podium.

"This is Andrea Atkins reporting live and we are about to hear from Detective Erica Barnes. Let's listen," she whispered.

"Thank you all for coming. I'm going to make a brief statement on our suspicions at this time regarding the assailant in the North case. From the victim's description of the physical characteristics of this man, we believe this was not a robbery attempt, but an attempt by Parker Emerson to break in and murder Ms. North. She fits the physical description of all of his previous female victims."

"What?" shouted Parker. "I would never! You lying bitch!" He slammed his coffee onto the table in front of him and threw the donut at the television.

"Fortunately, Ms. North had a weapon and was able to fend off her attacker. We know he was hit by at least one bullet, which was recovered at the scene; however, we are not sure how badly wounded he is. We urge anyone who may have treated this man in the last couple of days to come forward with this information. Remember, he is extremely dangerous. We urge all women to be diligent in taking safety precautions..."

Parker snatched the remote and turned off the television, pacing around the room He couldn't stand to listen to her any longer. It was her, the real one. All along, he thought she was a cop, but she was pretending to be a cop to throw him off guard. She was lying about him, just like she always did. He had to stop her. But how? He knew she had a gun. He'd seen it.

"Shit, shit, shit," he said, pacing faster. He started to shake and the headache was back. Blinding pain shot through his skull. "Oh, God, why won't she die? Why won't she die?"

He ran to the bathroom, making it just in time to spew sick into the toilet. He grabbed a washcloth running cold water over it. He put the cool rag on his face, rinsed it and then placed it on the back of his neck. It helped the nausea subside.

He needed to talk to Jordan. She'd know what to do. He'd bought a disposable cell phone when he went to get the supplies for his wound. No one could trace it, right? He'd get in his car and drive somewhere else, just in case. The FBI was after him and he wasn't sure how sophisticated their equipment might be.

Quickly he dressed, grabbed his keys and the new cell phone making sure to secure the deadbolt on his way out the door. He drove to Eagle Creek Park and found a remote spot before dialing Jordan's number.

"Hellooo," said a sweet young voice.

"Hi, sweet Mary. Is your mommy home?"

"Uncle Parker!" said his niece in a joyful voice. "Are you going to come see us again?"

"Not right now, sweetheart. But I really, really need to talk to your mommy right now."

"Okay. Miss you and love you."

"Same here."

"Mommy, it's Uncle Parker!"

He heard the clunk of the receiver on a hard surface, and then heard his niece yelling for her mom again. He tapped the steering wheel nervously with his free hand. He wondered if they'd coerced his baby sister into putting a tap on the line. Should he hang up? No, no, he had to talk to her. He had to know she was okay and to warn her about Mom. She wasn't finished torturing them. Jordan had to be warned about the pseudo cop. He had to make sure she didn't let Detective Barnes near her again.

"Hello! Parker! Is that really you? Where are you? I'm so worried about you." Jordan fired off each question in rapid succession.

"Yeah, Sissy, it's me."

"Parker, please, please, turn yourself in," she begged. "What you are doing to these women is wrong."

"No. You've got to listen. They're lying to you."

"Who's lying to me? Parker, Momma is dead. I found her myself. They think you killed her when you came to see me at Christmas. Did you?"

"Jordan. I thought I did, but she's not dead. She followed me here," he said, voice laced with panic. "Every time I turn around she's right there. Now she's pretending to be a cop and she's trying to turn you against me."

Jordan began to cry. "Honey, nobody could ever make me turn against you. I love you. I'm scared for you."

Parker heard a voice in the background say, "Mommy. What's wrong? Is he making you cry?"

"No, no. Mommy's just glad to hear from Uncle Parker. I want him to come home. Don't worry. Go on and watch your brother for me, okay?"

"Okay Mommy."

"Parker, please," pleaded Jordan. "Detective Barnes can help you. You need to go talk to her at the police station."

He was silent. What was going on? Was she keeping him on the line so they could find him? Had they already turned her against him?

"Parker, are you still there?"

"I'm still here. And I can't. I can't turn myself in because she's still out there. If I go to jail, who will protect you?"

"I saw her dead body, Parker. I buried her. She's in a coffin, in a cement vault, six feet underground. I swear to you our wicked, hateful mother is dead! She can't hurt us ever again."

Oh, God, they *have* taken over her mind. "I'm going to end this, Jordan. I'm going to take care of this once and for all. She's not going to take over your mind, I won't let her."

"Parker, what are you going to do?"

He didn't answer, but hung up. He knew what he had to do now. He'd have to call his employer to take more sick leave, but he would have his final revenge and he would have it soon.

Chapter 42

Erica had spent the majority of the day with Kendall making phone calls, trying to get a lead on Parker Emerson. Kendall had no luck the day before with the local hospitals, but they called each of them again to see if anyone fitting Parker's description came into their emergency rooms. Still no luck. Then Erica decided they should call all of the free clinics since Parker would probably want to keep a low profile. No Caucasian males came in with gunshot wounds.

"Well, he's either not as badly wounded as we thought or he's gone off into the woods to die like a wounded animal," Kendall said as she tossed her file folder on the desk and leaned back in her chair.

Erica kneaded her temples to ease the headache she'd developed. "Do you think he left Indianapolis to get treatment?"

"He may have," Kendall responded. "Maybe our little news conference will get some response. If he needed medical treatment, I wouldn't think he'd have left our viewing area."

"It'll air again on the evening news tonight." Erica's exhaustion wafted through her. "Holy crap. I told my dad I'd stop by tonight. I've got to grab a few groceries for him."

"Your dad seems to be in pretty good shape. Why doesn't he pick up his own groceries?"

"It's just something I started after Mom died. It makes me feel good to do it so he doesn't feel abandoned. Besides, it gives me an excuse to check up on him and make sure he's eating right. He was a tough cop taking care of the public interest, but we always knew who took care of things at home. After he decided to retire, he and Mom planned to see the world. Unfortunately, it wasn't meant to be."

"Life hands out some pretty nasty stuff sometimes," said Kendall.

"I think Natalie Ralston will verify that for you."

"How is she?"

"Jacobs said he stopped by the hospital this morning and got her to ID her assailants from a photo lineup," said Erica. "Turns out, they were the two guys the night shift found killed execution style in an alley off of Illinois Street."

"I'm sure it's a relief for her. They certainly won't be coming after her again."

"Amen, sister," cracked Erica. "I'm going to call it a day. It's after five already and I want to get home before dark tonight."

"Good idea. I'll see you tomorrow."

It didn't take Erica long to finish her shopping—bananas, grapes, walnuts, and some of Pop's favorite frozen entrees. In the parking lot, she felt the hair on the back of her neck stand on end, as if a chilled wind had blown on her. She looked around several times, but saw nothing out of the ordinary. She placed the two bags of groceries on the passenger seat, looked around again, and decided she was being paranoid.

The traffic turned a ten-minute trip from the grocery store to her Pop's house into a twenty-five minute trip. She took the groceries to the front door and rang the bell. Erica could have unlocked it herself, but she'd always given her father the courtesy of his privacy. After ringing twice, she became worried. Was he on the john and unable to answer the door? Something in the pit of her stomach told her to forget propriety and let herself in.

"Pop! Pop, it's Erica. Where are you?" Walking to the hallway, she could see the open bathroom door, lights out. Maybe he was napping. She advanced quickly to his bedroom. The bed was made and he was nowhere to be found.

"Maybe he's out back and didn't hear the bell." She decided to put the groceries away and investigate the possibility. However, when she entered the kitchen she saw her father lying face down on the floor and he wasn't moving. Panicked, she dropped the bags and ran to him.

Kneeling beside him, she touched his back, talking to him, trying to get a response. He was warm and breathing, but definitely unconscious. She ran to the wall to get the phone and called 9-1-1.

"9-1-1, what is your emergency?" said the dispatcher.

"This is Detective Erica Barnes of the IMPD and I'm at my father's house. I found him lying on the kitchen floor unconscious. I need an ambulance."

"I've transmitted your location. The EMTs are on their way. Is he breathing?"

"Yes. There's blood on the floor. He may have fallen and hit his head. I didn't want to move him."

"Excellent. The EMTs will assess him and decide how best to move him. Is the front door open?"

"Yes."

"I'll relay this to them, please stay on the line."

"Pop, don't you die on me," she said to him, her chest heavy with anxiety. "You stay with me, you hear me?"

"Detective, the EMTs should be there in less than two minutes. Does he seem to be in any distress at the moment?"

"No." She paused to get her cracking voice under control. "But I'm not a doctor. I can't tell if he's breathing the way he should be, or if his heart rate is correct."

"How's his color?"

"What?"

"Is he pale or cold and clammy?"

"No. Why?"

"If he were, it would be a sign he isn't getting enough oxygen. If his coloring is normal, that's a good sign."

Erica knew the 9-1-1 dispatcher was trained to stay on the line with the caller to help them stay calm in these stressful situations. She just wasn't sure she wanted to keep talking to her.

"The EMTs have arrived at your location," said the dispatcher. "I'll hang up now and you can show them where your father is."

"Thank you." Erica hung up the phone and ran towards the front door. Sure enough, the EMTs had lugged their cases, a gurney and a backboard up to the house. She showed them where he was and then stood back while they worked.

The female EMT unpacked her stethoscope and turned to Erica, while her male counterpart took her father's blood pressure. "Has he been like this long?"

"I don't know. I came by after work to bring him some groceries," said Erica about to burst into tears. "He was like this when I got here."

"Respiration is good; BP 140 over 90; pulse is 100." The male EMT took out a trauma collar and placed it around her father's neck.

"Is this bad?" Erica could hardly contain herself.

"He has a laceration on his head. I noticed some blood on the edge of this table, so I'm pretty sure he hit his head on it. Blood pressure and pulse are usually high when someone has a concussion. Now that I have the neck brace on him, we'll strap him to the backboard. They'll probably want to do a CAT scan at the hospital to make sure he didn't crack any of his vertebrae or have a skull fracture from the fall."

"Oh, my God." Erica covered her mouth with one hand, experiencing the same panic she'd felt years ago when her mother became ill. She wasn't ready to lose her father, too.

"Don't worry. We'll be very careful. His head injury is a concern, but his color is good. My best guess would be there's minimal swelling of the brain. At his age, one of the big concerns is broken bones."

"Will you be taking him to St. Vincent Hospital?"

"It's the closest, if it's alright with you?"

"Of course," said Erica. "All of his doctors are there."

Erica walked over to the phone and called her brother. It was only 4:00 p.m. in Seattle, so he wasn't home from work yet. Erica told Rick's wife what happened and promised to call later with news.

Once the EMTs had her father strapped to the backboard, they hoisted him onto the gurney and laid him there as gently as though he were a feather. They told her she could follow in her car.

At the hospital, of course, she wasn't permitted to go in with him until she took care of signing him in and promising them her first-born child if the bill wasn't paid. The nurse told Erica to have a seat in the waiting room, promising someone would call her back shortly. She knew all too well exactly what that meant. They'd get to her when they damn well pleased. Her nerves were on the brink of collapse when she saw a friendly face come through the emergency room doors.

Erica jumped up and threw her arms around Ben's neck. "How did you find out?"

"You know how fast rumors fly through the office," said Ben. "When a cop is down, everybody knows. How are you doing?"

"Not so good," she said breaking down. She didn't want to cry, but she just couldn't hold it back any longer. She could be vulnerable with Ben and not feel like he saw her as weak. He held her close and let her weep, hot tears soaking the shoulder of his shirt. When she'd wept to the point of exhaustion, he guided her to a seat and found a box of tissues. She dried her eyes and blew her nose, then explained what had happened.

"Miss Barnes," called the nurse. She and Ben jumped up and walked over to the desk. "Miss Barnes, they're going to take your father up for a CAT scan. It could be as long as an hour before you get to see him. You might want to go to the cafeteria and grab a bite to eat."

The nurse was being very kind, but Erica could feel nothing but irritation at having her father hauled off to another location. Logically, she knew it had to be done in order to find out what the damage was, but it still grated on her last nerve.

"Let's at least take a walk, sweetheart," Ben suggested. "It will help with your nerves. Maybe we can get something to drink. You don't want to get all dehydrated and pass out on me, do you?"

She gave him a half-hearted smile and agreed. They walked the halls for a bit then Ben convinced her to try to eat something.

She chose the chili—big mistake. It didn't taste bad; as a matter of fact, it tasted quite good. It just wasn't the right choice for someone with a knotted up stomach. She opted for eating her crackers and drinking her iced tea.

Ben was great. He tried to make small talk. He offered to make phone calls for her, but she declined. When they arrived back in the emergency waiting area, she looked imploringly at the nurse who simply shook her head.

"Look, Ben, you don't have to sit around here with me. This could take all night."

"I know I don't have to, I want to. I love you, Erica. Don't you know that by now? I want to be here for you when things are tough as well as when they're good."

"I love you, too. Thanks. You know how much I hate hospitals."

He nodded and put his arm around her shoulders drawing her close. She laid her head on his shoulder and closed her eyes.

The next thing she knew, there was a bright light. Erica stood up and walked toward it. Then Erica saw her standing there like an angel with her arms extended in a welcoming stance.

"Mom?" Erica knew it was her mother, but she couldn't believe it. "Are you for real?"

"Of course I am," her mother replied in the cheerful manner Erica remembered. "Are you alright, dear?"

"Mom, there's something wrong with Pop. It looks like he fell and hit his head." She looked at her mother and the panic ensued again. "You haven't come for him, have you?"

"Sweetheart, I don't make those decisions."

"Then who does?" Erica cried. "I want to talk to whoever is in charge. It's bad enough I lost you, I can't lose Pop, too."

"I didn't come here for your father, Erica. I came here for you."

"What?" Erica exclaimed. "Are you telling me I'm dying?"

"No, no," Clara laughed. "I've come to comfort you, just like I did when you and your brother were little. Nobody you love is going to die tonight. Just be patient. The doctor will be there soon."

"Really? How do you know?"

"I just know. Have I ever lied to you?"

"No. I miss you, Mom."

"You don't have to, you know. You may have decided to be a cop like your father, but you have a lot of me inside you. You have my eyes. All you have to do when you miss me is look into the mirror and you'll see me."

"Erica," she heard a male voice say. "Erica, wake up."

Opening her eyes, she realized she must have fallen asleep and was dreaming. She could hear the nurse calling her name. Shaking off the sleep, she stood feeling refreshed and approached the trauma station. The nurse buzzed them in and the doctor met them on the other side.

It was Dr. Foster, the same emergency physician she and Brent had talked to about Marilyn Novak's mother several weeks ago. At least she knew he was very concerned about the patients who came in on his shift.

"Detective Barnes. I take it Michael Barnes is your father."

"Yes, Dr. Foster. This is Ben Jacobs. He has my permission to hear whatever you have to tell me about my father."

"Well, the good news is, there is no swelling in the brain. As a matter of fact, your father regained consciousness during his trip to the hospital. He'll have a nasty headache for a few days, but the head injury was relatively minor. I had to put three stitches in his head wound, but it will heal pretty quickly. It looked worse than it was."

"Usually you don't mention good news like that unless there is some bad news," said Erica. "What else is going on?"

"The bad news isn't really very bad. He sustained a broken left elbow when he fell. He tells me he slipped on something, went down hard, and the next thing he knew he woke up in the ambulance."

"How bad is the elbow?"

"He'll have to see an orthopedic surgeon. He has no other broken bones, but we need to keep him for a few days for observation due to the concussion. I think the orthopedist will schedule the surgery while your father is still here. We'll be admitting him shortly. In the meantime, he's been asking for you. He's behind curtain number three," he said pointing to the only closed curtain in the trauma center.

"I'll sit out in the waiting room so you can have a private moment with him," said Ben. "I'll be there when you come out."

"Thank you," she said, kissing Ben on the cheek.

She peeked around the curtain. "Hey there, Pop."

"Kitten," he said playfully. "I was wonderin' where they was keepin' ya. Did I give ya a scare?"

"Yeah, you did."

"Sorry 'bout that. Musta spilled somethin' and took a nose dive."

"It's okay, Pop." She smiled at his ability to keep his sense of humor. Of course, once the adrenaline wore off, he'd be hurting and complaining. Erica doubted he'd receive anything for the pain until they were sure his head injury was no longer an issue.

"Your mother came to me while I was out," he said. "She told me I was goin' to be okay and to get my butt back here so you wouldn't worry none."

"Funny," she said, smiling lovingly at him. "I dozed off in the waiting room and she came to me, too. She said you'd be okay and she'd always be here for us."

"And she will, too," he said with confidence. "She never lied to us, you know."

Erica smiled at her father, and then kissed his forehead. "No…she never did."

Chapter 43

Chennelle had decided to get an early start so she could finish some paperwork and go over some of the facts of her current cases. She lifted her cup to take a sip of coffee when she saw Agent Morgan and SSA Zimmer practically running towards her. She set her cup down and stood.

"I thought *I* got up early," said Chennelle. "It's only seven something in the morning. Has something happened?"

Spencer gave her a serious frown. "We got a call from Peter Elliott a few minutes ago. He says he got a call from the guy who's committing these murders. He says something big's about to go down and he wants us to meet him at his place at 7:30. Are you in?"

"Of course. What about Erica?"

"Would you mind giving her a quick call so she knows to meet us there?" asked Zimmer. "It sounded like Elliott preferred for her to be present."

"Maybe he thinks this will make amends for giving her such a rough time," said Chennelle.

"Maybe." Morgan's demeanor seemed rather stiff this morning. "We need to make the call and get over there before he changes his mind."

"He may act like an ass," commented Zimmer, "but I don't think he'd protect a killer, do you?"

"Right now, I don't know what to think," Morgan replied. "With all the facts, he knew about the case, I think he was in communication with Emerson the whole time."

They continued debating the issue while Chennelle attempted to call Erica. She returned to the agents and found them quietly waiting, Morgan looking anxiously at his watch.

"Barnes didn't answer," said Chennelle. "I'll try again from the car."

***

Erica had hardly slept after she'd gotten home from the hospital. Despite the doctor's assurances, she was still very worried about her father. Every time she woke through the night, she'd call the nurses' station to find out if he was still doing okay. His nurse was kind, but at 3:00 a.m. told Erica to get some rest or she'd be in worse shape than her father would. Erica took the hint and decided she'd go over to the hospital at about 8:00 a.m. and check him out herself.

Erica woke at 5:30 and made a pot of coffee. Bleary-eyed, Ben had woken as well when he realized she was out of bed. She wondered if he'd gotten any sleep with her constantly getting in and out of the bed all night. He drank a cup of coffee with her and then headed over to his place after she promised to call in sick. It was an easy promise to make. She wasn't going to abandon her father in his time of need.

She was drinking her second cup of coffee when the telephone rang. Fearing it might be the hospital, she snatched it up before the second ring.

"Erica, it's Rick. How's Pop doing this morning?"

Relieved, she told her brother about the hourly conversations with the hospital through the night. There was no change and the orthopedist would be in this morning to examine Pop and schedule the elbow surgery.

"Geez Erica! You called them every hour? Are you nuts?"

"I'm sure they think so. Do you plan to come to see him?" Her question was met by a few moments of silence. She knew she was about to hear the same old crappy excuses.

"He's not dying is he?"

She rolled her eyes as he went on.

"We've got this big deal going. I can't get away right now."

It was her turn to be silent and she didn't care how uncomfortable it made him feel. He always had one more big deal, or maybe next month or next year. He'd only been back to Indianapolis three times in the years since their mother's death.

"Come on, Erica. Don't lay the guilt trip on me."

"I didn't say anything. If you're feeling guilty, it isn't because of anything I'm laying on you. You just go ahead and finish your business and when you have time for us, let me know."

"See. You do that every time."

"Whatever, I'll let you know how the surgery goes. Gotta go get a shower and get to the hospital. I'll talk to you later." She hung up before he could respond.

"At least he had the courtesy to get his ass out of bed early and call before he thought I'd be going to work," she said aloud, slamming the phone back in its cradle harder than she'd intended.

She'd been thinking about having a bagel and cream cheese, but had lost her appetite. A shower would be good. Something about the way the warm water flowed over her from head to toe always seemed to cleanse the mind as well as the body.

As she untied the belt to her robe and approached the bathroom, Erica stopped when she heard a noise. It sounded like the shower was already turned on.

She pushed the door open to see water pouring from the exhaust fan onto the toilet and splattering everywhere. *"Holy crap!"*

Grabbing some towels from her hall closet, she tossed one on the toilet and the others on the floor. At least the one on the toilet lid might stave off the splattering.

Turning, she walked quickly toward the living room, grabbing her telephone and calling the emergency maintenance number. The operator said Joe was on call and he'd be there within fifteen minutes. The water flowed so quickly, she was afraid she'd drown before he got there. However, she was grateful for the chance to put on her sweats before he arrived.

She heard a knock and peered through the peephole. Joe stood there smiling. She opened the door and stepped aside for him to enter.

"Good morning," he said. "Heard you've got a flooded bathroom. It's probably coming from the tenant above you. I'll take a look and...."

Joe never had the chance to finish his sentence.

A man dressed in black sweatpants, black hooded sweatshirt, and a pair of Thunder Kicks stood in her doorway swinging the *nunchaku* he'd used to incapacitate Joe. He had a bright orange backpack he tossed on the floor. The man was only about five-feet, ten-inches tall, and built like a prizefighter, muscles bulging. Parker Emerson didn't look much like his old photo. He'd shaved his beard and mustache and wore glasses. Something about his current looks though made her feel like she'd seen him somewhere before. Had he been under her nose the whole time? Had he been that *inconspicuous*?

She heard her cell phone ringing on the kitchen counter, sitting alongside her Glock. Even if she went for her Glock now, he was too close to her. She'd never be able to release the safety and get a shot off before he'd have her.

"You are very clever, Mama. How did you convince the police department to let you stage those TV appearances?" His eyes blinked erratically and his head twitched nervously.

"*What?*" Erica glared at him in disbelief. Trish Zimmer was right. Parker Emerson thought everyone was his mother. She dashed to the opposite end of the couch from where he stood.

"Don't run from me or try to fight me, Mama."

"I'm not your fucking mother, you nut job!" She shouted hoping to rouse the neighbors.

"I know exactly who you are," he said, smiling.

Erica saw a totally determined person in those crazed eyes. "And I know you're a crazy son-of-a-bitch who enjoys breaking women's necks and then raping them with whatever's handy. Can't get your dick up to rape them while they're still warm?"

"You're the one who taught me that little trick, Mama," said Emerson, moving a step closer.

She could see him becoming more agitated. Her attempts to snap him back to reality were not working. Why didn't the neighbors check to see what was going on? Had anyone heard the noise and called the police? Erica decided shocking him with put downs wasn't the wisest approach. He'd probably heard them all from *Mama*. She decided that a calmer approach might work better.

"Look, Parker, my name is Erica Barnes. I'm a homicide detective with the Indianapolis Metropolitan Police Department. You've been asking me to stop you."

"You stop that right now," he said, pointing a finger at her, face twitching constantly. "You always tried to make me think things that weren't true and now you're impersonating a police officer."

"Think about it Parker. Don't you remember going to your mother's house? You already killed her. She can't hurt you anymore."

Parker turned his gaze to the floor and started to shift his weight from one foot to the other. He was clearly confused and more agitated. Moreover, this twitching and blinking…what was going on with him? Erica was at a loss for what to say next, but she knew she had to keep talking.

"Parker, the women you've killed were *not* your mother. You know that, don't you? Otherwise, why would you keep seeing her? They had dark hair and brown eyes like she did when she abused you. Don't you see? Your mother isn't thirty-five any more, you are."

"No, no, no," he said beginning to pace. Parker's muscles jerked so violently she thought he might be going into a seizure.

No such luck.

"Think about it. These women are the same age as you are. I'm your age. I couldn't possibly be your mother."

"Oh, my." A weak voice floated through the apartment door. To Erica's horror, there stood elderly Mrs. Yates from across the hall. Why did it have to be she who heard the ruckus? Why didn't she simply call the police?

"Run, Mrs. Yates," Erica screamed.

However, before Mrs. Yates could gather her wits, Parker had turned, kicking her in the chest. As she stumbled across the hall, Erica heard Mrs. Yates hit the wall. She looked past Parker to see her neighbor crumpled on the floor, eyes open in a death stare.

"You sorry son-of-a-bitch! She was 83 years old."

"Probably would have died soon anyway." He sighed. "It appears to me we've made an awful lot of noise, so don't make this hard, Mama—unless you want me to do that to all your neighbors."

"No way." She knew she was no match for him. Erica wanted to keep as much distance between them as possible. The kick he had just given Mrs. Yates and the stomp kick to the heart he had administered on Keith Gray were obvious indications of his combative skills. She had to outwit him, to stay one-step ahead anticipating his every move. If she didn't, she'd be dead next.

"Why didn't you stop me?" His voice cracked, his eyes brimming with tears. "I needed you to stop me."

This strange shift was disconcerting. Erica stared at him wondering if she was talking to the same person. He'd gone from bold caveman to a whimpering child. This could definitely give her an advantage.

"Parker, I know you didn't mean to hurt anyone. When you realized they were someone else, you'd already gone too far."

"They knew me. I bagged their groceries. I didn't mean to kill the baby," he said blubbering.

Erica suddenly realized where she'd seen him. It was the grocery store where she stopped two or three times a week to buy groceries for her Pop. He must have seen each victim there and believed his mother had reappeared. Then he stalked them until he understood their routines.

Parker made a sudden move to the right and she responded by moving to the left around the end table. A lamp sat there. Perhaps she could use it as a weapon, if she could figure out how to unplug it. If she didn't get it unplugged with the first yank of the cord, then he might have a chance to make a move on her.

"I know," she said, her eyes fixed on his. "We've known about you since we consulted the FBI. Sounds like you've been doing this for a while—starting with your wife."

"*My wife?*" He peered at her with confused, blinking eyes. "My wife's a writer. She went on a tour."

"I'm sorry, Parker, but your wife is dead." Erica had reached the floor socket and started to push lamp plug with her foot. Parker still stood at the opposite end of the couch looking confused. He held his head and started squinting like people who have migraines. Erica maintained eye contact as she nudged the plug with her foot, hoping to pry it out.

"She can't be dead," said Parker. "Alecia went on a book tour. I know. I saw the itinerary. She won't be back until June. Her last stop was London. She's an international star, you know."

"Parker. Alecia never started the tour because you mistook her for your mother and killed her."

Parker stopped crying, rage in his eyes. "*You're lying!* You're trying to trick me." Then he jumped onto the couch attempting to get closer to her. Without having sufficient time to pull the lamp loose, she moved away quickly to avoid capture. She reached the phone, but instead of dialing 9-1-1, she threw it at him, hitting him square in his right eye, stunning him. She heard him scream in rage as she ran for her gun.

Erica barely touched the handle of her Glock when Parker had her from behind in a chokehold. Even Sensei Nakamura couldn't get out of this one. He was about to kill her.

Who would find her? Ben? Brent? Surely, one of the neighbors had heard all the commotion and had called the police.

"Parker. You don't want to do this," she said pulling at his arm so she could breath.

"I've wanted to do this for a long time. This time I'll be rid of you for good!"

His grip loosened slightly. Erica realized something held him back. She didn't believe he'd spent this much time talking to any of his other victims.

"Parker," she choked. "Parker, why don't we just sit down and talk for a while."

"No, no, no," he said with panic in his voice. She could feel him tremble. "You'll try to get away. You'll hurt me again."

"No, I promise. I don't believe you want to hurt me. I know I don't want to hurt you. I think you know who I really am."

She could feel each twitch of the muscles in his body along with his panic-stricken puffs on the back of her neck. Then his grip tightened and she knew she was about to die.

Chapter 44

Detective Kendall arrived at the apartment building with the Federal Agents at approximately 7:30. They had decided to take the stairs to the third floor. Peter's apartment was the last one on the left, just like Erica's one floor down.

"I wish I'd reached Barnes," said Kendall, gritting her teeth.

"Sorry, Kendall, but we just couldn't wait," said Morgan. "We need to get in there and get this information so we can stop this bastard."

The three walked down the hallway, Agent Morgan in the lead. He stopped and held up a hand. Peter Elliott's apartment door stood ajar. They each drew their weapons and stealthily approached the apartment. Zimmer and Kendall positioned themselves on each side of the door. Morgan looked at each of them in turn, and then nodded his intent to push open the door.

"FBI!" Morgan entered with Zimmer and Kendall bringing up the rear. They funneled out in different directions, each shouting 'clear' as they filtered through each room. At least until Agent Morgan entered the master bedroom. He nearly tripped over a writhing Peter Elliott.

Morgan yelled for the others. Seeing the situation, Zimmer called for an ambulance while Morgan tried to calm Peter.

"Detective…" Peter shook barely able to speak. "…Barnes."

Zimmer leaned down towards him. "Has he gone after her, Mr. Elliott?"

Before she heard the answer, Kendall turned and left the apartment without saying a word. She walked to the stairway and took them down as quickly as possible. When she opened the door to the second floor, there was an elderly woman crumpled like a rag doll at the end of the hallway across from Erica's apartment. She could see a light coming from Erica's doorway, hearing loud voices.

On her left, she heard the elevator door opening and Sergeant Jacobs exited from it. She bolted in front of him holding her finger to her lips then pointing to his weapon. He drew it quietly, and then saw the body in the hallway. His eyes widened with anguish. Kendall motioned for him to follow her.

At the door, the only thing in view was toppled furniture, a backpack and a man lying face down just inside the doorway. Jacobs looked at Kendall and mouthed, *when we go in, spread out*. Kendall nodded and they went in.

"Police! Freeze!" Jacobs saw a man who looked a lot like Parker Emerson with Erica in a choke hold.

"Look Mama, it's the police," sneered Parker while he stroked her cheek. "Back off Detectives. This is between me and my mama."

"You're holding Detective Barnes, Parker. It's over. Your mother's already dead." Kendall feared he was beyond reason, but she had to try. "Let her go. There's no other way out of this for you."

"I don't want her to hurt anyone else," said Parker looking up and down nonplussed.

Erica tried to rear her head back to hit his nose, but he held her too tightly. She mouthed to Kendall to *take the shot*.

"Come on Mr. Emerson." Jacobs moved further away from Kendall. "Listen to Detective Kendall. You've made a mistake. You're holding Detective Erica Barnes. You asked her to stop you, so you must be tired of killing women just to find out they aren't really your mother."

Parker looked at him in surprise. "She's supposed to be dead, but she keeps coming back. I have to do this."

"No you don't," said Jacobs as he continued to walk through the living area. "Talk to me about your wife, Alecia. Why did you think you needed to kill her?"

"I didn't kill Alecia." Parker looked perplexed, eyes blinking as though the light hurt them. "No, no. Mama wanted to hide me, to put me back in the closet. No food. No water." He was regressing again, pulling Erica a step toward the door.

"It was cruel," Jacobs said. He and Kendall spread out further causing Parker to look in different directions at them. "Your mother should never have been so cruel to you. I can understand why you thought your wife did the same thing to you, but I don't think she meant to hurt you."

"How would you know?" he said irritably. "You don't know what it's like."

"We know what your mother did to you. Exacting revenge on women who look like her doesn't stop the pain, does it?" Kendall asked, keeping her gun trained on him.

Parker looked at her frowning.

"That's right, Parker. We know everything your mother did to you." Kendall saw something in his eyes, a fierceness that made her heart race.

"You don't know squat!" Parker tightened his grip on Erica, jerking her closer to the door.

Kendall didn't want Parker to take Barnes into the hallway. She quickly responded. "We know it's not your fault, Parker. Your mother was horrible to you and to your sister."

Parker stared at Kendall, not noticing Jacobs moving again.

"You don't understand. No one but Jordan could ever understand. Tell me, Detective, how do you explain to a five-year-old his mother hates him so much she rams a broomstick up his ass to punish him for dropping a glass of milk?"

"I can't explain it, Parker," Kendall answered. "It wasn't right. She was wrong. It was cruel and never should have happened."

Parker looked at Kendall, his face brightening at her acknowledgement. His bottom lip trembled and his head and neck muscles jerked. Kendall kept eye contact. Parker looked like he was about to cry.

"Your mother is dead. Jordan told us so," said Kendall. "Jordan's a good person and a wonderful mother. She wouldn't lie to us, would she?"

"No." Parker's voice became more childlike.

"If you kill Detective Barnes, it won't really make you feel better and it will hurt Jordan. Wouldn't you like to see Jordan again?"

Erica looked imploringly at Kendall, and then at Jacobs. *Take the shot*, she mouthed again.

"No!" Parker's anger flashed again. "You're trying to trick me!" Parker tightened his grip on Erica who closed her eyes as he pulled her with his back towards the doorway. He'd placed her in front of him like a shield. He took her chin in his right hand like a vice grip. He was about to snap her neck...

Chapter 45

Then it happened. A shot rang out. Blood and brain matter flew towards the ceiling. Parker's grip on Erica loosened as he fell forward, pinning her beneath him.

Erica looked over her shoulder and saw Agent Morgan standing in the doorway looking down at the floor. SSA Zimmer knelt, frozen with her gun still pointed at an upward angle looking down at her target. Blood spatter dripped down her face and clung to the front of her clothing. Agent Morgan approached her cautiously. He touched Zimmer's shoulder and she relinquished her weapon to him. He gently helped her rise to her feet.

Erica had the breath knocked out of her. She could feel someone pulling Parker off of her. Able to breathe more deeply now, she could feel the warmth of Parker's blood and God knows what else sliding down the back of her head. Someone pulled her to a sitting position.

"Oh, baby. Oh, my God," said Ben helping her to her feet. "You're not hit, are you?"

Erica shook her head. Then she burst into tears and collapsed in his arms. He held her until the tears subsided. She whispered in his ear. "Did Agent Zimmer shoot him?"

"Yes, she knelt down so she could shoot him in the base of the head to avoid hitting you. She's pretty shaken."

Erica pulled back from him. She gave him a weak smile and turned to see Morgan rubbing Zimmer's arm as she trembled. For the first time, Trish Zimmer seemed human to Erica. She did have feelings after all. Erica approached the two FBI agents.

"Agents," she said in a hoarse voice. Zimmer turned, her cheeks lined with tears, her perfect makeup running. "I'd shake your hand, but right now we're drenched in evidence. Thank you Supervisory Special Agent Zimmer. You saved my life."

Zimmer smiled and nodded, appearing to be on the verge of more tears.

"This was the first time Trish has had to use deadly force," said Morgan. "I suspect you know what it's like."

"Yes I do, Agent Morgan. If you ever need to talk about it, Trish, I'll be there for you."

"Thank you," she responded.

Kendall was checking on Joe when a couple of patrol officers appeared in the doorway, guns drawn. She told them it was over and instructed them to start a log and secure the scene. Kendall checked Mrs.

Yates who had definitely expired then called for paramedics, forensics, and a death investigator.

The paramedics treated Joe first. He'd taken quite a blow to the head, but had regained consciousness. They took him out on a gurney, assuring Erica he would make a full recovery.

Another pair of EMTs had arrived and started checking Erica for injuries. She had a cut over her right eye where she'd banged her head on the counter when Parker grabbed her. They were trying to convince her to go to the hospital. They insisted she could have a concussion or internal injuries for which she may not show symptoms until it's too late. Erica only agreed as long as they took her to St. Vincent Hospital so she could see her father afterward. She also insisted they wait until the crime scene investigators did their collection of her clothes and took photos of her. She wanted to shower and change, but had to wait until CSI completed their examination of her.

Mark Chatham arrived with his double-team sending half of them to the third floor and the other half to Erica's apartment. CSI had to photograph her, and then take her bloody clothing. Fortunately, she was able to do it in privacy with Sophia Parelli. She then took a shower despite the water still leaking through her ceiling.

Erica came into the living room in time to hear Ben ask if he could go to the hospital with her. Kendall told him it was no problem since she had plenty of help to process the scenes.

Erica walked by and nudged his arm. "You coming, Jacobs?" She was anxious to get this exam over so she could tell her father what happened before one of his buddies called him.

Jacobs took Erica's arm and stopped in front of Agent Morgan. "By the way, how's Elliott?"

Morgan shook his head. "He didn't make it."

Chapter 46

Brent walked into the surgical waiting room and found Erica staring out the window. "What's going on? I take a little time off and my partner ends up fighting off a serial killer and becomes homeless."

"Shut up, Freeman," she retorted, glad to hear his voice. "You get on my nerves."

"Is that any way to talk to the friend who just brought you your favorite candy?"

"Are you kidding?" She turned, her eyes becoming larger. She'd been too nervous to eat breakfast before her father went into surgery, but her stomach was protesting now.

"I know better than to tease a woman about her chocolate. Don't forget I grew up in a house with four of them."

He handed her the box of her favorite Miller's Chocolate Covered Cherries. She sat down ripping the box open in no time.

"What? You're not going to offer me one?"

She glared at him for a moment, then softened her gaze and held the box out. After all, it was thoughtful of him to bring them.

"As soon as you swallow that one, could you tell me your version of what happened?"

She nodded and swallowed her third chocolate with a bit of ice water. "I was an idiot, Freeman. I was so focused on Pop I let my guard down."

"That could happen to anybody."

"I should have listened to Zimmer's profile. At first, I totally focused on Peter Elliott, because he looked similar to the photos of Emerson. Poor bastard."

"Poor Elliott? The asshole made your life miserable."

"I know, but he didn't deserve to die like that. He got a similar blow to what Emerson gave Keith Gray, only Elliott bled out slower."

"Damn. I see your point. Poor bastard indeed."

"Then we found out Joe worked for the landscaping company assigned to all of our victims. A little plastic surgery could have done the trick. Joe was in jail when Emerson killed Gina Haag. I'm just glad Emerson didn't kill Joe."

Erica stood up, pacing back and forth a couple of times. She stopped in front of Brent. "The thing is, Zimmer's profile said he'd be hiding in plain sight. He obtained a fake ID in the name of Grant Jordan after which he shaved, colored his hair, and got some glasses."

"I guess I missed all the fun."

"Barrel of laughs," she said sarcastically. "He was a bagger at my favorite grocery store. The one I use three or four times a week. I shopped there the day Pop took his fall. I didn't remember ever seeing him until he mentioned working there. Is that pathetic, or what?"

"Who registers the many pimple-faced baggers at any given grocery store?"

"*I will* from now on." Erica paced again. "I'll make sure I take a good look at everyone I come in contact with from this day forward." She stopped again. "You just don't know what it's like to feel totally helpless. When someone pulls a gun, at least I can pull mine too and have an equal chance. This guy had me around the throat. I still can't figure out why he didn't just go ahead and snap my neck like all the others."

"Kendall told me she talked to Jordan Collins. It seems he called her the day before. She told him she knew their mother was dead because she buried her. Maybe somewhere in his very screwed up mind he knew you couldn't be Wanda Emerson."

"You could be right," she said, sitting down and popping another chocolate into her mouth. "By the way, I'm going to be staying with Pop for a while. It will take weeks for my apartment to be refurbished. Between Emerson overflowing Elliott's sink so I'd have to call in the leak to Zimmer spraying his brains all over my ceiling, they've got their work cut out for them." She spoke about the incident as nonchalantly as possible, but she still shook inside.

"So. What's this I hear about you and Jacobs?" Brent asked, winking at her.

"We started seeing each other last fall. He's a nice guy. Lots of fun."

"Uh huh." Brent gave her the raised eyebrow gaze. "That's it? Nice guy, lots of fun?"

"You don't think I'm going to go into any further detail with you, do you?"

"Erica, look who's here." Ben walked toward them, Kendall and Morgan not far behind.

"Hey, look who's already here," Erica answered in a sing-song voice.

"Freeman," said Ben. "Guess you've heard."

"Sure have. You tell Mayhew yet?"

"He'd already figured it out," Ben answered. "Of course, he hasn't had too much time to hassle me about it. Jada's due to give birth the middle of next month so he's a bit preoccupied."

Erica cleared her throat to get their attention. "Agent Morgan, I don't believe you've met my partner, Brent Freeman. Brent, this is Spencer Morgan from the Indianapolis field office of the FBI."

Brent walked over and shook Spencer's hand. "Thanks for taking care of my partner."

"Actually, it was one of our profilers who saved Detective Barnes' neck, if I may coin a phrase," quipped Morgan.

Erica laughed and then took on a more serious tone. "How is she?"

"She's still shaken. Unless a person is a total asshole, the first time you shoot someone is pretty rough—especially when we have to shoot to kill. He had a lethal grip on you. She didn't want him to have enough strength to finish you off."

Erica observed Chennelle at the back of the group. "Kendall, you're awfully quiet."

"It's just the sense of relief we get when a case like this is solved. It's wonderful and exhausting all at once. Nothing a good night's sleep won't cure."

"It's a shame Peter Elliott didn't make it," said Erica. "Did you ever figure out how he was contacted by Parker Emerson?"

"Mark Chatham has people looking in every corner of Elliott's apartment for clues," stated Kendall. "He sent Elliott's computer to the lab so they can pull everything off of it for thorough examination. Stevenson's asking for a warrant to search Elliott's desk and computer at work. I'm sure the *Star* will give us some resistance, but we'll get it sooner or later."

"Has anybody talked to Jordan Collins since her brother was killed?" Erica asked.

"I called her the same day," said Spencer. "She was very upset, but I believe she knew this would be the outcome. We told her we can release the body in a couple of days so she's making arrangements to have him shipped to Lincoln for burial. She promised she wouldn't bury him next to their mother."

"At least she has her husband and children to get her through this," said Ben. "The families of his victims can be at peace now, knowing the person who robbed them of their loved ones is dead."

"And every thirty-something brunette can relax," said Brent.

"As long as they don't relax too much," said Erica. "As we all know, even when one falls there's always another one out there to take his or her place."

"Miss Barnes." Her father's orthopedic surgeon stood in the doorway, a friendly smile on his face.

She stood up and walked toward him. "Is Pop okay?"

"Your father did great. He's just as healthy and as much a fighter as he was during his hip surgery. I had to put a pin in the humerus just above the elbow. At his age, it will take quite some time to heal and he will need to start physical therapy in a few weeks. Will he have help at home?"

"Yes, I'll be staying with him for a while."

"Good. He'll just need some help adjusting to using one arm. We should be able to release him in a couple of days. Do you have any questions?"

"Not right now. Thanks, Doc."

The doctor nodded smiling as he turned, most likely on his way to see another patient.

"What a relief," said Ben.

"Yeah, but you don't know what Pop is like when he's not 100%."

"Kendall," said Brent. "I think you and I should head back to the office. You can fill me in on everything you two have been working on since I've been gone."

"And you can fill me in on how our lady prosecutor is doing," she responded.

Erica watched them go then realized they'd left poor Agent Morgan out of most of their conversation. "Thank you again, Agent Morgan, for your help on this case. We couldn't have done it without you and Agent Zimmer."

"Anytime, Detective," he said. "I'd better get back to my office as well. You take care now, and let us know if you need anything."

She nodded.

As he departed, she felt let down. All these weeks under so much pressure and now it was all over. Besides, she found she actually liked working with Agent Spencer Morgan. He was bright, thorough, and downright handsome.

"Hello," Ben said tapping her on the shoulder. "I'm still here."

"Sorry, Ben. Since Pop will be in recovery for a while, would you like to go down to the cafeteria with me? All I've had to eat today are a few of these chocolates Freeman brought me."

"Sounds like a good idea."

"Oh, by the way, I forgot to ask you why you came back to the apartment that day," said Erica.

Ben blushed and gave her an impish smile. "I left my badge on your nightstand."

Chapter 47
Two Weeks Later

"Look at old Brent cuttin' a rug," said Tyrone as he finished his last bite of wedding cake. "You'd think *he* was the newlywed."

"Must feel kind of weird being at your ex-girlfriend's wedding with your new girlfriend," said Ben.

Erica smiled to herself. Although she'd had misgivings about Brent getting involved with Natalie so quickly, she could see now that they belonged together.

She'd been thinking a lot about her own relationship. She loved Ben, but she'd found herself thinking way too often about Spencer Morgan. Would someone who was ready to commit to a relationship keep envisioning what it might be like to be with another man?

"Hey, what's got you off in another world?" Ben said, giving Erica a start.

"Just watching all those love birds dancing," she answered.

"Tyrone," said his lovely and very pregnant wife, Jada. "I know dancing with me is like dancing with a beach ball, but I do love this song."

"Anything you want, Sugar," Tyrone said. He stood and offered his hand to help Jada rise from her chair.

"Great band," said Brent as he and Natalie returned to the table.

"Sure is," said Ben. "Do you all want something to drink? I'm buying."

"In that case, I'll have whatever's on tap," Brent said as he took his seat next to Erica.

Natalie and Erica declined, and then Natalie excused herself to go to the bathroom.

"So, how are you, Erica?" Brent's expression of concern almost brought her to tears.

"Actually, I'm doing better since Stevenson insisted I take a leave and see the department shrink. It seems to be helping."

"How's it going with your dad?"

"Pop's been better than I expected. I think he's trying to put my needs first. He knows how it feels to be in a situation where you wonder if that moment is going to be your last."

"I'm glad to hear it. We miss you at work though." He paused. "You and Ben seem a little tense."

"Not sure where it's going right now. Almost having your life snuffed out with the flick of a wrist makes you rethink where you're going and what you're doing."

"You know I'm here for you if you need me."

"Sure do, partner," she said, her heart warming. Brent Freeman was one of the most sensitive men she knew.

Ben and Natalie arrived back at the table at the same time. He handed Brent his beer. When Tyrone and Jada made it back, Jada was breathing heavily.

"Mercy!" Jada proclaimed. "I forgot how much energy it took to dance with twenty-five more pounds on you."

"Well," said Ben. "I would like to propose a toast."

They all stood, taking their glasses of various drinks in hand.

"To wonderful friends and superb colleagues, may we always be together."

They all chimed, "Here, here." Glasses clinked and just as they were about to put them to their lips....

"Oh!" Jada put her glass on the table and pressed her other hand to her abdomen. "Tyrone, my water just broke," she said in a whisper.

Tyrone looked down at the floor and sure enough, there was a puddle. "Okay, darlin'. Stay calm. Suitcase is already in the car. Hold onto my arm, I don't want you slippin' in this stuff."

"Can we do anything to help?" asked Natalie.

"Just find somebody to clean up this mess before the bride and groom see it," pleaded Jada. "This is so embarrassing."

Tyrone took one of Jada's arms and Ben took the other. Erica grabbed Jada's purse and followed them out while Brent and Natalie looked for a hotel employee.

Jada had a couple of labor pains before she made it to the car. Tyrone voiced his concern that they wouldn't make it to the hospital in time. Each of their children had come in a shorter period of time, the last one coming forty-five minutes after Jada's water broke.

Ben helped Jada get into the back seat where she could lay down. Erica gave her the purse and wished her good luck. As Tyrone and Jada sped towards Methodist Hospital, Ben put his arm around Erica.

Erica started to tear up, confusion pounding in her head. She didn't want to cry, not here at such a happy occasion, but she couldn't hold back.

"Don't worry, honey," said Ben. "They're old hands at this. Jada and the baby will be fine."

Ben had misunderstood her tears. She nodded and brushed her cheeks with the back of her hand. Starting toward the banquet hall, she dropped her gaze and started to sob. She felt Ben take her arm, stopping her from advancing.

"This is more than what's going on with Jada, isn't it? These don't seem like tears of joy to me."

"You're right," said Erica. "I just can't pinpoint exactly what it is. I guess the wedding and now the baby...."

"A lot of good emotional stuff to add to the bad," Ben stated. He took her chin in his hand and raised her tear streaked face to his. "Erica, you do what you have to do to get through this. If it means…," he stopped and gulped. "If it means, I have to give you space, I'll do it. I love you and I'll wait as long as it takes for you to work this out."

"I don't deserve you," she said, hugging him and placing her head on his shoulder. She did need some time. Pop needed her to help him while he recovered from his broken elbow, so she'd stay with him until she found a way to get past what had happened.

Ben pulled back from her. He took the handkerchief from his breast pocket and wiped her face. "There now. What do you think? Should we go back to the party or would you rather go home?"

"Let's go back to the party," she said, smiling at him. "I'm not leaving until I've had my first Chicken Dance with you."

###

About the Author

M. E. May lives in the Far Northwest Suburbs of Chicago. The fourth of five children, she was born in Indianapolis, Indiana, and lived in central Indiana for the majority of her life. It is no wonder she chose the capital city of Indiana as the setting for the Circle City Mystery Series.

She attended classes at Indiana University in Kokomo, Indiana, studying Social and Behavioral Sciences. Her interest in the psychology of humans sparked the curiosity to ask why they commit such heinous acts upon one another. Other interests in such areas as criminology and forensics have moved her to put her vast imagination to work writing fiction that is as accurate as possible. In doing so, she depicts societal struggles that pit those who understand humanity with those who are lost in a strange and dangerous world of their own making.

The first novel in the Circle City Mystery Series, *Perfidy*, won the 2013 Lovey Award for Best First Novel at the Love is Murder Conference in Chicago.

Made in the USA
Charleston, SC
04 July 2013